Nik isn't looking for love

when he takes a summer internship at Hot Shot Sports magazine —in fact, it's the last thing on his mind – but when Tiernan, a handsome Olympic hopeful, offers a distraction from the stress of life, he has to decide if he wants to take full advantage, or if he's just using Tiernan as an excuse to forget about his problems.

After a disastrous Olympic trials four years ago, Tiernan is determined to stay focused this time around. He can't afford any distractions, but the cute photographer documenting his Olympic progress might just be worth the risk.

Also recommended…

You may also enjoy these other ForbiddenFiction works:

Vaulted by E.E. Grey

Dorian has been working his whole life to make the Olympic gymnastics team and win that elusive all-around gold medal. Just because he's the youngest, shortest and not the most socially savvy team member shouldn't warrant all the teasing, especially from Jules Gardner, the former Olympic bronze medalist and current teammate who he had a crush on for years. But can he resist Jules?(M/M)

Red and the Wolf by Kailin Morgan

Aidan is content. He's got a good job, nice house and is comfortable in the small town—far away from anyone who knows his secrets. Yet, he feels the prickle of something stalking him. It doesn't help when a stranger starts insinuating his way into Aidan's life. Newcomer Seth is attractive in a way that stirs something in Aidan he had thought long buried. Can he keep his secret and continue in his solitary life or will events conspire against him to drag the truth into the light and change everything? (M/M)

Backstroke

E.E. Grey

ForbiddenFiction
www.forbiddenfiction.com

an imprint of

Fantastic Fiction Publishing
www.fantasticfictionpublishing.com

BACKSTROKE

A ForbiddenFiction book

Fantastic Fiction Publishing
Hayward, California

© E.E. Grey, 2017

For more information, contact publisher@forbiddenfiction.com.

CREDITS
Editor: Lon Sarver
Cover Design: Siolnatine
Cover Art: Adapted from photo by S Photos at Shutterstock.
Production Editor: Kaye O'Malley
Proofreading: Jae Knight
Font: Wellrock Slab, by Manfred Klein

SKU: EEG-1.000308-01 FFP
ISBN: 978-1-62234-324-9

Published in the United States of America

DISCLAIMER

Dedication

Thank you, Ronan,
for letting me crash with you in Dublin
for a much-needed break from writing.

Contents

Chapter 1: On The Edge...1

Chapter 2: Heat Stroke...9

Chapter 3: Tiernan's Lament.......................................16

Chapter 4: Photographic Evidence..............................23

Chapter 5: Crossing The Line...................................30

Chapter 6: Instant Gratification..............................38

Chapter 7: Bibliophile..44

Chapter 8: Shared Interests.....................................53

Chapter 9: Gone To Trials...64

Chapter 10: On The Starting Block............................71

Chapter 11: Sinking In...78

Chapter 12: Favoritism..87

Chapter 13: Something New......................................94

Chapter 14: Through The Lens..................................100

Chapter 15: Runs In The Family...............................108

Chapter 16: Booze And Boys....................................116

Chapter 17: Rattlesnake Cove..................................123

Chapter 18: Something Old.......................................130

Chapter 19: Wedding Bell Blues................................137

Chapter 20: Lavender And Cream..............................145

Chapter 21: Something Borrowed..............................152

Chapter 22: Something Blue.....................................159

Chapter 23: Quelle Surprise.....................................166

Chapter 24: Homecoming...173

Chapter 25: Religion of Avoidance............................180

Chapter 26: Inevitability...187

Chapter 27: The Deep End.......................................194

Chapter 28: Drowning...201

Chapter 29: Butterfly Bandage.................................209

Chapter 30: One Stroke..219

Author's Notes:...229

About the Author...231

About the Publisher...233

Chapter 1:
On The Edge

"You ready, kid?"

Nik shouldered his camera bag and shoved down the butterflies in his stomach. They'd been there since that morning, and no amount of coffee had drowned them. Instead, it just made him twitchy. He shoved his hands in his jeans' pockets to clamp down the nerves, though it didn't stop him from swiveling his chair and trying to tune out the bustle of surrounding reporters, the clacking of keys, beeps of the copier, phones ringing constantly. Interns darted around in a flurry of papers.

"As I'll ever be," he said. He wouldn't admit (out loud anyway) that he was nervous, but he was sure Jennifer knew. In the whole week they'd known each other, Jennifer had already picked him dry of mundanities including where he was from (New York City), where he was going to college (Chicago), and if he was seeing anyone (no). Nik supposed that was normal for a journalist. They were supposed to ask questions.

Jennifer raised an eyebrow, her eyes skimming down his body. "You're gonna get heatstroke, kid. It's a hundred and ten degrees out there."

Nik frowned at his feet, black converse and skinny jeans, a faded dark blue t-shirt underneath his black jacket. "It's cold in here."

"Because the AC is blasting seventy degrees," she pointed out. "At least lose the jacket. I can't be responsible for the intern dying."

Reluctantly, Nik pulled off his jacket and slung it over his chair. He'd been given the tiniest cubicle in the whole building, but he supposed he should be grateful he got a desk at all, since he and Jennifer were only guests while they did their story.

He felt naked without his jacket, vulnerable, but the minute they stepped out the doors, he knew Jennifer had been right. Arizona was the worst place ever, he decided as they headed for the car. Why would anyone choose to live in this place? He couldn't see any beauty in the weirdly cloudless sky, the strange spiky plants that lodged themselves in your skin if you got too close, everything a sickening shade of beige. It almost made him miss New York. Almost.

"How long are we here for?" Nik asked as they reached the car and he opened the door to a blast of hot air that would have withered a plant. He could *see* the heat radiating from inside.

Jennifer grinned at him over the hood. "Until the Olympics or until Pace gets himself knocked out of the running."

"What are the odds of that?" Nik forced himself into the car, eternally grateful when Jennifer turned on the AC full blast. He still couldn't believe he got to cover the 2024 Olympics. The last few weeks had been like living in a dream, but now it was real. He had to meet the swimmer and get to work.

"He's ranked number one in the nation," Jennifer replied, backing up and pulling out of the parking lot. "He's almost guaranteed a spot on the Olympic swim team."

"So we'll be here a while then." Nik looked out the window as downtown Phoenix rolled by, a sea of gray buildings and silver cars.

"Thought this was your dream job."

"The weather leaves something to be desired." *To say the least.* He hefted his camera bag into his lap and fingered the strap. It had taken him a lot of work to get here. He shouldn't be complaining about the weather, but he was used to New York, to school in Chicago, where an all-black wardrobe didn't garner him funny looks on the street. The looks reminded him of home; his brothers always had something to say about his clothes. Or his hair. Or school. Or the fact that he never played sports. Or that he left.

"You want to be a photojournalist, you gotta get used to uncomfortable situations," Jennifer said, tugging on a kinky curl as she turned onto another street. She wasn't what Nik had expected when he'd gotten the internship and they'd told him he'd be helping a journalist cover an Olympic journey story.

Jennifer was young, probably only mid-thirties, and she was cool. Her hair was dyed half blue, its natural dark brown on top, and she had a tattoo on her collarbone of a bird. The black ink was dark, even against her brown skin. Nik had been thinking about getting a tattoo. Maybe this summer, he'd actually do it.

She had a point about uncomfortable situations, though Nik was pretty sure he'd lived through plenty of those already.

"So what are we doing today?" he asked. If he was going to suffer through this heat, he wanted to learn as much as he could. He could have been back at the New York office, copy-editing pieces or memorizing coffee orders. This was the opportunity of a lifetime for Nik, and he wasn't going to fuck it up.

"We're just going to meet Pace," she said, darting around a slow car. Nik grabbed the dashboard, heart jumping into his throat. He hadn't spent much time in cars growing up — the subway was much safer in his opinion — and Phoenix traffic moved so fast. "Introduce ourselves, get some of the background so we can start. We'll be shadowing him up to trials, then to Paris."

Paris. There'd been a time when Nik hadn't ever thought he'd get out of the Bronx, let alone to Paris.

"Have you been?" he asked, turning from the window.

"To Paris? Once, in college," she said. "I just remember a lot of wine and waiting in line forever to go up the Eiffel Tower. Hot guys, though."

Nik definitely wasn't going to Paris to pick up guys. This internship was a huge break. When this was over, he'd have photographs published in a national magazine, in print and online, with his name on them. That alone was worth its weight in gold.

"We're here," Jennifer said a moment later as they turned onto another long street that led towards what looked like a college campus to Nik. The sign at the entrance read, "Ahwatukee Olympic Center" and underneath that, arrows: "Elite Gymnastic Center" and "Swim Center."

"What is this place?" He craned his neck as they drove down the driveway, past meticulously landscaped desert — a vast garden of beige rocks filled with carefully placed desert plants along cement walkways.

3

"It's an Olympic training center," Jennifer replied, taking the turn towards the pool. "They do gymnastics, swimming. A lot of athletes come here."

When Jennifer had said 'pool,' Nik had pictured an outdoor pool surrounded by beach chairs and people drinking drinks with little umbrellas, like they did at the apartment he was staying at. Walking into the Olympic-sized pool, his mouth fell open a bit. Chlorine and humidity hit him like a brick as they went inside, the air almost as hot as outside. The pool was massive, far bigger than the public pool he'd only ventured into a few times as a kid at home. Each lane was separated by floating buoys, with starting blocks lining one end of the pool.

Pulling himself together, he hurried after Jennifer, shouldering his bag and glancing around. The bleachers around the pool were empty, and only a few people were in the pool. A grey-haired man in a sweat suit blasted his whistle, a shrill sound that echoed off the walls.

"That must be him," Jennifer said, nodding at the guy in the pool. He was moving fast enough that all Nik could really see was the blur of his backside. Jennifer already had her phone out, flipping to an app to record and transcribe.

The man in the sweat suit blew his whistle again as he caught sight of them. He reminded Nik of an army general, with his close-cut salt-and-pepper hair and broad shoulders.

"You're the reporter?" he asked, voice gruff, shaking Jennifer's hand firmly.

"I am," she agreed. "Jennifer Morton. This is my photographer and assistant, Nik."

The man merely nodded at him and turned to the pool. "Tiernan, get out of there! The press is here." He glanced back at Jennifer, eyeing her carefully. "We don't have tons of time to wax poetic about his abs, got it?"

"Yes, sir," she replied with an easy smile that seemed to appease him. Nik wasn't sure he'd ever seen anyone so serious in a sweat suit.

The man, the coach, Nik supposed, ambled away as Pace hauled himself out of the pool.

To say it wasn't a movie moment would be a lie. Nik turned and watched the guy lift himself out of the pool, water cascading off his tanned back, over his tiny shorts and dripping onto the floor as he straightened up. His dark hair was plastered to his head but stuck up as he shook it once. He wiped water off his face, his sea green eyes landing on Nik. Nik could swear he smiled slightly, just for a second as their eyes met, but then the guy grabbed a towel and ran it over his chest as he stepped towards them.

Nik hadn't seen many swimmers in his life, and it had definitely never been a *thing*. Until now, apparently. He couldn't help watching the way water slid down Pace's chest, down to the V cut at his hips and those *tiny* swim trunks. He could see pretty much everything and he wasn't disappointed.

Pace didn't seem self-conscious at all about the fact that he was wearing practically no clothing. Instead, he smiled at Jennifer and offered a hand.

"The reporter?"

"Jennifer Morton," Jennifer supplied, completely professional whereas Nik wasn't sure he'd be able to form a complete sentence if this guy spoke to him. "This is Nik Cali."

Pace smiled at Nik and Nik struggled to describe it to himself — dreamy was the only thing that came to mind, as stupid as that was. It was a very good thing he wasn't the journalist here.

"Tiernan Pace," Pace introduced himself.

"Tiernan?" Nik repeated, the only thing he could think to say. It was probably better than saying, *holy shit, you're hot.*

"Irish," Tiernan explained. "My parents, well, they fucked in Ireland once and here I am. I guess they thought it would be sentimental."

Nik didn't know what to say. Luckily, Jennifer jumped in.

"It's nice to meet you, Tiernan," she said, giving Nik a gracious reprieve as he struggled to remember what he was doing here. Oh, right, photos. Fumbling with the strap on his camera bag, he got it open and pulled out his camera. "We're really just here to introduce ourselves. We'll be following you on your journey to trials and to the Olympics. The magazine wants weekly articles for our online section."

"And what's your job?" Tiernan asked Nik, gazing down at him. Tiernan was a good five inches taller than him, which wasn't all that surprising since Nik barely cleared five-seven. He'd always been small — scrawny, his brothers used to say.

"I, I take photos," Nik stuttered finally, feeling a flush creeping up the back of his neck. He was acting like a twelve-year old kid with his first crush. He was twenty years old for fuck's sake. He had to get a grip.

"Make sure you get my good side." Tiernan winked at him cheekily and the flush deepened. What the fuck was wrong with him?

Jennifer's eyes were on Nik and she raised that eyebrow of hers again. "We'll just let Nik do his thing," she said, and for a moment, Nik was confused. Photos. She was talking about photos. He couldn't remember the last time a guy had made him feel so stupid, blindsided almost. It was ridiculous. Just because he was good-looking. Okay, he was the hottest guy Nik had seen in a long time, at least in real life. The last guy he'd hooked up with had had huge ears that stuck out past his hair and made him look like an elephant.

He wasn't here to ogle swimmers. He was here to work, he reminded himself as Jennifer talked to Tiernan. That meant taking photos.

Photography was something Nik was good at. Hell, it was the *only* thing he was good at. English? Terrible. Math? Even worse. But photography, that he could do.

It wasn't great lighting in the pool. Everything had a blue hue to it, but Nik tried a few shots anyway. They'd have to get him outside if they wanted anything decent. Maybe they could set up a real shoot. He'd pitch it to Jennifer.

He caught Tiernan's eyes on him a few times but tried to ignore it. It would be too much to hope he was more than just a flirt. Besides, Nik had way too much shit in his life right now to worry about a guy. It was the last thing he needed.

"I'll give you a hint," Tiernan said as Nik changed camera angles. "My good side is back there." He pointed at his back and Nik's mouth twitched.

"I'm not so sure about that," he muttered, gazing up past Tiernan's straight nose to the way his eyes crinkled as he smiled.

"Not sure if I should be insulted or flattered."

"Let's go with flattered," Jennifer interjected. "You must have people throwing themselves at you all the time."

Tiernan shrugged, watching Nik again. Something fluttered in Nik's chest at his gaze but he looked away.

"I guess. I don't really pay much attention."

Jennifer laughed. "I bet you don't. Well, it was nice meeting you. We'll be seeing a lot of each other. I'm gonna go ahead and set up our first official interview."

"You'll be there?" Tiernan asked Nik and Nik ran a hand through his messy hair, making it even more of a mess than it usually was. The humidity in here wasn't helping.

"Uh, yeah," he agreed, putting his camera away and not meeting Tiernan's gaze. "I'm the intern."

"Okay," Tiernan said and Nik only chanced a look at him when Jennifer was busy picking a time and a place to meet.

He didn't know what was going on. No one as hot as Tiernan had ever hit on him. Most guys thought he was a little weird, with the all-black ensembles, shaggy hair that never seemed to do what he wanted, and bony stature — sharp angles everywhere. Tiernan looked smooth everywhere.

He managed to make it out of the pool without making a fool of himself, but he could tell by the look Jennifer gave him that he hadn't been completely successful.

"That was interesting," she said as they got in the boiling hot car.

"Yeah."

She kept looking at him until he started to feel uncomfortable.

"What?"

"Nothing." She started the car and pulled out of the parking lot. "Just I've never seen you blush."

Nik stiffened, staring hard out the window. "I didn't blush."

"He smiled at you and you fell hard." She sounded amused, shaking her head at the windshield, a smile on her lips. "Not that I blame you. He is definitely on par with celebrity hotness."

Nik said nothing. Talking about guys wasn't something he did, especially with people he'd only known a week.

As they drove, his phone vibrated in his pocket. Pulling it out, he frowned at the name: Rae. Ignoring the call, he shoved the phone away. He'd call her later. The phone vibrated with a text a second later. He didn't read it.

"You think you can keep it in your pants and be professional?" Jennifer asked and Nik nodded quickly.

"Of course." If there was one thing he was good at, it was repressing.

7

"Good 'cause we're going to be spending a lot of time with Tiernan in his Speedo and I want a good story out of this."

"Me too," Nik agreed, letting out a deep breath as he turned to the window and watched Saguaros whip past.

Chapter 2:
Heat Stroke

Nik scrolled through the image search on his phone as he curled up on the couch in his tiny apartment. The air conditioner was on full-blast, but it still wasn't cold enough for him.

His eyes flicked from image to image on the screen, pictures of Tiernan at varying stages of his career. In every one, his eyes seemed to stare at Nik, stormy green like the ocean. Fuck, he was hot.

This wasn't how Nik had intended to spend his evening (stalking Tiernan on the internet — his Instagram had proven to be a wealth of jack-off material. The only thing hotter than one Olympic swimmer was apparently several in the same tiny swimsuits, all hanging onto each other like they were the best of friends). He'd intended to do some research on the Olympics, considering he'd never actually watched one. He figured it was probably a good idea to at least pretend he had an idea.

Wikipedia had led to Olympic swimmers, which had led to Tiernan's page (one sister, grew up in Las Vegas, went to University of Arizona on a swim scholarship) which had led to Tiernan's social media profiles and many pictures of Tiernan half-naked in his suit, grinning at the camera.

He wasn't even supposed to care about how hot Tiernan was. His job was to take great photographs so he'd get noticed by the editors, get great recommendations, and go into his junior year of college with some experience under his belt. He could just hear his academic advisor now.

"What did you do this summer, Nik?"

"Spent the whole time staring at a swimmer's ass."

Yeah, he didn't think that would go over too well. He already had enough to worry about with student loans piling up, and everything else. Disappointing his advisor when he'd worked so hard to even get to this point wasn't something he was interested in. She was one of the few who actually believed in him.

That didn't stop Nik from gazing at the full-size picture of Tiernan taking up his screen. It didn't hurt to look.

The phone ringing interrupted his creepy stalking and he sighed at Rae's name on the screen, blacking out Tiernan's face. He supposed he couldn't ignore her forever.

"Hey," he greeted her a second later, curling further into the couch as though that might protect him from what she was going to say. Despite being 3,000 miles away, it was like he could feel her presence the minute he answered the phone.

"You didn't text me back," she said immediately.

"I was busy." It was only half a lie. He'd been working, sort of.

Her silence said more than it needed to and Nik sighed. He could practically see her, sitting in their old room, the window a tiny square that faced a brick building and a flashing red sign, horns blaring outside, police sirens in the distance. Unlike all his brothers, Nik and Rae looked similar, with the same dark hair and olive skin, dark brown eyes, but Rae didn't have the bags under her eyes like Nik always did. Maybe it was because she slept more. Maybe it was because she hadn't spent her life getting pushed around by their brothers. They had protected Rae. They had punished Nik.

"What?" he asked finally when she was silent too long. He was pretty sure he knew what, but he asked anyway.

"It's Mom," she said, ignoring Nik when he butted in with, "It's always Mom." "She's getting worse."

He was supposed to feel bad, to feel worried, but he only felt annoyed.

"So? What am I supposed to do about it?"

"*Nikos.*" She used that tone he hated, the one where she reminded him that she was, in fact, older than him. By ten minutes. Whatever. It hardly mattered.

"*Rae,*" he echoed in the same tone, shoving a hand through his messy hair and staring out the window. It was a different view than he was used to. Buildings didn't tower here, and the sun cast a golden haze over everything as it sunk. It was almost pretty.

"She's our mother," Rae reminded him, as if he needed a reminder. He'd spent most of his life wishing his mother would remember that fact.

"She abandoned us," he pointed out flatly. "You, me."

"She was — "

"I don't want to hear the excuses again." He'd heard them enough times. She was depressed. She couldn't handle their dad leaving her with five kids.

"Fine," Rae said sharply. "But Andre keeps asking where you are and why you're not here."

"He knows exactly where I am and why I'm not there." Nik crossed his arms. "He never helped me."

"He raised us."

"We raised ourselves," he pointed out. "Or have you forgotten all the times we went to the shelter for food, walked home from school 'cause we didn't have money for the subway, how about the time Andre said I was the reason Mom drank?" Nik didn't have much sympathy for Andre's needs when it came to their mother.

He heard Rae sigh on the other end. "Fine, you're right, Nik. We had a shitty childhood, but they need you now."

"They only want me there so I won't be here, actually doing something with my life." Andre wanted everyone to be as miserable as he was, to stay in the city forever, to deal with Mom's drinking, the liver cancer that had reared its ugly head last year. He wanted Nik to suffer like he had, having to take on four younger siblings.

As true as it was, Nik still felt bad when he thought about Rae stuck in New York with his mom and his brothers. She deserved to get out like he had.

"You haven't been home since you left for college," Rae said, her voice softer now. "You didn't come last summer, and now you're gone again."

Nik didn't want to come home. It wasn't home anymore and he hoped it never would be again. Rae was the only thing about it that he missed. He felt bad about leaving her behind, but he had to get out of there before he became his brothers, working a dead-end job and drinking too much on the weekends.

"I just wanted to tell you that her liver is getting worse. They're looking for a donor, but I don't know if we'll be able to pay for the surgery even if they do find one. It'd be nice if you came home."

11

It was only because it was Rae that Nik even considered it, just for a moment. If it had been Andre or Seth or even Dan, he would have said no right away.

"I can't," he said finally, tugging his jacket closed. The air seemed suddenly cold and he shivered.

Rae didn't respond for a long minute, but he could tell she was disappointed. Nik wouldn't say it out loud, not to Rae, but his mother deserved what she got. She'd abandoned them, left them to be raised by older brothers who blamed Nik for their dad leaving. Not Rae, just Nik. She'd spent her days drinking, occasionally finding it in her to pay for things like food or rent when they were so behind there was an eviction notice on the dilapidated door. Now she had liver cancer, from all that drinking he'd caused just by being born. He didn't owe her anything.

"Yeah, okay," she said finally. "So how's the internship going?"

"You don't have to ask," Nik told her, picking at a loose thread on the couch. The apartment was pretty bare without even a TV, but he'd never watched much TV. The beige carpet had unknowable stains under the table that had come with the place and the kitchen was barely big enough to turn around in, just enough space for a small fridge and an easy-bake oven. The lamp in the corner didn't quite reach into the corners, and darkness seeped in through the windows.

Rae didn't really want to know and telling her made him feel like he really was shitty for leaving when she couldn't.

"Well, I want to ask," she said. "You're still my brother even if you are a stubborn little shit. Andre says you're being selfish, but maybe sometimes you gotta be."

It didn't make him feel any better that Andre thought that. He didn't want to argue about what was selfish and what wasn't. Andre hadn't cared anything about him until he wasn't there to pick on anymore. "The internship is fine. Arizona is hotter than hell."

"Meet any cute swimmers yet?"

Nik immediately thought of Tiernan and his perfectly tanned skin. "Don't be stupid."

"Just asking. I've seen some of those athletes. They're not terrible looking, you know. You could do worse than hook up with one of them."

12

Nik shifted uncomfortably. He didn't like to talk about guys, even with Rae, though she was the only one of his siblings who didn't use it as an excuse to tease him.

"I'll remember that," he said dully.

"You should," she said seriously but sighed. "I have to go. Text me back next time, okay?"

"Yeah, yeah," he replied, if only to appease her. It would be better if he could just pretend that home didn't exist. His life would be so much easier.

"I love you, you idiot," she said a moment later and Nik smiled to himself.

"I love you too, Rae."

She didn't say anything else as she hung up and Nik set down the phone. Next time, it might not be Rae calling him, asking him to come home. They'd sent out the nicest one first; a good strategy if Nik knew anything about the art of war. It might be Dan next or Seth, or Andre if he was really pissed off. Nik wasn't looking forward to it.

For now, he had better things to think about, and he only hesitated a second before bringing up the picture of Tiernan again and sinking into the couch.

Considering Nik had practically memorized Tiernan's face, it was so much better in person. He had to force himself to focus on the camera, on the photographs he was supposed to be taking.

The pool was outside this time — apparently the Center had more than one pool. That only meant it was a thousand degrees out. Nik almost couldn't be annoyed, though, when the sun sparkled off the water dripping down Tiernan's shoulders as he propped himself against the edge of the pool, arms on the ledge and chin resting on his hands, gazing up at the camera in Nik's hands.

Tiernan tilted his head to the side as Nik snapped the photo. He wasn't wearing the swim cap and his dark brown hair stuck up oddly from when he'd shaken it dry. Nik followed a drip of water that slid down his cheek.

"So you're the intern?" Tiernan asked, eyes following Nik's camera.

13

"Mhm," Nik replied. He stayed behind the camera so at least it wouldn't look like he was just memorizing the color of Tiernan's eyes — green with a thin ring of blue around the outside. The camera also hid the inappropriate amount of time he let his gaze rest on Tiernan's mouth while his mind wondered what his lips would feel like on his skin.

"You're going to be following me around this summer?" Tiernan asked it with a hint of a smile, eyes searching for Nik's behind the lens.

"Me and Jennifer." It would be too easy to let himself get distracted by Tiernan, though he wasn't doing a good job of not being distracted at the moment.

Jennifer was fiddling with her recorder as Nik got a few pictures in before the interview. She didn't seem to be paying them much attention, for which Nik was glad.

"Aren't you hot?" Tiernan asked after a minute and Nik lowered the camera, eyebrows furrowed.

"What?" Did Tiernan just call him 'hot?' Nobody had ever called him hot, that he could recall. Weird, short, punk. That, he'd been called. But never hot.

Tiernan nodded at his outfit. "You do know you're in Arizona?"

Oh. Nik raised his camera again. "I'm fine."

"'Cause if you were hot," Tiernan went on, licking his lips slowly, "you could always jump in."

"And ruin the camera? No thanks." This was an expensive camera and Nik wasn't about to get it wet. Not even when Tiernan smiled at him and an intriguing thrill ran through his stomach. Very few people had outwardly hit on Nik in his life. His usual hook-ups came from eyes met over drinks at some dimly-lit cafe, or the rare times it had happened in high school, from behind stacks of books at the library. Nik wasn't used to this very obvious flirting Tiernan was doing. If Nik hadn't been the only one there, he might have thought it was for someone else.

"Leave the camera out," Tiernan said simply. "I'll get you out of those jeans."

It was smooth, Nik had to admit that, and he even smiled as he snapped a picture of Tiernan's grin.

"You hit on all photographers?" he asked, trying to be just as smooth, though he wasn't sure he succeeded. He was all too aware that Jennifer had stopped messing with her phone and was watching them now. If she hadn't been there, maybe he would have given in to what Tiernan was clearly suggesting.

"No," Tiernan replied, a mischievous glint in his eye.

Fuck.

Nik didn't know what to say, and he cursed his body for responding without his permission, a flush creeping up over the back of his neck, blood rushing to his cock as Tiernan held his gaze. He had to stop thinking about the idea of Tiernan pressing him up against the edge of the pool, warm water enveloping them as Tiernan's hand slid down — Standing up, he took a step backward, practically running into Jennifer.

"Careful there," she said, guiding him out of the way. "You ready to get to business?"

"Yes," he said quickly, looking away from Tiernan. He needed a distraction, a distraction that wasn't Tiernan in tiny shorts, hardly anything left to the imagination as he hauled himself from the pool and grabbed a towel.

"Okay," she said with a quick look his way, but she turned to Tiernan. "This will be quick and painless, I promise."

He merely smiled and took a seat on the bleachers with Jennifer while Nik busied himself checking his photos. He didn't have to, but he worried if he didn't, he might do something stupid like jump Tiernan right there, and that would be far from the professional image he wanted to project during this internship. When he did sneak a peek, Tiernan appeared to be answering Jennifer's questions easily, but he met Nik's gaze and smirked a second before looking away.

Oh yeah, Nik was definitely fucked.

Chapter 3:
Tiernan's Lament

"Your butterfly slipped."

Tiernan glanced over as he let the cable weights fall. Straightening his back, he wiped the light sheen of sweat off his forehead. Good posture was essential to good stroke technique, Coach always said. Weight training wasn't Tiernan's favorite activity, but it was better than the days Coach made him go over old meet videos and do "mental preparation."

Dylan crossed behind him and grabbed a weight off the floor.

"Stalking me now?" Tiernan asked, pulling the weights up again. The swimmer's gym was a much smaller facility than the gymnastics facility, with mostly free weights and other strength-training equipment. The walls were painted a sad shade of grey, with very few windows, replaced with mirrors so Tiernan could see himself everywhere he turned.

"You wish someone would stalk you," Dylan scoffed, rolling his eyes, pushing back his sandy blond hair. He leaned towards Tiernan, as though they were sharing secrets, but Tiernan knew better than to trust Dylan with any of his secrets. Dylan had been a thorn in his side since he'd moved to Phoenix. "You sleep with that reporter yet?"

He really had been keeping an eye. Tiernan shook his head. Tiernan didn't keep tabs on the other guys who trained at the Center. They each had their own coaches and used the facilities separately. He didn't have time to wonder how they were doing — his only concern should be himself, Coach always said. Unless he was swimming relays.

"She's not exactly my type," he said, thinking of Jennifer's warm smile, a smile that made him feel like she wasn't a journalist. Probably a dangerous thing to think of a reporter as a friend. That was how they got you to reveal the things that should have been kept to yourself. He'd have to keep that in mind for future interviews.

Dylan snorted and hoisted the weight up. It was too much weight, probably only to try to impress (or intimidate) Tiernan. "Like you could land someone as hot as her. I was talking about the scrawny one, with the camera permanently glued to his hand."

Nik. Tiernan almost smiled but Dylan was right there, watching him in the mirror, waiting for something he could use to get under his skin. Just because they trained at the same facility didn't mean they were friends. When it came down to trials, it was every man for himself.

Tiernan didn't answer Dylan's question, swiveling to the side of the bench. Across the room Sam entered, crossing to the pull-up station. He tossed his towel aside and stretched his muscles.

"Jealous a hot journalist isn't following you around, Dylan?" Tiernan knew how to get under Dylan's skin when he had to, though on the whole, he tried not to. "Maybe if your ranking was higher."

Dylan glared, eyes narrowing. "It would be if you hadn't stolen that heat at the Championships."

"Steal would indicate you'd had it in the first place," Tiernan said simply. "Which you didn't." He was pushing his luck, but he wasn't in much of a mood to listen to Dylan complaining.

"Fuck you, Pace," Dylan spat, dropping the weight and glaring at him. "Trials are in a week. We'll see who's better then."

Tiernan didn't reply as Dylan stormed out of the gym. Sam turned to watch as the door slammed shut.

"What's he upset about now?" Sam asked, turning from his station.

"The usual." Tiernan crossed to the pull-up bar and leaned against it, gazing at himself in the mirror. He could probably do with a little more weight-lifting, if he was honest. He wasn't as buff as Dylan or Sam, but mere power wasn't everything. He caught Sam watching him in the mirror and flashed him an easy smile.

"What was he saying about the journalist?" Sam asked, grabbing the bar and pulling himself up. He made it look so easy. "Personally,

I don't think I'd want one following me around. Too distracting with trials coming up."

"It's good exposure," Tiernan said, shoving his hair back. "Good opportunity for more sponsors."

Sam smiled slightly. "I don't know that you need any more sponsors. Save some for the rest of us who can't pay our bills."

Sponsors were the only reason Tiernan *could* pay his bills. Without them, he'd be just as poor as everyone else. "Make the Olympic team and we'll get you set up with some athletic company. You could be the next Ryan Lochte."

Sam rolled his eyes. "Yeah, okay. First I gotta make the team."

"Top two, come on, we can do it."

If Dylan was the person Tiernan got along worst with, Sam was the best. Sam was a big guy, but he was more relaxed than the other swimmers at the Center. He had dark skin, broad shoulders, a square jaw. He was handsome in his own way, not that Tiernan had ever thought about Sam like that.

Sam didn't look convinced, and he pulled himself up and down again. For such a big guy, he didn't act like it. "You didn't make it the first time you went to trials," he pointed out.

"Don't remind me," Tiernan said, frowning. He tried not to think about that moment four years ago, when he'd fucked up everything. It would be different this time.

"So how *is* the reporter thing?"

Tiernan smiled this time as he thought of Nik's wide-eyed confusion every time he hit on him. He hadn't gotten much further than flirting, always inconveniently interrupted by something or someone. There was just something about Nik — his insistence on wearing all black in one hundred degree weather, all the sharp angles of his body, the natural pout to his lips that made Tiernan think of shirts tearing and hands grabbing in dark rooms.

"It's nice to be appreciated," he just said and Sam snorted.

"Says the number one swimmer in the country."

It may have been true, but a title was only as good as his next win. He grabbed a couple of weights and settled onto a bench, lifting them slowly up and down. Sam continued with his pull-ups, slow and steady.

"Maybe they can do a feature on you," Tiernan suggested. Sam deserved it as much as anyone, and he was a hell of a lot nicer guy than Dylan. He'd been world champion in breaststroke last year, but press hadn't seemed to notice. Tiernan was fucking lucky to get all the media attention that he did. He was pretty sure it had to do with his green eyes and six-pack, but still. No one ever accused an athlete of being smart.

"I don't want it," Sam said dismissively, dropping down from the bar and grabbing his towel. He wiped the sweat from his brow and shot Tiernan a smile. "Some of us don't need constant attention."

"I don't need constant attention," Tiernan argued as the weights grew heavier in his hands. "But that doesn't mean I don't enjoy it."

Sam shook his head. He grabbed a weight and joined Tiernan in lifting. For a moment, the gym was silent. Tiernan had lost count of how many reps he'd done, probably not enough. He didn't know if there was enough preparation in the world to get him ready for Trials, really ready.

"Whatever happened to that cooking class thing you were doing?" Sam asked. "You promised me dinner once you became a fancy chef."

Tiernan laughed and let the weights fall to the floor, pushing himself up. He'd forgotten about that. It had been months ago, a whole lifetime ago. Months felt more like years during the run-up to Olympics.

"I finished the class," he said. "But I never took the next one because I have this little thing called constant training, so basically, I can make you bread, but only, like, four kinds, so take your pick."

Tiernan had taken the class as something to do other than training, and he'd found out he was really good at mixing things. Not the most impressive discovery, but cooking had always been something he really wanted to try. He could *cook*, basic things and some recipes, but he wanted to be like those annoying people on TV who never looked at recipes and always had perfectly set tables. He didn't even have a table in his apartment. He figured he had a ways to go.

Maybe after the Olympics, he could get back to it. He'd have more time then, time to take a break.

"Then you owe me bread," Sam said simply, and Tiernan laughed.

"I'll get right on that."

Sam didn't reply, and Tiernan rose from the bench and headed for the locker room. He had more work to do.

Two missed calls from his sister and one from his mom. Tiernan made a face at his phone. Who called anymore? Just send a text or passive-aggressively subtweet. He'd get the message either way. But no, three missed calls instead and they would expect him to call back. No matter that he was busy training most of the time.

His fridge was practically empty when he opened it, but he grabbed a beer and headed to the balcony. His balcony, if you could call it that, being two feet wide and four feet long, overlooked the pool, which shimmered under the sun. Sometimes Tiernan slipped into the pool after dark, when there was no one there, so he could really think. The water was the best place for him to find peace sometimes. A palm tree grew too close to the building, its leaves pushing into what little space he had. Plopping into the cheap lawn chair he had out there, he cracked open the bottle and pulled out his phone. If he didn't call Ella back, she'd go crazy.

"Ella, my favorite sister," he greeted her when she picked up. "I see you clogged my inbox again."

"I'm your only sister," Ella said in a deadpan, and Tiernan grimaced. She was in a mood today.

"Which means you're the favorite by default," he pointed out. He knew he shouldn't have called. One of the good things about training in Phoenix was that it was far away from Ella's drama.

"Stop joking, Tiernan," she said, and he spent a second trying to remember a time she hadn't been constantly on edge. Probably before she got engaged. Well, maybe not. She'd always been type A. "You know why I'm calling."

He sighed. "The wedding." It was always the wedding. Nothing else could possibly matter except her wedding right now.

"It's in three weeks," she said, her voice annoyed. "I need to know if you are coming. Michael said he couldn't wait so he's picked his best men already."

Tiernan didn't care about being a best man to a guy he barely knew. He'd met Michael twice in the last two years and he didn't think they'd even had a complete conversation.

"You do realize," he said for what felt like the millionth time, "that Olympic trials are next week. Then I'll have to be training constantly until the Olympics." Why had she picked this date? Of all the dates, three-hundred and sixty-four other days in the year and she had to pick one in July on an Olympic year.

"*If* you make it," she replied. "You didn't last time."

It was low blow, and Tiernan winced and gritted his teeth, staring unseeingly at the cars on the road in the distance. The sun glinted off the metal.

"I'm going to make it."

"Because you've changed," she said and Tiernan could hear the doubt in her voice. "You stopped partying and drinking and sleeping with everything that moves."

Tiernan didn't want to talk about this again. He hadn't been smart four years ago — he'd been young and in college and away from his parents for the first time. He hadn't focused like he should have.

There was only one way to get Ella off his case, and that was...

"Fine, I'll be there. Tell Michael and Mom and Dad that I will be there." He would be there, but he'd be flying home immediately afterwards to get back to training because he *would* make the Olympic team this year.

Ella let out a relieved sigh. "It didn't have to be this hard, Tiernan."

Everything was this hard when it came to his family.

"Do I need to bring a date?" he asked because he didn't want to hear the big sister lecture on priorities. He knew what his priorities were, and they weren't weddings, especially not this month. Any other month and he would have been thrilled to buy an expensive tux he'd never wear again, attempt to bond with Michael over strippers and shots, and even listen to Ella's constant back and forth on hydrangeas or lilies (personally, he'd go with peonies. Much prettier and more expensive).

"You can," she allowed. "Just not — "

"A guy," Tiernan finished, already knowing what she was going to say.

He heard her sigh again, as if he was making things difficult. "You know how Mom and Dad are. They like to pretend you're not gay."

"Right. This has just been a ten year phase."

"Tiernan, it's my wedding," she said in that tone she used when she was about to hit him. "So play nice. They're paying for it, you know."

"It's nice they pay for one child's happiness, at least." He shouldn't have been so bitter, and he tried to shake it away. Dwelling on his parent's favoritism wasn't something he liked to think about. Yet another distraction. "I will be a good son, how about that?"

"Just come to the wedding," Ella said, as though she was exhausted already. Tiernan felt the same. "They'll be happy to see you."

As long as he didn't bring up the 'gay thing.' Then they'd make it through just fine.

"Fine, but I'm buying you a dildo as a wedding gift."

"Tiernan!"

"Bye, Ella!" He hung up the phone and groaned out loud. One more thing he had to do between now and August.

Taking a swig of his beer, he ignored the missed call from his mom. She'd probably called for the same thing.

If you make it. You didn't last time.

A pit formed in his stomach as Tiernan watched someone get in their car and pull out of the lot. It was nice to know she had so much faith in him. He knew he'd blown it last time, but that was last time. Things were different now.

His biggest problem now was figuring out a way to tell Coach he had to take a weekend off in the middle of Olympic training. He wasn't looking forward to that.

Chapter 4:
Photographic Evidence

As much as Tiernan hated to admit it, Dylan was right. The butterfly was not exactly his thing. It never had been, but he did it well enough to qualify and well enough to place in world championships, so it was on the roster. He was much better at backstroke.

Water slammed into his face with every stroke and he could barely hear the coach's whistle above the splashes as he swam. Coach had been pushing the butterfly hard since it was his weakest event, which meant Tiernan spent hours practicing his technique. He'd gotten his time down, but not enough, according to Coach.

"Fifty-three point fifty-five," Coach said when Tiernan reached the stop and pulled his goggles off. Water ran into his eyes and he sucked in air, his heart sinking. Coach stood above him, blocking the overhead light. He cut a tall figure, intimidating even in his track suit.

Tiernan cursed at the time. That was good enough for tenth place.

"We need to get you down to fifty-one seconds if you want to qualify," Coach said, writing down the time on his spreadsheet. That was two extra seconds Tiernan had to lose somewhere.

"Can I just cut off a limb?" Tiernan joked, but Coach didn't smile. Tiernan wasn't sure he'd ever smiled, but he was former military. That was part of the reason Tiernan had picked him as a coach. He didn't give a shit what was going on in Tiernan's life; he was only there to train him and make sure he didn't fuck up like last time.

"Let's run it again," Coach said, and Tiernan didn't complain, climbing out of the pool and taking his place on the starting block. They'd run it until he got it right.

He waited for the whistle, but instead, all he heard was, "Pace."

E.E. Grey

Coach had his arms crossed, the whistle hanging on his chest, and he was watching someone approach from the doors. Dropping from the starting block, Tiernan smiled as he caught sight of Nik with his camera bag slung over his shoulder. He didn't see Jennifer anywhere; a good sign.

Coach turned to him before Nik could reach them. "I understand the necessity of this… venture, Pace, but don't let it get in the way."

"No problem, Coach," Tiernan promised. "It's just a few photographs."

"You got an hour then back to training." Coach left before Nik could reach them.

"I'm ready for my close-up," Tiernan greeted Nik, winking as he arrived. Nik seemed not to react, busy fiddling with the camera bag. Or maybe he was trying not to, judging by the way his eyes flicked up, too brief to really look at Tiernan.

Nik was in his black jeans again, the ones that hugged his hips so tightly that Tiernan wondered how difficult it would be to get them down. His shirt was faded, the picture on the front practically gone. Tiernan was glad he'd dropped the jacket this time — he didn't want him to die of heatstroke, even though the jacket made him look like an adorable punk kid.

Most of the time, Tiernan tried to focus on swimming. It was guys like Nik (well, guys and alcohol) that had caused him to lose focus last time trials rolled around. He was smarter this time, though, older. He could play a balancing act this time.

"No Jennifer?" he asked, taking off his goggles and swimming cap. He pushed his hair down, though it wouldn't make much difference.

"Nope," Nik said, still not meeting his eyes. "Just me today."

Good. Tiernan let his eyes wander over Nik while he wasn't looking. Most guys he slept with were the athletic type — he just seemed to attract them, the ones who cared about muscles and toning. He liked that Nik wasn't like that. He was small and lean, tight like a bow string.

"I was thinking maybe the locker rooms," Nik said after a minute of surveying the pool. His voice sounded a little tight, but Tiernan didn't comment on it.

"Sure," he agreed, falling into step with Nik, who kept his eyes straight ahead. It was different from all the other times, when Nik

24

hadn't seemed to be able to focus on anything else. "You want me to change?"

"We could... I don't know," Nik said, shaking his head. "Let's just do some test shots first."

They entered the locker room, a long rectangular room filled with rows of lockers, with showers at the end. Everything in here always seemed very grey to Tiernan. There were a few high windows, but not much natural light aside from that.

"Harsh lighting in here," Nik muttered, taking out his camera and pointing it at a row of sinks.

"Why aren't we doing this in a studio somewhere?" Tiernan had some experience with photographers, for his sponsorships, and they usually had a whole studio set-up, complete with bright lights, makeup, and a photographer who complained about the background the whole time.

Nik tossed him a look and dropped his camera bag on a bench. He seemed looser now that he had the camera out. "That's not what photojournalism is."

Tiernan adjusted his suit, lycra cutting into his hips, and raised an eyebrow. "Where do you wanna start?"

Nik blinked a few times before he spoke, cutting his gaze away from Tiernan to his camera. "Maybe the shower."

It was almost too easy, but Tiernan knew what he looked like, and how many guys were turned on by that. Nik was no exception.

The showers stood in a long row of stark showerheads and spigots. A long, narrow window overlooked the room. Tiernan turned on one of the showers and turned to Nik.

"Ready?"

"Let's test some," Nik muttered, gesturing Tiernan under the water.

Tiernan stepped under the flow, closing his eyes for a second as the warmth swept over him. The showers were luke-warm on their best days, but after so much time in the pool, he hardly noticed. He heard the click of the camera and opened his eyes.

"Step forward," Nik directed him, backing up for a full shot. "Keep your face out of the water."

Tiernan knew somewhat what to do. He'd done photo shoots for sponsorships before, but it was different. At those, there were ten people watching. Someone was doing makeup and adjusting his suit as if they had no problem groping him in public. Nik was more reserved. He didn't try to touch Tiernan, simply directed him around and moved to get a better angle.

When Nik lowered the camera, Tiernan stepped out of the shower, water dripping down his shoulders. "How was that?"

Nik bit his lip as he flicked through the photos, and Tiernan watched his fingers move through the camera roll.

"Not bad," he said finally, meeting Tiernan's eyes for the first time. Tiernan felt something pass between them then, something dark and heated in the look that he couldn't pinpoint. Not for the first time in his life, he wished the swim suits had a little more give.

Nik cleared his throat finally and nodded at the lockers. "Let's try some over there."

Tiernan wasn't sure how long he could keep standing here in his suit with Nik, all alone, watching him finger his camera and avoid his gaze.

They moved to the lockers and Nik reached out, tentatively nudging Tiernan's shoulder towards the locker.

"Right there," he said quietly, hiding behind his camera again.

Tiernan obeyed Nik's commands — "Turn towards your left, a little more. Smile a little more. Not that much. Pretend I'm your best friend."

The click of the camera was always followed by another suggestion. Nik moved him easily around the space, keeping him focused, like a professional photographer.

Nik had him up against the sinks, the mirror behind him, hands gripped onto the counter.

"Now pretend you want to sleep with me," Nik said, the words muffled behind the camera.

Tiernan arched an eyebrow and smirked. "Don't have to do that."

The camera clicked again as Nik lowered it. He held it loosely in his hand as he stared at Tiernan, emotions flickering through his eyes that Tiernan couldn't categorize.

Tiernan wasn't the kind of guy who waited for what he wanted, and he didn't wait for Nik to respond as he stepped forward and kissed him.

Tiernan's hands found Nik's waist, hauling him up, turning him around against the counter top. He felt Nik's legs press to his side,

Nik's free hand pushing in his hair as their mouths met for a hard, burning kiss. He hadn't expected Nik to be so hard, to respond so well, pushing his tongue in Tiernan's mouth as Tiernan groaned.

"Wait," Nik gasped a second later, pulling away, cheeks flushed, a hand still tangled in Tiernan's hair. "We can't do this."

"Why not?" Tiernan asked, dragging Nik's bottom lip into his mouth and sucking. He thought Nik might almost just let him until he pulled away again.

"I don't — I don't know," Nik mumbled, eyes falling to Tiernan's mouth.

Tiernan took that as a yes, and Nik didn't protest again as Tiernan brought their lips together.

"Mmm, wait, the camera," Nik panted a minute later, pulling the strap over his head. Tiernan took it from him and set it on the counter then yanked Nik towards him. Nik slid off the counter, barely balancing on his tiptoes as Tiernan kissed him.

If Tiernan had expected Nik to be soft and shy, he was mistaken, judging by the way Nik grabbed at him, kissed him back hard with lips and teeth and tongues. It wasn't fair, Tiernan thought vaguely as Nik's hands skimmed down his bare back, that he had so little clothes on, and Nik so much.

Tiernan shoved Nik up against the lockers, hearing the rattle echo down the row. Nik's muffled noise caught in his throat as Tiernan shoved his hands under Nik's shirt.

Jesus, it was good. Tiernan felt the heat rushing through his body, blood rushing to his cock as it stiffened against Nik's hips. He wanted more, all of Nik beneath him, but right now, all he had was his rib cage, fingers skimming under his shirt as Nik keened against him.

"Shit," Tiernan panted, cupping Nik's jaw to pull him closer, sucking on his tongue, pushing against him with his hips. They didn't have long. Coach would expect him to be back in the pool after the shoot. He didn't have time, but fuck, he wanted it anyway.

Nik's hands slid down Tiernan's sides, his skin dry now from the shower. His touch was light but not fumbling, like he knew what he wanted and was just waiting for Tiernan to give him the go ahead.

Tiernan moved first, reaching for Nik's belt and yanking it open. The buckle clinked as it fell and Tiernan went for Nik's jeans.

E.E. Grey

"Fuck, these are tight," he muttered, momentarily distracted by Nik's tongue in his ear as he shoved the zipper down. Jesus, he hadn't been prepared for this, not for the way Nik melted into him, seemed to know exactly what to do to leave him weak.

"Hurry up," Nik panted in his ear. His breath ghosted hot over his skin and Tiernan groaned and pushed his hand under Nik's waistband.

They didn't have time to do this right, but Tiernan didn't care. He wanted to get off and he wanted to get off now. His swim shorts had long since failed to hide his excitement and he didn't have to give Nik the go ahead to pull his cock out.

Nik's hand moved steadily, long fingers stroking him, a little bit rushed, but Tiernan wasn't complaining. He had Nik's cock in his hand, squeezing lightly and drinking in the noises Nik made when he moved. He shouldn't have been going so slowly. An hour had to have passed already. He was pushing it.

Moving forward, Tiernan pushed Nik's hand away, ignoring the blink of confusion that followed. They didn't have time, but they couldn't stop now.

Tiernan took both of their cocks in his hand, pushing them together. Heat rose against his skin, and he could feel Nik's flush, the way Nik's fingers dug into his shoulders as he jerked them both off.

"Oh, fuck," Nik breathed, hips pushing into Tiernan's hand, their cocks rubbing together. Tiernan could feel every ridge, every muscle. This was what he'd been missing. This was what he needed. He was so close.

"Five minutes, Pace!"

"Shit — shit!" Tiernan cursed under his breath, trying to pull away but Nik's grip tightened.

"No," he breathed, that one word setting him off and Tiernan came, gasping as panic filled him.

Tiernan looked toward the door, but Coach didn't come around the corner. Between the tightening in his gut, Nik dragging their mouths together, Tiernan gasped for breath. He'd been caught with his pants down before, but he didn't think Coach would take it as kindly as other people.

Tiernan's stomach was sticky with come, smeared on his hand and Nik's shirt when Nik pulled away, both of their cocks softening.

Coach hadn't come in. Tiernan's heart rate went back down as he let go of Nik. The last thing he wanted was Coach accusing him of not being serious. Maybe the locker room hadn't been the best idea. When he looked at Nik, though, with his messy hair and flushed cheeks, he reconsidered. He'd fuck Nik anywhere if he got that look in return.

"I gotta get back to training," he said, pulling his suit back on properly and washing his hands. When he turned back, Nik had gotten his pants back up and was shoving his hair aside, eyes on the floor again.

Moving over, Tiernan reached into Nik's back pocket and pulled out his phone. He entered his number and handed it back despite Nik's questioning look.

"Text me," he said, squeezing Nik's ass before he left. He wasn't sure Nik would do it, but Tiernan was willing to take a chance for a little more of what had just happened.

Coach stood at the pool, checking his watch impatiently. He didn't look impressed as Tiernan approached him. Tiernan couldn't tell by looking if he'd known he was in the locker room.

"Lateness doesn't gain you points, Pace," he merely said as Tiernan reached him. "Up on the block. We've got more butterflies to practice."

Tiernan climbed up as Coach reset the stop watch. As he stood up, he caught sight of Nik leaving, his back to Tiernan as he pulled open the door. Nik paused and glanced back, only half a second, before he left. The door snapped shut behind him.

Coach didn't pay the slightest attention to it. He blasted his whistle instead. "On your mark."

Tiernan turned from the door and took his position. He wiped the smile from his face as Coach said, "Get set." Now it was time to focus. He'd think about Nik later.

Chapter 5:
Crossing The Line

Nik stepped in the break room, glancing around quickly, but it was empty; sad white tables facing the faded counter top, which held a microwave and a coffeemaker in desperate need of a good scrub. The fluorescent lights flickered above him. He stepped in, feeling a little awkward. It had been a few weeks but he still couldn't shake the feeling since he wasn't an intern for the paper, but they were using their office as a sort of base of operations. It almost felt as if he shouldn't be using the break room or drinking the painfully bitter coffee.

Grabbing a mug, he poured out a cup of coffee anyway. Bad coffee was better than no coffee.

"Any left?" A girl popped her head in behind him, a friendly smile on her face as she entered. Her bright blond hair, darker at the roots, fell in perfectly styled waves down her back and she wore a trendy dress under her jacket. She reminded Nik of all those girls he saw in typical college movies, but then everyone in Arizona seemed to look like that.

The girl, one of the interns at the paper, stepped up next to him and reached for the bag of coffee in the cupboard.

"I swear, people in this office drink more coffee than all of Seattle." Her smile was soft, easy, welcoming.

Nik hadn't really spoken to any of the interns much. They were usually busy with their own work, and since Nik and Jennifer were only borrowing space, he hadn't really seen the point.

"Maybe it's all the sun," he suggested, and the girl laughed.

"Coffee doesn't keep you hydrated. It just keeps you perky."

Clearly Nik wasn't drinking enough coffee then. He didn't think this girl needed any, though, from the way she bounced in. He hesitated a second as the girl filled the pot and started another batch. He'd never been good at the small talk and making friends of life. It had been easier with Rae, who was more outgoing, who knew what to say to people.

"I'm Nik," he offered finally as she wiped down the counter with swift, purposeful swipes of a towel.

She smiled. "Brooke." Someone called something from the main room, and she wrinkled her nose. "That's me. Back to work."

She tossed the towel in the sink and breezed out of the break room as easily as she'd come. Nik allowed himself a second to envy her easy ability to talk to people, but he returned to his desk without waiting for another intern to introduce themselves awkwardly in the break room. He had a lot of photos to edit.

Nik sat down at his desk, the borrowed computer open to the editing software where pictures of Tiernan were splashed across in various stages of editing.

"How'd it go?" Jennifer stepped up behind him, sipping a cup of coffee that had obviously not come from the break room.

Nik's mind flashed back to Tiernan's hands on his hips, fingers brushing against his rib cage, and his heart thudded at the memory. He hadn't really analyzed what had happened the other day. He didn't want to analyze it, beat it to death with questions and uncertainties that didn't mean anything in the grand scheme of things. He'd wanted it; Tiernan had wanted it. That was all that mattered.

"Fine," he managed to say, looking away. It didn't help that the only other thing to look at was his computer and Tiernan's face.

"You get there okay?"

He shrugged. "The light rail lets out close but not that close when it's a million degrees out."

"I said you could borrow my car," Jennifer pointed out, bending over to look at the pictures.

"Can't drive. Don't have a license anyway."

She tilted her head to look at him. "You don't have a license?"

"Don't need one in New York or Chicago." Phoenix had the light rail, which had been extended to most of the surrounding areas outside of downtown. He heard rumors from people at the paper

31

that the plan was to extend it all the way to Carefree, wherever that was. It definitely wasn't the New York subway, but it was better than nothing.

"God, it's like a porno," she said instead of answering him. Nik's heart jumped in his throat.

"What is?"

"He really is pretty." Jennifer sighed, straightening up. "And I guess it's a credit to your skill that you made him look so good."

"He already looks like that," Nik muttered, thinking of Tiernan's abs under his hands, the bulge in his swim suit.

He hadn't texted Tiernan, though it had only been a couple days. He wasn't sure what he would say aside from, it was good getting off with you — want to do it again? That might not be too bad. Tiernan might not even mind for all he knew.

The only problem was work. Or, well, his image at work. Even though he would spend most of the summer with Jennifer, he was actually interning for *Hot Shot Sports* magazine. It was one of the biggest sports' magazines in the country, and Jennifer's articles were already appearing online with his photos. If he impressed them, maybe he could turn this internship into a job. Maybe he could start freelancing while he was still in school. In order to do that, he had to be professional, and jerking off the magazine subject in a locker room was not professional.

On the other hand, no one as hot as Tiernan had ever so much as looked at him, and wouldn't he be an idiot not to hook up with him? He wasn't at school or at home where people would care. Fuck, he didn't know. He needed to focus on the internship.

Jennifer smirked at his answer and took a sip of her coffee. "I bet."

Nik chose to ignore that. "So trials are next week?"

"Mhm," she agreed, pulling up a chair from a nearby desk. "We leave for Florida on Saturday. Trials last all week."

"So after trials, then what?"

"If Pace makes it, there'll be a three week training period before he leaves for France."

"If? I thought he was the best in the country." Nik frowned, glancing at the photograph of Tiernan leaning against the sinks. That had been minutes before he'd jumped Nik.

32

Jennifer took another gulp of coffee. "That doesn't always mean they make it. Pace went to trials four years ago and he didn't make it then."

"He didn't? What happened?" Apparently Nik hadn't read his Wikipedia page closely enough.

"He finished seventh in two of his events and tenth in another. Only the top two make the team in each event."

"So he just wasn't good enough?"

She shrugged. "I heard he was partying too much back then. He was only nineteen. You do stupid things when you're younger. I think he has a better chance this time. The alcohol rumors have stopped, anyway."

Nik wasn't sure what to make of that. He'd been under the impression that Tiernan was one hundred percent committed to swimming, but even Olympic athletes had lives, he supposed.

"You've met him," she said. "He seems like he's in a good place, doesn't he?"

Nik couldn't say. People could hide a lot, that he was sure of. "I guess." He wondered if the other day had been Tiernan's toned down version of 'partying.' He almost didn't care. It had been good.

His phone vibrated with a text and he pulled it out.

Call me now Nikos

A text from Andre. Nik ignored it and shoved the phone away. It was the third text today that Andre had sent him. He had no intention of calling his brother. He could already hear the (very one-sided) conversation where Andre would call him a selfish little bitch, and demand he come home and "contribute" to the family.

Nik's chest tightened every time he thought of calling, of Andre saying he was useless and Dad should have taken Nik when he left. Sometimes he wished he had.

"Booty call?" Jennifer joked, finishing her coffee and checking the time on her phone.

"I wish," he muttered. "Just my brother." *Being an asshole.* There was no need to drag other people into his problems. That was something that would have gotten him thrown in foster care as a kid.

"Well, I'll let you get back to your editing and your brother. Tell him hi."

Nik wouldn't, but he nodded anyway. She left him at the computer and he ignored his phone buzzing again. Andre would still be pissed later and Nik had work to do.

Andre's pissed

Nik rolled his eyes at the text Rae sent him as he stood waiting for the light rail. Even though the sun was low, it was still hot out, an oppressive heat that made him want to tear all his clothes off and jump in the first pool he saw. He'd just missed the train so he would have to wait another five minutes to get out of this heat.

What else is new? He typed in response. He hadn't read the four other texts he'd gotten from Andre since that afternoon. It couldn't be anything good. Rae always said that avoidance wouldn't solve his problems, but so far, it was a hell of a lot better than lying down and taking it.

Leaning against a pillar, he wiped sweat off his forehead. He'd thought that, being a dry heat, he wouldn't sweat so much in Arizona, but apparently it didn't matter how dry it was when it was a hundred and eighteen degrees out.

He says you're being an inconsiderate fucking dickbag

Nik wasn't that surprised. Pursing his lips, he typed in his response slowly. *Why are you telling me this?*

It wasn't Rae that wrote back but another text from Andre.

Listen you little shit mom's sick and its your responsibility to help we helped you stop being a self centered fucker and come home screw your stupid art school and get with the real world nick

The lack of punctuation was enough to drive Nik crazy. He ignored the misspelling of his name for auto-correct, but he couldn't ignore the anger bubbling inside him as he read Andre's text. Andre helped him? Andre had pushed him around, called him names, locked him in the closet for four hours once. Rae said that was what brothers did, but they'd never done it to her.

Fuck you Andre, he typed, not caring about the consequences. *You helped me sure. You helped me realize I had to get the fuck out of there. Take good care of mom like you never did me.*

He sent it with an angry jab at the screen. When would Andre get it through his head that Nik wasn't coming home? He didn't owe

Andre anything for bothering to make sure they didn't die growing up. He hadn't done much more than that.

Anger tingled under his skin as Nik glared at the screen, and he found himself opening a new message instead. He wasn't sure what made him do it, but he pulled up Tiernan's number.

You free?

The screen above his head told Nik the next train was two minutes away. No text came from Andre or Tiernan and the train screen changed to one minute away. For a second, he wasn't sure Tiernan was going to answer him, if he'd even saved his number. He might have thought Nik was some random person texting him.

As a bird, came Tiernan's response a second later. Nik let out a breath he didn't realize he'd been holding.

The train pulled around the corner and Nik bit his lip as he typed in his response.

Wanna meet?

It was crazy. He was crazy. He barely knew Tiernan; they'd hooked up once in some weird fluke of the moment. Nik still hadn't quite explained the last time, the desperate urge he'd felt when Tiernan had kissed him. It had felt good to be wanted, though, for just a moment. It had felt good to stop thinking about everything in his life. He wondered if he could have that again.

The train screeched to a stop in front of him and a blast of cold air hit his face as the door opened. He didn't get inside, waiting for Tiernan's reply.

It came a few seconds later and Nik's heart jumped excitedly.

5038 Hardy Dr

Pulling up the address, Nik checked the maps on the light rail and turned, crossing to the other side of the platform instead.

Tiernan's apartment building looked like it came straight out of a magazine, much nicer than the apartment Nik was staying in for the summer. Palm trees surrounded the whole lot, a volleyball net was set up over lush grass, and the pool glistened, white umbrellas hovering over empty chairs. Jennifer had said some professional swimmers had sponsors, which meant they got paid a hell of a lot more than a magazine intern did. Nik was lucky to get paid at all. Tiernan must have had some good sponsors.

Nik checked the apartment number Tiernan had sent him. It wasn't an apartment building like Nik was used to — towering over the street with a buzzer. Instead, it sprawled in separate buildings with four apartments in each. The landscaping he passed was pristine and the pool sparkled beyond the fence in the setting sun.

Near the pool, Tiernan had said, around the back of the complex. Number twelve two-oh-seven. Second floor. There were only two floors in each building.

Nik found it with only minimal confusion. All the buildings looked identical, from the beige stucco to the same exact number and position of windows in the front.

Nik knocked on the door, stepping back to wait. He didn't let himself second-guess why he was there. If he did that, he would turn around and leave, letting Andre get the best of him. Luckily, he didn't have to wait long. Tiernan opened the door a minute later, an easy smile on his face.

"Come in," he said, stepping back to allow Nik inside.

It was nice and cool in the apartment, and Nik took a moment to take in the main room. It was bigger than his apartment, with nicer furniture. Beige carpet spread from the living room to the hallway. A large TV faced the squishy brown couch, and the blinds over the sliding glass door clacked against each other as Nik stepped over and pushed them aside. The balcony overlooked the pool, sunlight glittering off the water, palm trees swaying in the breeze.

There was no pretense this time. Nik wasn't here to take photographs, or do an interview, or wonder who painted the picture on the wall. He could feel Tiernan behind him as he stared out the window, but Tiernan didn't speak. They weren't there to talk.

Turning, Nik took in Tiernan for the first time, really looked at him, since arriving. Tiernan didn't seem surprised that Nik was there. He simply stood in the middle of the living room, having followed him halfway to the balcony window.

"You look… different," he said finally.

"It's the clothes." Tiernan smiled and Nik realized he was right. He'd never seen Tiernan wearing actual clothes. They weren't fancy — just a faded blue shirt and a pair of jeans — but it made him look more human, less god-like than he did when he only had on his suit. Tiernan tilted his head to the side. "You want a drink?"

"No," Nik said simply, reaching for the hem of his shirt and pulling it off. He hadn't come here to drink.

Chapter 6:
Instant Gratification

Nik dropped his shirt on the floor, catching the way Tiernan's eyes followed the movement. A thrill ran through his stomach at Tiernan's heated gaze. There was no question there.

Before his shirt hit the floor, Tiernan's hands were on him. Tiernan crowded him up against the wall, just past an opening that probably led to the bedroom, but Nik wasn't thinking about the bedroom. His mind was on Tiernan's hands, smooth fingers gripping his waist, pushing him up. His mind was on the way Tiernan's mouth collided with his, hot and hard, everything Nik wanted from this. He didn't want soft, slow, questioning.

Tiernan's knuckles grazed over his rib cage, drawing out a moan that Nik didn't try to stifle, hands gliding over his pounding heart then sliding down his back, tracing the notches in his spine. Nik pushed into him, taking what he wanted, biting at Tiernan's mouth as his hands scrambled for his shirt. He had to work harder this time to get Tiernan undressed.

Tiernan was pliant, letting Nik strip off his shirt, get him down to half-dressed.

The way he should be, Nik caught himself thinking as his hands dug into Tiernan's waist, eager to feel his body again.

He'd thought a lot about Tiernan's body since that first time they'd met; replayed the way water dripped down his chiseled abs, slid down his long, tanned torso to his cock trapped inside those tiny shorts. His hands followed the V cut in Tiernan's stomach, to the swell of his ass under his jeans. He pulled Tiernan in closer, biting back a gasp as their hips met in a harsh clash of fabric, rough against his hard cock.

"Fuck," he cursed, distracted from the throbbing in his dick as Tiernan nipped at his jaw, a hot, wet tongue sliding down his neck, teeth following in a way that made him ache with want. It had been so long since he'd been able to just let go.

Tiernan's hands on his ass pulled them into an unsteady rhythm, Nik's cock pressed to his thigh, still too confined in his jeans, but he wouldn't last long if Tiernan didn't stop the frantic way he rutted against him.

Everything was too hot, the air radiating heat between them, heavy and frenetic. The way Tiernan kissed him, mouths sliding together recklessly, a slip of tongues and lips and teeth biting and sucking. Nik never pushed him away, only pulled him in. More, he wanted more.

Nik tugged at Tiernan's jeans, getting a hand between them, stopping the thrust of Tiernan's hips, buying himself more time. He didn't want to come in his jeans. No, he wanted to come with Tiernan deep inside him, fucking him until he couldn't breathe, until he couldn't think.

"Fuck me," he breathed, pulling away from Tiernan's mouth, and Tiernan followed for half a second, eyes half-closed, breath hot against Nik's cheek. "Now."

Tiernan mumbled something that might have been a curse, but Nik didn't have time to ask as Tiernan pushed him away from the wall, past the opening and backwards into a bedroom. He didn't get a good look at the interior before he fell backwards onto a bed, soft and fluffy, the duvet billowing up to envelope him.

There was no slow-down, no pause where Tiernan took him all in, no steady tease of dropping his pants. Tiernan shoved his down as Nik kicked his own off, leaving him naked, all sharp angles exposed, cock hard and dripping in his hand as he reached for it and Tiernan climbed over him, stretching to the box of condoms under the bed. Tiernan's stomach brushed over Nik's prick, and Nik sucked in a sharp breath. He wanted to see Tiernan's mouth around his dick, see Tiernan spread out beneath him, begging for Nik to suck him off. But they didn't have time.

Tiernan's warm hand smoothed over Nik's side when he came back, pushing him over onto his stomach. Nik's cock was trapped between his stomach and the silky softness of Tiernan's duvet — seriously, what the fuck was it made out of? It was like some high-end hotel shit. He squirmed as a thrill of anticipation stole over him when Tiernan's fingers played down his spine, the pop of the lube cap, Tiernan's cock pressing up against the back of his thighs.

Nik closed his eyes. For once, he wasn't thinking about home, about Andre, Rae, his mom. It was just him and Tiernan, alone in his apartment, seconds away from being fucked. He pressed his face to Tiernan's pillow, breathing in the smell of him — remnants of chlorine and something tropical.

Tiernan didn't ask how he wanted it, and Nik was glad. He just wanted it, anyway Tiernan was willing to give it. Nik wanted Tiernan spreading his thighs, sliding in between them, the crinkle of a condom wrapper over their panted breaths. He wanted Tiernan's fingers opening him up, quick but steady, no time to guess, to wonder.

His cock throbbed and he shuddered as Tiernan slipped a finger inside. He groaned, pushing back into Tiernan's touch, impatient for more. He heard the air conditioner kick on, but he felt hot, a flush on his skin, sweat on his brow as Tiernan slid his finger out and pushed in against him, the tip of his cock teasing his entrance.

The air pressed in around him as Tiernan pushed inside, slowly once then harder. Each thrust made Nik's toes curl, the tight heat crawling up his skin until he could only moan into Tiernan's pillow and clench the sheets in his fists. He was glad Tiernan never slowed, fucking him so deliciously that his stomach curled and he bit the pillow as he cursed, "*Fuck.*"

His breath came in short gasps, panting as he ground his hips back, riding Tiernan as much as he could with his face pressed to the mattress. He heard Tiernan's exhalations, sharp and short, a stream of curses falling from his mouth as he stroked Nik's back, fucking him into oblivion.

"Fuck yes, Nik, *God,*" Tiernan muttered, thrusting deeper inside him until Nik couldn't feel anything other than the fullness of Tiernan's cock inside him, the pressure in his ass, a burn he'd feel tomorrow.

His prick twitched painfully, a reminder of how hard he was, how much he needed to come. Reaching down, he jerked, sucking in a sharp breath at the pressure building in his cock.

Tiernan moved quickly, mumbling praises about his ass, fingers pressing into his spine, grip tight on his hip. Nik closed his eyes, listening to Tiernan's words, hand tight on his cock, desperate now. He wasn't Nik the weird art kid here. He wasn't Nik the disappointment, Nik the reason Mom's fucked up. He was Nik *your fucking ass is so fucking hot — shit, God, I'm gonna come.*

Tiernan came first. Nik could feel the push of his hips, the way his hands tightened on his skin, leaving bruises for the next day. Arching back, Nik's hand moved faster. Jesus, he just needed to come, and he did, all over Tiernan's ridiculously soft duvet cover.

Cursing, he gasped for breath as his release coursed over him, tight and hot and sudden, like a bottle uncorked. He dropped to the mattress with a sigh, his body relaxed and loose. He heard Tiernan flop down beside him and it took effort to turn over to look at him.

Tiernan had his hands behind his head, gazing at the ceiling, half a smile on his face. He glanced over when Nik turned.

"You're good," he said simply, like he told everyone that after sex.

It was nice to just relax, to not think for a little while. Even if it was here, with Tiernan, doing the one thing he'd promised himself he wouldn't do.

"You talk a lot," Nik said finally.

Tiernan laughed briefly. "So I've been told. I figure people like the compliments." He paused, then rolled into Nik, cupping his jaw and pressing a kiss to his cheek. "You really do have a great ass."

Nik couldn't help smiling at that. It wasn't true, of course. He hardly had much of an ass at all, especially compared to Tiernan, whose ass Greek sculptors would have worshiped. He didn't bother correcting Tiernan, though, and only stretched.

"What the fuck is this duvet?" he asked, running his hand over the dark blue fabric. "It's, like, the softest thing I've ever felt."

"Egyptian cotton," Tiernan replied, smoothing over a few wrinkles. "Heaven on a mattress."

"Guess your sponsors pay well enough for Egyptian cotton," Nik said. He'd probably have to work six extra shifts to even afford something like that, and if he was working extra hours, it would go towards paying for school.

"Actually, my sister bought these last year when she came to visit. She said it was disgraceful for a twenty-two year old to have the same sheets from high school. She also got me a vegetable peeler, which I have yet to use." Tiernan sounded amused. Nik caught him watching him, green eyes flicking down his face.

He'd stayed too long, he decided, sitting up and looking around for his jeans. Tiernan didn't follow.

"Maybe you want that drink now?" he said from behind Nik, a hand brushing over his back, and Nik tensed for a second.

Nik hesitated. He really should get back to his apartment and pretend he had a pinch of self-control. A vibrating sound reached his ears and his eyes fell on his jeans on the floor. The vibrating didn't stop — someone calling. His heart contracted painfully. Probably Andre to yell at him.

"Okay," he said, slipping off the bed and grabbing his jeans. He silenced the phone without bothering to look. Tiernan rolled off the bed as Nik pulled on his jeans and shoved back his hair from where it fell in his eyes. He could already tell he'd be sore tomorrow.

Nik left Tiernan to pull on his pants, wandering into the living room. The sun had set but it wasn't quite dark yet. Lights had come on around the pool and a few girls in bikinis lay out around it. Behind him, Tiernan crossed to the fridge and pulled out two beers, cracking them open against the counter top.

Nik grabbed his shirt from the floor, pulling it on as he turned. He took the bottle Tiernan offered.

"Thought athletes weren't supposed to drink."

Tiernan smiled, collapsing on the couch and taking a swig. "Swimmers need to carbo-load," he said, tipping his beer to Nik.

"Not sure that's what they mean." Nik took a sip and gazed at the large painting behind the couch — some southwest scene. He wondered if it had come with the place.

"It's not," Tiernan assured him, propping up his feet on the coffee table. "Though I have used it as an excuse before."

Nik didn't ask about four years ago, though he wanted to. It wasn't really his business after all.

Tiernan had left his shirt off, and Nik could see the marks left by his fingernails, red and angry on his skin.

"Will your coach get mad?" he asked, nodding at the marks.

Tiernan glanced down. "They'll be mostly gone by tomorrow."

Nik moved over to the couch slowly, sinking down on the opposite end. It felt weird now that they weren't clawing at each other's clothes, just sitting here talking. He could still feel Tiernan's hands on him, Tiernan's mouth on his neck, the warmth of his thighs. He shivered, but blamed it on the air conditioning.

"You train every day?" Nik had to admit that he didn't know much about swimming or the Olympics or how any of it worked. He'd never really watched; never really had the time (or cable) to watch. He remembered vaguely watching bits and pieces in the summer library programs he'd gone to so that he didn't have to be home.

"Pretty much," Tiernan said, nodding slowly. "At least six hours a day, not including gym time."

"Is it worth it?" Nik couldn't even imagine swimming for six hours a day. He could barely doggy paddle, let alone swim a one hundred meter race in fifty-one seconds.

Tiernan drained his beer. "Completely."

In his pocket, his phone vibrated sharply. Nik jabbed at it, annoyed. Couldn't Andre just leave him alone? For a few hours at least?

"Work?" Tiernan asked lazily, looking completely relaxed as he stretched out. Nik wished he could be so relaxed.

"My brother," Nik muttered, taking a long drink of his beer. He grimaced at the sourness and set it aside. He'd never been much for beer, not after growing up with his mom.

"Pissing you off? I know the feeling." Tiernan didn't meet Nik's gaze when he looked over. Nik didn't ask how he knew. Tiernan's life wasn't any of his business.

"I should probably go," Nik said at length, glancing out the window. The sky was steadily darkening now with the sun gone.

Tiernan made an agreeing noise, but he didn't say anything until Nik pushed himself off the couch.

"Let me know when you're ready to go again." Tiernan smirked at him, getting to his feet and heading for the door.

Nik was surprised at the casual way Tiernan offered, but he said nothing about it.

"I, uh, I'll see you," he managed to say as Tiernan opened the door for him.

"You will."

When the door was shut behind him, Nik smiled to himself. For something he'd said he wouldn't do, he certainly didn't regret it.

Chapter 7:
Bibliophile

Nik stared unseeingly at the images on his screen, pictures of Tiernan staring back at him. Around him, the office lacked its usual bustle, too late for the regular employees to still be hanging around; a copy machine beeped somewhere in the depths of the office. Out one of the distant windows, the sun cast an orange and pink glow inside, gilding over the empty desks and chairs.

Nik blinked at his computer. He was supposed to be editing, but he kept getting lost in thoughts of Tiernan, the memory of Tiernan's hands on his hips, shoving him down onto the mattress, pushing inside him. Normally, he wouldn't have lingered over the memory, but it was the second time it had happened. Second was a big number, one Nik never usually reached with guys. He kind of preferred it that way.

He hadn't called Tiernan yet. It had been two days. He didn't know what he was supposed to say.

It wasn't that he didn't want to do it again. Tiernan was the hottest guy who'd ever talked to him, let alone wanted to sleep with him. Nik had too many other things to worry about, though. There was Rae, who never outright asked him to come home, but it was always there when they talked. There was the internship, where he was supposed to be acting like a professional. Professionals did not sleep with their subjects. Well, Nik admitted to himself as he stared at Tiernan's chiseled abs on the screen, some photographers did. Some photographers only became photographers so they could sleep with models. Nik had heard plenty of jokes to that affect when he told people his major.

That wasn't why wanted to be a photographer.

He needed to call Tiernan or something, just to let him know... Nik didn't know what. He wasn't really sure what was going on, and he didn't want to think about it too hard, or too many questions would pop up, questions he didn't want to know the answer to.

"You staying late?"

Nik looked up from his monitor at a voice behind him, swallowing down the momentary surprise.

Brooke stood behind him. She had already taken off her work jacket, leaving her in a brightly-colored dress that fell to her knees, exposing the watercolor dandelion tattooed on her upper arm.

"Gotta finish these," he replied, nodding at the screen. He had to get these edited for the next update Jennifer put out. The magazine wanted at least weekly updates.

Brooke leaned in over his shoulder and Nik caught a whiff of sweet perfume. "They look good to me. Unless you're planning on 'shopping in some more abs. Not that he needs it." She smiled and Nik wondered briefly if she was hitting on him. That would be a first. "Hey, so some of us are going to hit Mill Avenue if you want to come."

Over her shoulder, Nik saw a group of interns, mostly people he hadn't spoken to, lingering by the door.

"Um," he said, hesitating. In college, he never had time to really go out — after classes and work, he was generally just too tired to drag himself anywhere else. His roommates were usually entertainment enough. Ty did performance art, and often practiced in the living room.

He did have editing to do, but as he stared up at her bubbly expression, he didn't want to do it. For once, he'd been invited out, and there was nothing stopping him from going.

"Sure."

"Great." Reaching over him, she clicked save and closed the program. "Let's go."

Nik didn't have much of a choice but to follow her and leave his work behind.

"No Long Island Iced Teas!" Madison called after Ryan as he left to get the drinks. "Right, Alyssa?"

One of the girls Nik didn't know, a brunette with short-cut hair and a flat nose, scowled across the table at Madison.

"It was one time, shut up."

"You're from New York, right?" Brooke asked Nik, ignoring the bickering going on beside her. The rest of the group crowded around a table near the stage.

Nik wasn't sure what kind of place this was — a bar or a club — but the guy at the door had barely glanced at his ID. The bar was dimly-lit and sconces with brown and yellow glass hung on the walls. The floor was stuffed with tables around the edges except for a small square cleared out in front of the stage. Nik shifted on the uncomfortable wooden chair. The walls were all wood-paneled, which only added to the dimness and feeling of a 1970s living room.

"You made out with half the bar," Madison said with a smirk, and a guy next to her snorted. Alyssa only glared in return.

"Sort of," Nik answered Brooke. "I go to school in Chicago." 'Sort of' didn't really cover New York, but Nik didn't want to get into it with total strangers.

"Ryan's from Chicago," Madison piped in as he returned and passed out the drinks.

"I moved here when I was five," he replied blithely, sliding into his seat. "I don't remember anything."

"Which school?" Brooke talked over them, pushing a bottle towards Nik.

Nik took the drink, a bottle of sour-tasting beer that he set down quickly. The top of the table had been scratched in several places from years of use. "School of the Art Institute of Chicago."

"Fancy," she commented, twisting the tiny red straw in her glass, something clear and topped with cherries. "I'm up at Northern Arizona. Not impressive but at least the weather's better."

Nik wouldn't know. He hadn't been out of Phoenix and he doubted he'd ever get anywhere up north. He couldn't help thinking he shouldn't be there, surrounded by interns he didn't know. He'd never been great at making friends.

"NAU sucks," Ryan declared. "Everyone knows U of A is way better."

"Tucson smells like trash," Madison said to the agreement of several people around the table. "ASU is clearly the best."

"Yeah, all those videos shot in the locker rooms sure are appealing," Alyssa drawled.

"That was, like, twenty years ago. Is no one ever going to get over that?"

"They discovered Pluto in Flagstaff," Brooke piped in, to which Madison scoffed.

"Which isn't even a planet."

"So you're from here?" Nik asked Brooke. He didn't want to get in the middle of a school rivalry, which was clearly a big deal.

"University of Arizona is a public ivy," Ryan pointed out to Madison, who rolled her eyes. "And we've had eight Pulitzer Prize winners."

"My parents live in Chandler," Brooke said, taking a sip of her drink. "Which is why I'm taking an internship here instead of somewhere cool like New York or LA. Free room and board. Can't really complain."

What it must be like to have supportive parents, Nik couldn't imagine. On stage, a band was setting up, guys in dark clothing, their hair too long. The bassist shoved his hair back as he plugged in his instrument and plucked out a low melody.

"You're lucky," Brooke told him. Madison and Ryan had stopped arguing as the band started and they slid away to listen in closer. Nik felt less awkward now that it was just him and Brooke. She didn't appear to be interested in the band.

"Lucky?" Lucky was not something Nik had ever been. Luck hadn't gotten him where he was. He didn't believe in it.

"You've got this great internship. You get to travel. You got to choose your college. I really wanted to go to UCLA."

"Why didn't you?" Nik wouldn't call any of that luck. He had never thought of it as fortunate, since he'd worked so hard for all of it, and kept working to keep it.

"Because it cost a fortune," she said plainly. "But it's okay. More money for books."

Nik perked up. "You read a lot?" Most people he knew thought books were a pointless waste of time when there was the internet. Andre always said Nik needed to stop living in fiction and live in the real world.

"Oh my God, way too much," she admitted. "I just can't resist new books, you know? It's like they're calling me. Have you read the new Asbury Series book?"

"Wait, there's a new one?" Nik had read the rest in high school, tucked away in the library, devouring every page, getting lost in Grace Asbury's adventures in her kingdom, where she was the rightful ruler by birth. In the first two books, she'd been deposed before she could even take the crown and had her memory wiped by the evil ruler who took her place. Nik had often longed to have his memory wiped so he could start new.

"It's the third in the series," Brooke said eagerly, and Nik wouldn't have pegged her for a fantasy reader, not with her perfectly curled hair and bubbly personality. "It's amazing. You have to read it, like, right now. I will lend you my copy."

"Sure," Nik agreed, slightly surprised. She was so eager to share with him, so different than what he was used to. "That'd be great."

She beamed, tossing her hair over her shoulder. "Then I'll have someone to talk to about it. I love Grace so much. She's so smart and independent and resourceful. I probably would have died already if I were in the book. And, of course, I love Cam. He's so dumb, but I love him anyway."

"He's like Ron," Nik said without thinking. Normally, he didn't reveal to strangers his weird love of young adult books. They'd always been his escape, but Andre had always mocked him for reading, so he'd taken to hiding it. Now, it was just a habit.

"Ron from *Harry Potter*?" Brooke asked, eyes lighting up. "I *love Harry Potter*. It's so good."

Nik smiled at her enthusiasm, so much more than he'd ever allowed himself to show when talking about books. Rae read sometimes, but usually it was just books about the human psyche, which bored Nik to tears. He'd rather read about fantastical lands and pretend he could live there instead.

It was just nice to talk to someone about it without having to hide how much he really cared. It was something he could do with Rae, but lately, he couldn't talk to her without feeling the heft of guilt on his conscience afterward.

"Pretty sure it's my favorite book ever," Nik admitted. "I can't believe it's been four years since the last *Fantastic Beasts* movie came out." He'd sneaked into the theater to see it, dragging Rae with him, and he'd watched in awe and slight disappointment that this was probably the last Harry Potter they'd get, unless JK Rowling finally did write a Marauders prequel.

"What House are you in?" Brooke asked immediately, and Nik couldn't help smiling.

"Slytherin and Wampus."

"Ravenclaw and Horned Serpent."

From the little he knew of Brooke, it made perfect sense. He found himself smiling as they talked. It was so easy to talk to her, almost like talking to Rae. For a moment, it felt as though a weight had been lifted, one he hadn't even known he was carrying, a brief respite from the heaviness of everything, the confusion over what to do about Tiernan, the worry about Rae, the anger at Andre. It was all gone as Brooke grinned and talked about how she was probably more of a Slytherclaw.

"So do you sell your photos?" Brooke asked a minute later, changing the subject and pulling out her phone, bringing up his Instagram.

Surprised, Nik watched her swipe through his pictures. How had she found it? He guessed he shouldn't have been surprised. After all, he had looked up Tiernan's, too.

"Sometimes," he said as she scrolled past a shot of a sad homeless man Nik had taken back in Chicago. "I have a website."

"Find it for me," she said immediately, switching to the internet browser and handing him the phone.

Nik typed in the address and handed it back. "It's nothing special, just some code I threw together."

"These are awesome," she said, sincere, taking back the phone as the website came up.

Nik didn't keep it as updated as he should — most of his photos just went on Instagram instead — but he had a couple years' worth of photos there, since high school.

"I run a blog," Brooke said, skimming through the photos. "It's mostly current events stuff, opinion pieces, pop culture, but people really like interviews and features. Maybe I could feature you and your work."

"Why?" Nik asked before he could stop himself. It was a habit he needed to break.

Brooke smiled at him, miffed. "Because you're good." She scooted her chair closer and Nik's nostrils filled with her perfume. For a second, Nik froze, unsure. Was that what all this had been?

"Um, Brooke," he said finally when she didn't move back, gazing at him with her eyes wide. "I'm not really... I'm kind of... gay."

She laughed, surprising him. "I know," she said, flipping her hair back and crossing her legs. "I'm actually trying to get David over there to ask me out." She jerked her head toward the stage, just barely, to where one of the other interns was watching them, a crease in his brow.

A wave of relief washed over Nik and he laughed. "I thought you were hitting on me."

"Don't get me wrong," she said quickly. "You're great, and you've got that Goth, artsy, don't-talk-to-me vibe that's very Big City, but I'd much rather geek out with you about Grace Asbury than date you."

He laughed. "So, David, huh?" He glanced at the guy still standing by the stage. He wasn't watching them now, but he glanced over every few minutes. He was good looking, Nik supposed, with short-cut brown hair and a skinny nose. Not Nik's type, but did he even have a type? Tiernan was the exact opposite of the guys Nik usually hooked up with, but finding an athletic guy in an art school was like finding a needle in a haystack.

She took a sip of her drink. "It's been a month and he barely responds when I talk to him."

"Maybe he's shy," Nik suggested. Giving advice about guys wasn't his strong suit. He was usually the one who needed it.

"Or he doesn't like me," she said simply, finishing her drink and pushing it to the center of the table.

"You should ask him out," Nik said instead. Brooke was as pretty as any girl he'd seen in Arizona, and she was nice to boot. There was no way David could be that stupid.

"Oh, right, because it's so easy," she said, chancing a glance at him, but David seemed focused on the band playing.

Nik couldn't really help. He wasn't sure he'd ever been on a real date, and he definitely had never asked anyone out on one. The thought of facing rejection head-on made his stomach turn. "What would Grace Asbury do?"

Brooke shot him a look, lips twisting against the smile there. "I think I'll stick to the slow method," she said. Nik paused a minute before sliding an arm over her shoulders and ignoring her surprised expression.

"Maybe we can speed it up a little."

She smiled after a second and leaned into him as Nik gestured to the bartender for another drink for her.

"So tell me about Chicago," she said, and Nik smiled as David frowned at the stage.

"Gummy bears and lemon sorbet?" Brooke asked as they walked down the street. Even after dark, the heat was oppressive, like it weighed them down, pressing into their shoulders. "You're very strange."

Nik licked the ice cream off his spoon as a group of college-age kids pushed past them, loud and rowdy, and he stepped aside to let them pass. The street was busy, filled with kids their age, heading for clubs or shopping in the too-brightly lit stores they passed.

"I almost never had ice cream growing up, so I get to put whatever I want in it."

"How could you not have ice cream?" she asked, affronted. "It's a kid staple."

They passed a clothing store and kept walking. Nik had no idea where they were going. They weren't going anywhere in particular, and it felt nice to just wander around with no destination in mind. It felt like when Nik was a kid and he'd disappeared to the park for hours just so he wouldn't have to be home.

He shrugged. "Not in my house." He didn't want to go into how they'd barely had food let alone treats like ice cream. Almost out of habit, he checked his phone, but there were no texts from Rae. She hadn't texted since the other night.

I'm eating ice cream, he texted her after a second, avoiding a pole as they walked.

Lemon sorbet? came her reply just as quickly and Nik smiled to himself. It was nice to pretend, at least for a minute, that things could be normal.

"Who's that?" Brooke asked as they turned a corner. The lights were dimmer here, a little less welcoming.

"My sister," he said, typing in his response: *Anything else would be a sin.*

"Older? Younger?"

They took another turn and Nik recognized the parking lot. The rest of the group had gone off to some dance club, but flashing lights and techno-pop wasn't really his idea of a good time. Brooke had thankfully offered to drive him home.

"Technically, older, by ten minutes."

I've got the churro guy in the park wrapped around my finger. Free churros, came Rae's text.

A+, he texted back and tucked the phone away as they reached the lot.

"Cool," Brooke said. "I always wanted a sibling. I got a dog instead, named her Luna."

Nik smiled as they reached her car and she unlocked it. The lights flashed in the dark parking lot and he slid inside. His phone vibrated again with Rae's response and he pulled it out as Brooke started the car.

I miss you.

Nik stared at the words on the screen, a sinking feeling in his chest and he put the phone away without replying. He couldn't explain how three words could bring him down so quickly.

"What kind of dog?" he forced himself to ask, and Brooke flashed him a smile.

He wasn't listening to her reply, though, as they pulled out of the dark lot and onto the street. His hand curled around the phone in his pocket and it didn't vibrate again.

Chapter 8:
Shared Interests

"Are you seriously torturing yourself with that?"

Tiernan clicked out of the video on his tablet as Sam rounded his chair. It wasn't usual that Tiernan was at the pool before anyone else, especially Coach, but he hadn't been able to sleep last night. He'd woken up before sunrise and lay in bed until he couldn't stand it anymore. He'd rather be in the pool than thinking about trials in a few days. He was better when he didn't think.

That hadn't stopped him from pulling up the old video of last Olympic trials. He didn't know why he still watched it, watched him finish sluggishly, in tenth place when he should have been first. He still remembered the sinking in his stomach, the nausea that wasn't solely due to the large quantity of alcohol he'd consumed the night before.

Last time, the night before trials, he'd gone out to some bar in Charlottesville, gotten drunk off Jaeger bombs, and picked up some guy with a tongue ring. He barely remembered that night, but he'd never forget the day after. Not his finest moment — and there was always seemed to be a never-ending stream of people to remind him of it.

"That's debatable," he said, tucking the tablet away. He preferred not to talk about his previous failures, even with Sam, who might have understood. "You're here early."

"Could say the same." Sam gave him a look that Tiernan didn't particularly appreciate, as though Sam was trying to figure out if he was okay. Sam knew him well enough by now to know when things were off, but Tiernan brushed off his concern with a smile.

"Just thought I'd get some laps in before everybody else crowds the lanes." Really, he just wanted an excuse not to answer his phone when his sister called him for the fourth time about his tux measurements and to drill in the importance of bringing an "appropriate" date, as she called it.

Tiernan had bigger things to worry about than who his date would be.

He needed to get his times down, to perfect his technique, and he didn't have much time left to do it. That was what kept him awake at night, not the lament of Ella's bridesmaid dress color choices.

"You ready?" Sam asked, rubbing his head. Sam kept his head shaved so as not to deal with the hassle of swimming caps. Tiernan thought he had a point some days, but he liked his hair too much, even if it always smelled of chlorine.

Sam's knee bounced as he sat across from Tiernan, looking as not-ready as Tiernan felt, a nervous twitch to his fingers that Tiernan rarely saw. It happened to everyone around this time, and Tiernan didn't like seeing it in Sam. It made him feel even more nervous.

"Of course I'm ready!" he said instead, reaching over to hit Sam's knee. "I've been training for this my whole life. Don't worry, Sam. Trials are simple, just like any other meet."

It was a total lie, but it helped the knot that had been in his chest all morning. If he could keep reminding himself of that, everything would be fine. He just had to make it through trials. It would be smooth sailing after that. Well, relatively-speaking.

Sam was silent for a moment, nervously rubbing his hands over his knees, like Tiernan's words hadn't eased his worries at all.

"Do you regret it?"

"What?"

Sam nodded at the tablet. "Last time."

Most of the time, Tiernan tried not to think about it. It didn't do him any good to dwell on his past mistakes. He still remembered the looks of disappointment on his parents' faces when he'd turned up at their house, drunk from the plane ride, after trials had ended. It was almost as bad as when he'd come out to them the year before, but as usual, they sucked it up and pretended it didn't happen. That was even worse.

"Live and learn," he said, brushing Sam's question aside. "Come on, let's get in a few laps. Twenty bucks says I'll beat you."

Sam shook his head but hauled himself up from his chair. "You're on, Champ."

Tiernan smirked, following Sam to the pool. At least in the pool, he didn't need to think.

"Trials are in three days," Jennifer said, setting her phone between them on the table, the app already recording. Tiernan tore his eyes from Nik across the cafe, waiting at the counter for their drinks. He hadn't seen him since that night, and the memory lingered as Nik glanced at him. "On a scale of one to ten, how prepared are you?"

"Ten," Tiernan answered confidently. It wouldn't do to give the press any reason to doubt. As nice as Jennifer was, she was still a journalist and Tiernan had been burned before by reporters. "I've done everything I can to prepare."

According to Coach, he was about ninety-nine percent where he needed to be, but a lot could change between now and Sunday. Tomorrow, they flew out to Florida to get an early start, the lay of the land, and to beat out any potential jet lag.

"I'm still amazed how much work it really takes," Jennifer said, scribbling down some notes and shooting a brief smile at Nik as he returned with the drinks. Nik slid into his chair next to Jennifer, across from Tiernan, eyes darting to him quickly. "You've been training practically your whole life."

"Since I was thirteen," he said with a nod. "You can't just do it half-assed, if you want to really make it."

"What did your parents think of the whole swimming thing?"

He smiled behind his coffee. "I think they were just glad I was out of the house. They were really supportive in high school."

"But not now?"

Tiernan cursed to himself. He probably shouldn't have said that with a journalist recording his every word. Sometimes he forgot who he was talking to. Jennifer made things so easy, and with Nik sitting right there, it didn't feel like an interview.

For a long time, he'd been wary of press, especially after the last trials when he couldn't go online without seeing his name splashed somewhere, speculating about what had gone wrong. He supposed he hadn't been wrong to stay away from them the past couple years; he had only agreed to this spotlight as a way to turn things around. If he got good press this time, if he erased the memory of four years ago, he could change things.

"They're supportive still," he said quickly. "It's just they've got other things to think about. I'm not the only Golden Child."

Tiernan's gaze drifted to Nik. He wondered if he had supportive parents.

Nik looked the same as Tiernan remembered, with the dark circles under his eyes, like he never got enough sleep, shoulders hunched slightly, one hand wrapped around the strap of his camera bag. He didn't look like the kind of guy who would demand to be fucked, who would dig his fingernails into Tiernan's skin then worry about it afterward. He looked more like he'd rather be sulking in a dimly-lit bar than chatting in a bright, sunny coffee shop.

Nik's teeth closed over his bottom lip as Tiernan watched him, worrying it between sips of his iced coffee.

"You mean your sister," Jennifer asked, checking something in her notes. "Ella?"

"Yeah, Ella."

Jennifer scribbled something while Nik tapped his cup with his fingernails. He seemed preoccupied, as he turned his gaze to the window.

"So is your family coming to trials?"

"No," he said, turning back to Jennifer. "They don't usually come out for trials. Maybe if I make it to the Olympics."

"Your sister went last time," Jennifer said. "Are you two close?"

Tiernan hesitated. "We have our differences, but what siblings don't? For the most part, she's been supportive. She's getting married next month, though, and it's been a bit of a nightmare."

"Really?" Jennifer asked curiously, and Nik's eyes went back to Tiernan. "You don't like weddings?"

Tiernan finished his coffee and wished it was something stronger. He could use it after all the phone calls he'd been through with Ella. Why she couldn't ask their mother's opinion on flowers and appetizers was beyond him. "When your sister is the Bridezilla, not so much."

"What's she doing?"

Tiernan sighed. "What isn't she doing? First, she scheduled it the week before I would leave for France, then she wants opinions on colors, and flowers, and flower arranging. Like I know anything about that. Being gay does not automatically make me a wedding planner."

"So are you planning on going?" Jennifer asked, an eyebrow raised as she pushed her phone closer to him.

"Think she'd kill me if I didn't," he joked. "On top of everything else, now I've got to find a date."

"I doubt you'll have a problem," Jennifer assured him. "If I put that in, you'll probably have a hundred people fighting for that privilege."

Tiernan laughed. "Please don't. I've never done well with set-ups."

His parents had tried a few times after he'd come out, and they constantly dropped hints about some neighbor or other's daughter.

"I'm sure we could find you a cute guy, even on short notice. You've been out for several years now," Jennifer said. "Has that affected your career at all?"

Tiernan always expected this question. It was usually the only one people were interested in since he'd come out officially. Coach had said it was no one's business but his own, but if he was going to do it, he might as well go all the way. That had been four years ago, after trials, when everyone had wanted to know what went wrong. He had felt so alone then, hiding who he was from the world, ignored by his parents. He'd overcompensated with guys, sex, alcohol so he wouldn't have to think about their disapproval, though he'd never admitted that to anyone out loud.

The press had lapped up the 'gay thing' as Ella called it. They'd chalked up his failures in trials to emotional distress, which was at least better than saying he just wasn't good enough.

Nik looked up sharply at the question, a slight crease to his eyebrows, like he was worried. He didn't need to worry. Tiernan was much more discrete about his private life these days. He didn't need the press getting wind of any relationships; they always ran them into the ground.

Tiernan shrugged. "Everybody always wants to talk about it, as if it changes the way I swim or how I train. It doesn't. All it changes is the way people perceive me, and sometimes they underestimate me, which can be a good thing. I'm definitely not the first. The first time I heard of a gay athlete, it was the Olympic Diver, Tom Daley. I was only eleven. I didn't even know they existed. I didn't even know that's what I was. But gay athletes have been around forever. The gymnastics coach here, Coach Stuart, he's well-known as a gay athlete and that hasn't stopped him from having a great career."

Jennifer nodded. "Do you get to talk much with Coach Stuart?"

Tiernan shook his head. "I've heard he's a little intense, which is saying something considering my coach is an ex-Marine."

Jennifer smiled. Beside her, Nik tapped his fingers on the table, drawing Tiernan's gaze.

Tiernan hadn't texted Nik, though he had his number saved in his phone now. He hadn't texted, but he'd spent a lot of time replaying that night as he lay in bed, a hand grasping his cock. He retraced the smooth planes of Nik's back, sharp shoulders flexing as he pushed inside him, the muffled moan into Tiernan's pillow when he came.

Yes, that memory had gotten him through several stressful days.

"I'm sure my readers are curious," Jennifer said, glancing between him and Nik, "if you have a 'type.'"

Tiernan laughed, looking away from Nik's fingers wrapped around his cup. He really shouldn't have been thinking of Nik's hands around his cock right now, with a journalist staring at him, searching for every little secret.

"No type," he assured her, shoving a hand through his hair. "I don't have that much time for dating these days. I'd rather just spend time with someone who shares my same interests."

As Jennifer nodded and wrote something down, Tiernan caught Nik's eyes. Nik said nothing, but Tiernan could swear he caught a smile there as Nik looked away.

"What interests do we share exactly?" Nik panted, lips red and swollen as Tiernan's mouth slid to his neck.

Smiling, Tiernan pulled back to let himself take a second to enjoy Nik underneath him on the couch, down to his boxers already. The blinds to the balcony were half-opened, afternoon sunlight filtering in. This was Tiernan's favorite time of day, just before sunset, when even the heat seemed to dissipate and everything turned gold.

He liked this view, he admitted, with Nik's body open to his. He ran his hands over Nik's hip bones, enjoying the way Nik squirmed. It hadn't taken long, just a few steps from Tiernan's front door to here.

"This," he said simply, swooping down to take a nipple in his mouth and suck as Nik cursed above him. He worried the skin, soothing it with his tongue a second later, pressing Nik's hips down with his hands. Nik never fought him, only pulled him closer, hands on the back of his head.

Nik's skin was smooth and soft, a fresh scent on his body, unlike the chlorine smell Tiernan could never seem to get rid of, no matter how much he showered. It was just part of the job. But Nik, Nik smelled like sweat and plain soap and something that distinctly reminded Tiernan of a big city, though he couldn't pinpoint what.

Moving down, he let his mouth trail down Nik's sternum, over his slim waist, nipping at his hip bone as Nik groaned. He'd thought about this, about getting Nik like this, less rushed than last time, for a couple days now. He hadn't thought it would be this easy.

Nik was willing enough, eagerly responding to his touches, arching into his hands, grabbing impatiently at his shoulders when Tiernan took too long lavishing his tongue on his stomach.

"Too slow," Nik growled, hauling Tiernan up to his mouth, kissing him hard, biting, messy.

Tiernan's cock twitched in his boxers, as eager as Nik's hands were against him.

"Don't be so fucking impatient," he panted, pulling away from Nik, brushing a thumb over his reddened lips before he reached down and pushed him over.

Nik rolled onto his stomach easily. "Then don't be so slow."

Tiernan smirked, pressing a kiss to Nik's spine, smoothing his hands down his sides, not bothering to hurry up. He pulled down Nik's boxers, getting them over his thighs and onto the floor.

"What's your rush? Hooking up with another swimmer after this?"

"Fuck you," Nik said, but it came out breathless as Tiernan slid his mouth down his spine, tracing each ridge with his tongue. He could feel the strain in Nik's body and wondered if he was always this tense. He wanted to make him loose, to make him forget whatever was causing him stress, just the way this worked for Tiernan.

"I'd rather fuck you," he murmured, nudging Nik onto his hands and knees, spreading his legs. He smoothed his palms over Nik's ass, admiring the curve, spreading his cheeks to reveal his entrance.

Nik tensed at the first swipe of his tongue over his entrance, then cursed under his breath and relaxed into it.

Tiernan wasn't going to brag, but he was pretty fucking good at this, if previous partners had anything to say. He lavished attention on Nik, tongue sliding inside him until Nik was panting harshly into his arm and pushing back against him. Tiernan smoothed his hands over Nik's thighs, digging into the soft flesh as he fucked Nik's ass with his tongue.

Tiernan pulled back only once to lick his palm and slide it to Nik's cock, thick and hard, hot to the touch. At this, Nik's body shuddered and he heard a quiet, "Fuck."

Tiernan's cock throbbed, ignored. He squeezed it with his free hand, for just a second. Tiernan moved back in, licking and sucking, listening to Nik's strained gasps. From the way Nik's breaths came in sharp pants, he wouldn't last long.

Moving back, Tiernan shoved off his own boxers and grabbed the condom he'd tossed on the coffee table earlier. He was more prepared this time, spreading lube on his cock and lining himself up with Nik's ass. The first push squeezed tight around his prick, and he closed his eyes at the heat enveloping his cock. Sometimes he forgot how good this was — he'd significantly cut down on his fucking around since buckling down on his training the last year. No fuck was worth an Olympic medal, his coach would say, though not in those particular words.

Tiernan wasn't even embarrassed when he only made it a few minutes before coming, a hand tight on Nik's thigh. He rode out the climax deep inside Nik, hips pushing against him. Nik groaned beneath him, reaching down to jerk himself off, coming with a shudder a minute later.

Nik slid into the couch, letting out a long breath, as Tiernan pulled out and tossed the condom in the trash. Tiernan collapsed against the couch, arms spread over the back. He didn't care that the blinds were open.

Nik moved after a minute, pushing himself up next to Tiernan. His face was red, a flush running down his shoulders, a sheen of sweat on his neck, and Tiernan smiled to himself. Frowning, Nik grabbed a few tissues from the box on the coffee table and wiped himself off.

Tiernan was too content to do anything other than watch Nik fuss. Nik stopped after a minute, sinking back into the couch.

They were silent for a moment until Nik shifted, reaching for his boxers and pulling them on.

"Your family's not coming to trials?" he asked, absently rubbing the spot on his neck where Tiernan had left a mark.

"Nah," Tiernan said, stretching out instead of getting dressed. He wasn't embarrassed by his body; he was practically naked most of the time anyway. "It's a long way to go for something..." He stopped before he could say, 'something that might not happen.' That wasn't going to happen this time.

Nik didn't probe him, looking preoccupied as he glanced out the sliding glass door. "You get along with your sister?"

He shrugged. "Most of the time, when she's not being a pain in the ass." He was sure he had about a million messages waiting for him about colors of vests and ties and things he couldn't care less about. "Why she had to get married in July, I don't know."

Nik glanced at him. "Didn't she know you'd be competing?"

"Yeah," he said with a frown. She knew. Everyone knew, but they didn't seem to care. Her wedding was more important than the thing he'd been working towards since he was thirteen. Buying her a silver tea kettle (that she would never fucking use, Tiernan knew perfectly well) was more important than the Olympics. They all expected him to fail again, he knew it. It wasn't exactly the confidence booster he would have liked at this stage of the game. "What about your family? Just the brother?"

Nik made a face. "Three brothers, twin sister."

"Jesus." Tiernan could barely deal with one sister, let alone three other siblings. "How do you do it?"

Nik almost laughed. "I moved halfway across the country from them. That's how I do it."

"Must be nice to have a big family," Tiernan said, thinking out loud. "When you're pissed at one, you just go hang out with another." Growing up, he'd wished several times to be an only child, but there were times, especially when his parents insisted on setting him up with yet another friend's daughter, that he was glad he had Ella to be the buffer and stop their hare-brained schemes.

"I mostly only talk to Rae," Nik muttered, frowning at the sofa. "She's the only sane one."

Tiernan smiled. "Do you have, like, a twin bond?"

"Fuck off," Nik said, rolling his eyes, but Tiernan could swear he caught a smile.

"I bet everyone asks you that, huh?" he asked, propping his chin on Nik's shoulder and watching Nik sigh.

"Everyone," he agreed with a frown.

"But you like your sister? Get along with her?"

Nik shrugged, and Tiernan followed the line of his jaw up to his mouth, the bump in his nose, his dark eyelashes brushing against his cheeks when he blinked.

"Usually. She was kind of my only friend growing up."

Tiernan's eyebrows furrowed and he pushed Nik's hair back. "That's kind of depressing."

"No, it was a good thing," Nik assured him. "If you knew my family, you'd understand why."

The way he said it, Tiernan didn't think he should ask, though he wanted to. He wanted to know what made Nik's forehead crease like that.

"I think you deserve lots of friends," he said instead, pulling Nik to him and pressing a kiss to his lips. "Everybody does." He kissed him again, deeper. He really needed to pack for the flight tomorrow but he'd rather stay on the couch with Nik, pretending he didn't have to face his fate in a few days.

Nik kissed him this time, tongue sliding against his until Tiernan felt his cock stirring with interest.

"I'll work on it," Nik said, pulling away, his fingers falling down Tiernan's cheek. He climbed off Tiernan and grabbed his jeans off the floor.

"So I'll see you in Florida?" Tiernan asked, watching Nik pull on his shirt. He put it on backwards, but Tiernan didn't say anything.

"Yeah," Nik said, heading for the door, but he paused as he opened it. He glanced back, teeth pulling at his bottom lip again. "Good luck."

"Thanks."

The door shut behind him. Tiernan sat back. Nik was the first person to say it, he realized as he sat there. He wasn't sure what to make of that, so he rolled off the couch and went to take a shower instead. He had a lot of packing to do.

Chapter 9:
Gone To Trials

"You don't fly much, do you?" Jennifer asked from beside Nik. She had arranged her tablet, water bottle, and phone on her tray, pushing in her wireless ear buds already. They'd only been in the air ten minutes.

Nik forced himself to let go of the armrests and take a breath. He purposefully didn't look out the window, keeping his eyes on the 'seat belt' sign overhead instead as his heart hammered.

"This is the first time," he managed to say. Was the air thinner up here? He felt a little like he was suffocating. Humans were not meant to fly.

"How did you get to Arizona?" she asked, eyebrows furrowing.

"A bus."

"And how do you get to school from home?"

"A bus." Nik had never had money to fly anywhere, and even if he had, where would he go?

"I didn't know busses still drove across the country," she said, shrugging to herself. "Well, this is an airplane, and you don't need to freak out. Just take a deep breath and we'll be there in no time."

Nik couldn't convince himself they weren't going to crash despite how smoothly everything *seemed* to be going. He'd heard about plenty of plane crashes before.

'No time' was about five hours, which was far too long to be up in the air for Nik's tastes, but he didn't have a choice. Part of this job was traveling, and if he wanted to be a photojournalist, he'd have to learn to travel on much longer flights. Besides, the flight to France would be a lot longer than this.

"So, when we get there," Jennifer said, pulling up the schedule on her tablet, "trials actually start tomorrow at nine AM at the aquatic center. Tonight, we have a dinner with Marion, so after we get to the hotel — "

"Wait," Nik interrupted as sudden panic seized him at her words. "We're meeting with the editor?"

"Yeah, I told you," she said, but Nik shook his head.

"No, you didn't."

Jennifer looked confused for a second but shrugged. "I must have forgotten. Well, anyway, she's going to be down to watch the trials, so she wants to meet, go over our progress, you know, normal stuff."

It wasn't normal for Nik. He had never even met Marion. The most he knew about her was that she'd played in the WNBA for many years before retiring and becoming the editor of *Hot Shot Sports*. When he'd gotten the internship, someone from HR had called him and told him to be in Arizona on May twentieth. Probably Marion didn't even know who he was.

"You know," Jennifer said when he just stared at his tray table, wordlessly processing what she'd said. He would have to meet the editor. Shit. "You worry a lot for someone who hasn't done anything wrong."

Growing up, Nik had gotten in trouble plenty of times for things he hadn't done. He'd learned to stop asking why and just accept it.

"I just, I don't know," he muttered. He'd never met an editor. What if she didn't like him? What if she said his photos were terrible?

"Maybe you have an anxiety disorder," she suggested, scrolling through her music.

Nik frowned but didn't reply. It wasn't a disorder. It was just his life.

Trying to relax, he sat back and took a deep breath. He'd make it through this flight then he'd deal with meeting the editor.

He closed his eyes and tried to focus on the sound of the plane, the rumble of the engines, blocking out the random conversations around him. His first thought was Rae, the last text message she'd sent that he still hadn't replied to.

I wish you were here so I wouldn't be alone with Mom.

It had dropped like a hot stone into his stomach, but it was exactly what Nik had predicted. If he was there, it would just be him and Rae, taking care of Mom while Andre and Seth and Dan were off working or drinking or whatever the hell it was they did when they weren't home. Andre said it was to take care of them, but he'd never been there when Nik needed him.

He didn't need Andre anymore. He didn't *need* anyone.

It didn't change the fact that Rae *was* there all alone, and Nik couldn't help feeling like he should be there too, even if the thought of going home made his stomach curl.

The only good thing about a plane, he decided, was that he could turn his phone off without feeling guilty. For the next few hours, there would be no messages, no voicemails. Who left voicemails these days? People born in the 80s, like Andre.

If he didn't have to get messages from his family, he didn't have to think about them either. He could think about anything. It was harder than it sounded, and he grabbed the arm rest as the plane jolted around. Beside him, Jennifer merely raised an eyebrow and went back to typing on her tablet.

Must be nice to have a big family, Tiernan had said the other day, like the more siblings you had, the better chance you had of getting along with them. Nik wished it had been only him and Rae. Life would have been so much easier. Tiernan was lucky he only had one sister.

Tiernan was lucky in general, Nik admitted. He had what he wanted — a career, a goal, a life. If he wanted to do something, he could just do it. Nik envied him.

Nik would be seeing Tiernan at Trials. He'd see him in his tiny competition swim suit, skin wet and glowing with water. He'd never seen a real race — Jennifer had made him watch some online, so at least he would know vaguely what was going on. It seemed pretty straight-forward, but what did Nik know? He'd be able to watch it in person, see the way Tiernan's body cut through the water like a torpedo. He could already see Tiernan's smile when he won, big and bright and something so genuinely happy that it made Nik's chest ache.

He wondered if Tiernan would come to him after, hyped up on a win, if he'd take him rough and demanding, make Nik suck him off, come on his face, dirty and wet.

Nik shifted, willing down the blood rushing to his cock. Cutting the fantasy short, he glanced at Jennifer as if she could hear his thoughts, but she was absorbed in writing her latest piece.

Nik liked the time he spent with Tiernan. For just a few hours, he didn't have to be Nik the poor kid from the Bronx, Nik the disappointment, Nik the intern. He didn't have to be anything, and Tiernan didn't ask him to be.

The plane jostled again and Nik shut his eyes, taking a breath and willing himself to let it out slowly. He'd be glad when they were back on the ground.

Well, he didn't die, although there had been a moment when they'd landed and the plane had pitched forward, like it might tip over on the nose. No one else had seemed concerned about the feeling of being thrown forward. Apparently it was normal, but Nik wouldn't say so.

His knuckles were white when they finally got off and he could have sworn he was going to have a heart attack, but Jennifer had merely herded him along with the crowd to pick up their bags. Nik wasn't looking forward to the return flight.

He had other things to worry about first, like dinner with the editor. He'd dug through his suitcase, but he hadn't found much that might be appropriately nice for a first meeting. The nicest thing he owned was a pair of slacks, and those were back in Chicago. Photographers weren't really expected to dress up most of the time. So Nik had to settle for his cleanest pair of jeans and a shirt that wasn't black.

If he'd thought the Arizona heat was bad, it was nothing compared to Florida. The minute he'd stepped off the plane, even in the walkway, his shirt had stuck to him, humidity choking him as sweat beaded on his skin. He remembered how much he hated humidity. It reminded him of summers in New York, laying on the couch in front of the window AC unit and praying for death.

Despite being past sundown when he and Jennifer headed to the restaurant, everything felt muggy. He didn't get two steps outside without sweat drenching his clothes.

The heat was the last thing on his mind as they arrived, though, and Jennifer spotted someone through the crowd.

"There she is. Come on," she said, taking Nik's arm and tugging him in the right direction.

Nik's stomach turned over as they weaved around tables and ended up near the middle of the room at a table with a tall woman sitting there. She was even taller when she stood, but her smile was genuine and she shook Nik's hand as Jennifer introduced them.

"It's good to finally meet you," Marion said, taking her seat. Her hair was held back in a tight ponytail over high cheekbones and makeup darker than her warm brown skin. Her arms were much longer than Nik's and she had a star tattooed on her muscular bicep. She was younger than he'd expected too, probably only late-thirties, early forties. "I try to meet all the interns, but you're a bit of a special case."

Nik wasn't sure what to make of that. He fiddled with his fork. "I am?"

She nodded, unfolding her napkin as the server set down glasses of water. The restaurant was nicer than most Nik had been in with dim lighting and dark carpet underfoot. The servers seemed to glide around unseen.

"Most of our interns are back in the New York office, making copies, proofreading. You're out on assignment. It's a rare opportunity."

Nik's heart thudded in his chest but he nodded. Beside him, Jennifer wasn't listening, perusing the menu instead. Very helpful.

"Our photography editor has been very impressed," Marion went on, sipping her water. Her lipstick didn't come off on the glass. "I, of course, see all of Jennifer's work come through. By the way, Jennifer, I'm very pleased with the direction you've taken with the pieces."

Jennifer smiled. "Thanks. It's been great working with Nik too. He's very professional, for a college kid."

She nudged Nik's side playfully, but he couldn't relax yet.

"I think you may have a real future in sports photography, Nik," Marion said casually, as though she wasn't telling him everything he'd ever dreamed about. "After this summer is over, I'd like you to talk to our photo editor. He may be able to give you some helpful tips."

Nik nodded, unable to speak, emotions overwhelming him. No one had ever wanted to help him, not really. His adviser at school was just trying to make sure he took the right classes.

"That, that would be amazing," he managed finally, feeling breathless.

Marion smiled. "We like to encourage our interns to reach their full potential."

Nik couldn't even describe the gratitude he felt. This was possibly the best moment of his life.

"I am starving," Marion said a minute later, reaching for a menu. "Nik, what are you having?"

Nik blinked as though coming out of a trance. He couldn't voice how he was feeling, and if he did, it would probably come out all jumbled up. For the first time, someone believed in him. He felt lightheaded, dizzy with happiness. He couldn't think about food. He could only see his future, and for once, it looked... good.

Beside him, Jennifer merely laughed and handed him a menu.

Nik was too wired to sleep, pacing his hotel room, skin thrumming with excitement. Fuck, he wanted to tell somebody, anybody, what Marion had said. She thought he was good. She thought he had potential. She wanted to help him. It was incredible.

He started to call Rae, but he stopped, thumb hovering over her name. If he called her, it would be five minutes of reliving the most amazing night but it would soon turn back to Mom and Andre and everything else that was going on at home.

The bubble in his chest deflated slightly at the thought. He wanted to tell her, but nothing was ever about him for long in their family. Plus, he wasn't sure he wanted to give her any good news when she was stuck in New York. He didn't want to brag or make her feel bad, which it surely would.

Sitting on the edge of his bed, he scrolled through his contacts instead. There weren't many people in there, aside from his family and a few friends he'd made at school. Those friends were all off enjoying their summers, drinking on lakes or partying in Europe.

The only other person in his phone was Tiernan. Not his first choice, but not his last choice either. Maybe he would even understand.

You busy?

He sent the message, glancing at the time. It was already well past ten. Nik should have been asleep — they had to get up early to get to trials. He was pretty sure there was no way he was sleeping tonight, though.

He didn't get a response, his message sitting as 'delivered' but not 'read.' Maybe Tiernan was asleep. He did actually have to compete tomorrow.

Nik waited five minutes, but no response came. His excitement wore off the longer he sat there, and, at length, he tossed his phone aside and pulled out the copy of the Asbury series Brooke had lent him.

> "It took me a year to find you," said Cameron, barely avoiding the branch Grace let spring behind her. He crashed through the underbrush, dogging her steps. "And now you want to walk back into the kingdom and face the man that took it all away?"
>
> Grace stopped so abruptly that Cameron smacked into her and fell back, stumbling over a log behind him. In her eyes, determination glinted, fierce and stubborn.
>
> "I know who I am," she said. "And I'm not afraid of what the Viscount will do." She reached out a hand and pulled Cameron off the ground. "You've been the only one who's always been there for me, Cam, but you don't have to come with me."
>
> Cameron sighed a long-suffering sigh. "You just love making my life difficult, don't you? Of course I'm coming with you. You'd still be lost without me."
>
> Grace smiled and together they headed into the woods.

Nik closed the chapter and glanced at the clock. It was far past bedtime, so he set the book aside. As he lay down and clicked off the light, he thought of Cam's unwavering loyalty to Grace, even after the last book and everything he'd gone through to find her. It seemed unfair that he would go through all that only to see her risk her life again.

Nik rolled onto his side and stared out the window at the tiny pinpricks of the light. He didn't know anyone who would do that for him, except maybe Rae. Instead of making him feel better, he clutched to the sheet and pulled it tight. He didn't need to share his good news with her; it just would have been nice.

Chapter 10:
On The Starting Block

Tiernan was supposed to go to bed early. Coach had sent him to the hotel at eight o'clock with strict instructions not to watch trashy reality TV or home decorating shows, just go to bed.

Tiernan had fully intended to, but then his phone rang.

He knew he shouldn't have answered it when Ella's name popped up, but maybe she was calling to wish him good luck. His parents had sent a brief text, like they were too busy to actually pick up the phone and call. They probably were considering the monstrosity that was Ella's wedding.

"If you're calling to wish me good luck, I don't need it but thanks anyway," he answered the phone cheekily, but the cold silence he got in return was enough to quash his good mood.

"I don't suppose you read those articles that reporter writes about you," she said sharply. A minute later as an unpleasant pressure grew in his chest.

"Not really," he said. He preferred not to know what people wrote about him. There'd been a time after last Trials when he'd read every article speculating on his defeat. They'd guessed everything from alcoholism, to emotional distress, to plain he just wasn't good enough. He'd stopped completely when the articles left a permanent pit in his stomach and made him want to quit swimming. It didn't matter what other people thought of him, his coach said. He knew what he was capable of.

"But you're there when you give the interview, right? So you hear what's coming out of your mouth?" She sounded more pissed than she usually did.

Oh fuck. What had he said now? It had been days since the last meeting with Jennifer, and between then and now, all he'd thought of was training. That was all that mattered right now.

"Generally, yes," he agreed carefully. It couldn't be said that he *always* thought before he spoke.

"So when you called me a Bridezilla, you meant to do that?" It wasn't a question so much as an accusation.

Shit. It was coming back. He hadn't meant it like that, exactly.

"Ella, I — "

"Do you know who reads this?" she interrupted. Tiernan rubbed his face as he sat down on the bed. He was sure she was about to tell him.

"You?"

Tiernan could almost see her glare.

"*My friends,*" she practically hissed through the receiver.

"So not you." It would have been too much to assume his own family would read something like this.

"You called me a Bridezilla, and now it's all over the internet! I'm sorry it's such a hassle for you to be *involved* in my wedding."

"It's just an article, Ella," Tiernan pointed out. He felt suddenly exhausted. He wasn't supposed to be having this argument, not tonight, not ever. "No one will remember tomorrow. I don't have time to do this."

"*You* don't have time?" she scoffed. "The wedding is in two weeks, Tiernan."

The wedding. That was all she cared about. Her stupid wedding; a giant party that could have been scheduled for any other day of the year.

"I'm very aware," he said, voice deadly calm. He was tired of this. "Are you aware that Olympic trials are tomorrow? I know you don't care about my career, but I do, and I'm sorry I said something stupid to a reporter, but I have bigger things to worry about."

He was sure Ella's wedding would go off without a hitch. She was so focused on controlling every detail that things would be fine, but he didn't have to be dragged into the drama.

"I came to trials last time," she said angrily, and Tiernan sighed.

"Yes, I remember. I remember that disappointed look on your face when I fucked it up. That was four years ago and yet everyone still treats me like I'm that stupid kid who's just gonna fuck it up again. That's why you're not here."

He knew that was why his parents hadn't come. He knew that was why Ella hadn't even bothered to talk about it. They were afraid he was going to disappoint them again. A part of him didn't blame them; last time, they'd had their hopes up so high and he'd crushed them. Didn't they think he'd punished himself enough between then and now?

"Maybe if you stopped acting like a kid, people would stop treating you like one," she said shortly.

"You're saying that biting my head off over one word in an article isn't childish?"

He could hear her growl over the phone. "I'm so tempted just to tell you not to come until you've grown up a little."

"Don't do me any favors," he snapped. It was too late for this. He might have tried to be a little more diplomatic if it wasn't the night before trials. He might have tried to be a little more understanding, but he'd been understanding since they'd announced the wedding date. He'd agreed to go when he'd probably be neck-deep in training. He'd humored her questions about hydrangeas versus lilies. He hadn't told her that Michael was a pinheaded idiot. What more could she want?

"I won't," she replied sharply. "You're coming to my wedding, with an *appropriate* date, and you're going to be the best guest possible. No getting drunk. No groping the ushers. No bringing up this article."

"I wouldn't dare," he said, rolling his eyes. Only his sister made him like this. Growing up, she had always been the perfect one, of the two. He'd been a close second up until trials last time. They'd always tried to outdo each other, or well, Tiernan had tried to be as perfect as her for a while. It hadn't worked out.

She seemed to sense his sarcasm. "I'll be at the Olympics if you go, you know," she said. "Because I'm your sister, and I care about you."

For a second, Tiernan felt bad for getting mad. At least she said it. It was nice to hear sometimes. The momentary guilt wasn't enough to erase his annoyance, though.

"And not because it happens to coincide with your honeymoon?"

"Ugh, you're so frustrating, Tiernan!" she snapped. "Why couldn't I have had a sister?"

"'Cause she wouldn't look as good as me in a Speedo," Tiernan pointed out, and he wasn't really surprised when Ella growled and hung up the phone.

Tiernan turned his phone on silent and collapsed back on the bed. He didn't want any more calls tonight. He was never gonna get to sleep anyway.

He lay there for a second, frowning at the water stain on the ceiling before standing up and grabbing the keycard off the table.

The hallway was eerily silent as he padded down a few doors. If Coach caught him out, he'd flay him alive. Around the corner, Tiernan knocked on a door, quietly, almost too quiet, but the door cracked open a minute later.

"Aren't you supposed to be asleep?"

"Could say the same to you," Tiernan said as Sam opened the door wider.

"Fuck it, come on," Sam said, stepping back to let Tiernan in.

All the lights were on in Sam's room, which led Tiernan to believe he'd been no nearer sleep than Tiernan. As much as Tiernan told himself that tomorrow was just another meet, it was a total lie.

Sam followed him in, flopping down on the bed. He hadn't even bothered to pull down the comforter.

"Too bad there's no mini-bar in here," Tiernan said, only half-joking.

"I'm sure both our coaches would love that," Sam replied, pushing two pillows behind him as he leaned against the headboard. "Turning up hung over on Trial day."

Tiernan shrugged. "Not something I haven't done before." He smiled, but the joke fell flat even as he said it. He couldn't deny that he was nervous. He couldn't sleep because memories from last time kept running through his head, like a movie reel of all his mistakes. Just thinking about it made his stomach knot up. "Fuck, let's talk about something else."

"What else is there?"

"Anything else," Tiernan said, climbing on the bed, crossing his legs and facing Sam. "What are you going to buy when you make the Olympic team and get yourself a great sponsor?"

"Not everyone gets sponsors, you know. We're not all as pretty as you."

As pretty as Tiernan was (he accepted that), he wasn't going to take that as an excuse from Sam. Sam was better than he thought. "Come on," he said, shaking Sam's knee. "Dream a little, Sam. Anything you want, what would it be?"

"I'd just like to pay my rent," Sam said, shaking his head. "Or maybe pay my parent's mortgage. They've done so much for me."

Tiernan knew he was lucky to have sponsors. A lot of people didn't, but if they didn't, they usually had family who supported them. Tiernan didn't have that anymore.

"They coming tomorrow?"

"Yeah. Drove down from Virginia. I just hope I don't disappoint them."

"If anyone's the disappointment in this room, it's me," Tiernan assured him good-naturedly. "And I know that you won't because they love you. You can't disappoint people who really love you."

Sam picked at a string on the comforter and nodded. Tiernan wished Sam believed in himself as much as Tiernan did. He'd seen Sam swim. When he was on, he was good. He just let doubts get in the way.

"Your sister coming this time?" Sam asked, and Tiernan shrugged.

"She's busy wedding-planning. Biggest day of her life, you know."

Sam hummed in agreement. Tiernan would have thought that the day she'd gotten her Master's degree would have been bigger than this since it had taken so long to get — growing up, she'd never sat around and gossiped about boys with her friends (Tiernan would know; he'd spied on her every chance he got) — but it wasn't. Apparently her wedding trumped everything.

"So are you ready?" Sam asked finally and Tiernan laughed.

"Fuck no," he said, smiling at Sam, "but that's not gonna stop me from doing whatever I have to win."

"Whatever it takes, huh?"

Tiernan nodded. It wasn't going to be like last time. "Whatever it takes."

Sam smiled, finally, and Tiernan felt better too. They could get through this.

"Guess I should go try to sleep," Tiernan said after a minute, sliding off the bed reluctantly. He doubted he would, but if he didn't at least attempt it, Coach would know.

"Hey," Sam said as Tiernan reached the door. "Good luck."

"You too." He really meant it and pulled the door open. Back in his room, he shoved his silent phone aside and climbed into bed, pulling up the thin top sheet and listening to the hum of the air conditioner. He was never going to fall asleep.

"Did you sleep?" Coach asked suspiciously, peering at Tiernan, like he could see into his brain.

Tiernan scoffed. "Of course." He adjusted his goggles on his forehead. The air was humid and sticky. He hadn't even gotten in the pool but he was damp all over from sweat. The pool was outside, and the sun beat down on his shoulders as the stands filled with spectators.

"Lying to me does you no favors," Coach said, lips pressed together, eyes narrowed.

Tiernan had slept, just not very well. The room had been too hot, so he'd turned down the A/C. Then it had been too cold. It didn't help that he couldn't stop thinking about the conversation with Ella. Any time he hadn't spent being angry about what Ella had said, he'd spent dwelling on tomorrow, the trials, his second chance.

"Are you nervous?" Coach asked matter-of-factly. That was what Tiernan liked about him. He was a straight-forward, to the point kind of guy.

He swallowed down the lump in his throat and huffed out a breath. "No," he said. He had to believe it. He had told Sam that it was just like any other meet, he had to believe the same or he wouldn't get through it. He shook out his fingers and purposefully didn't search the stands for Nik. He hadn't gotten Nik's text until the morning, too late. He probably wouldn't have texted back even if he'd gotten it the night before.

Coach set a hand on his shoulder, turning him away from the crowds. "I wasn't your coach last time, Pace, and I'm not going to tell you what you did wrong. That was then. This is now. All that matters is what you do today."

Tiernan nodded. Coach was right. He had to let go of last time. He had to stop letting it hold him back.

"You're going to make the team," Coach told him, slapping his shoulder. "I've got the utmost faith in you."

"Thanks, Coach," Tiernan said, a weight lifting off his chest. It was just nice to hear from someone.

Coach nodded once. "Let's get to the block. Butterfly first. Fifty-one seconds."

"Fifty-one seconds," he repeated, climbing up onto his block and pulling down his goggles. It was time to prove everyone wrong.

Chapter 11:
Sinking In

"I'm a little confused," Nik said, for what felt like the hundredth time this summer. "What is this one?"

They'd been ushered in the Press area, a little roped off area near the pool. Nik could see Tiernan talking with his coach, but Tiernan didn't look for him. He'd never gotten a response to his text, but he figured Tiernan was probably busy or sleeping. His excitement about what Marion had said had worn off, and the need to tell someone had dwindled with sleep. There was no need to get anyone's hopes up, least of all his.

Jennifer was scribbling notes down on her pad, jostled into Nik by some other press person trying to get a better spot. She shot them a glare and rolled her eyes.

"It's a Heat. In the Heat, everyone who prequalified for trials competes. In some events, the top fifteen or sixteen go to the semi-finals. In longer events, four hundred meters or longer, they just go to the finals. Top two in each event gets a spot on the Olympic team."

"So if Tiernan isn't in the top two, he won't go to the Olympics?" Nik glanced over to where Tiernan had climbed on his block.

"No," she agreed, squinting against the sun. It was hotter than sin and sticky as a, well, something Nik shouldn't have been thinking about in public. "But this isn't his only event. He's still got the hundred meter backstroke and the hundred meter freestyle."

"Oh. I hope he makes it."

Jennifer laughed. "Yeah, or else you and I are headed back to New York for the rest of the summer."

"I really hope he makes it," he muttered. It would be much harder to avoid his family in the same city.

"They're about to start," she said, touching his arm. "Get your camera ready."

Nik lifted the viewfinder to his eyes, searching out Tiernan on his block. He could see the rise and fall of his chest, the steely glint in his eye as he bent to take his position. Tiernan had never looked like this in any practice Nik had seen. His body was taut, like a bow string, ready to spring into action.

Jesus, that was hot, Nik found himself thinking as he snapped the photo.

The gun fired, and the swimmers shot from their perches, hitting the water in smooth dives. Around them, the crowd went wild, screaming and yelling, and Nik couldn't help glancing behind him. His school didn't have sports teams, and he'd never been to any kind of game as a kid. He'd never really thought about what it would be like, never thought about the frenzy that rose in large groups of people.

The swimmers raced towards the other end of the pool, and Nik could barely see Tiernan amongst the splashing, his form marred by other swimmers. The screen across the pool had an aerial view, but by the time Nik figured out which lane Tiernan was in, the match was over.

"What? Did he win?" he asked Jennifer, who seemed to know exactly what had happened.

"He got first place, so he'll go to semi-finals," she said, "but there's still a bunch more heats to go. I mean, there are over a hundred people who prequalified for this event."

"Holy shit," Nik breathed, but caught himself. Jennifer didn't seem to notice.

"Either way, the semi-final is this afternoon. Maybe we can get a comment for an update. Come on."

She muscled her way out of the press area, and Nik followed. Tiernan was pulling himself out of the pool as they got closer, shaking hands with other swimmers, accepting their congratulations, but he didn't really smile until his coach shook his hand and said something Nik couldn't hear.

Somehow, Jennifer sneaked past the barriers, and Nik darted away from the gaze of security. He didn't think they were supposed to be by the pool. The officials were already shunting everyone off so they could do another heat.

"Tiernan." Jennifer caught him as he turned for the locker room. His coach didn't look happy at her arrival, crossing his arms with a disapproving look. "Congratulations. Anything to say before the semi-finals?"

Tiernan merely smiled. "Just want to thank my coach is all, for always believing in me." He grinned at Nik for a moment before his coach hauled him off to the locker rooms.

"That's good enough," Jennifer said, tugging Nik in the other direction. "I'll get this written up. Send me that photo. We'll make it a bulletin on the website."

Nik watched Tiernan disappear in the locker room. Tiernan would have understood last night, because he had someone who believed in him.

Nik wasn't going to ask this time as they crowded into the press area for the semi-finals. Jennifer would probably smack him if he asked what the difference was between the semi-finals and the finals. The only thing the internet had told him was that the top swimmers from the semi-finals went to the finals, and competed again. Then the top two from the finals went to the Olympics.

It was, if possible, even hotter out than it had been before. He was going to have to shower *again* just to feel clean. His shirt stuck to his skin in uncomfortable places, and he plucked at the neck.

"Top four," Jennifer said over the rumblings of the crowd, drawing Nik's gaze away from where Tiernan was adjusting the waist on his shorts, fingers skimming under the skin-tight fabric. It already sat as low as possible on his hips, the V clear-cut at his hips.

"Huh?" He really should have been paying more attention to taking photos than ogling the swimmers.

"Top four move on to the finals," she said as if she knew he didn't know.

He nodded and took a few photos of Tiernan at the edge of the pool. He looked as focused as before, rolling his shoulders and stretching his arms. His coach was there again, talking into his ear as Tiernan nodded repeatedly.

"What are his odds?"

"Pretty good," she allowed, "but it's not his best event."

Nik turned back to the pool as the swimmers mounted the blocks. Glancing up at the big screen, he made a note of Tiernan's row this time. Fourth down from the top.

The gun went off and the crowd screamed behind Nik as the swimmers dove into the pool. He watched the overhead monitor closely this time, as Tiernan pulled ahead. It was mesmerizing, the way the swimmers moved, a rhythm as they reached the other end and pushed off again. His attention was locked on Tiernan, his heart racing as he reached the end of the pool and slapped the marker. Immediately on the screen, numbers popped up over rows.

"Third place!" Jennifer yelled over the crowd, grinning at Nik. "He's in the finals."

Nik couldn't help smiling as he watched the screen. For a moment, the camera focused on Tiernan's face, bright and happy as he shook people's hands and took the towel his coach handed him. Nik could only imagine that feeling. Maybe someday he'd know it too.

Nik's hotel room was eerily silent, aside from the hum of the air conditioner, and he couldn't find anything decent on TV to watch. For a moment, he considered calling Rae, to pretend for just a moment that everything was okay. They could talk about the internship, about how hot swimmers were, how amazing it was to see his photos on a real magazine's website. Mostly, he just wanted to talk to her, but he didn't call; it wouldn't be like that if he did. It had been, the first year he went away to school, but it couldn't be now with their mom's sickness hanging over everyone's head.

He felt restless, sitting in his room. He couldn't sit there and keep thinking about Rae, so he left his room and wandered downstairs, past the gym where he caught sight of a several swimmers working out. Outside, the pool was empty. Probably closed.

It seemed the only place in the hotel that wasn't bustling with people, so Nik ducked out the back door and wandered over to the edge of the pool. As he stood there, he realized it wasn't as empty as he'd thought. Someone was floating in the dark, drifting slowly. He caught sight of Nik, though, and quickly righted himself.

"Sorry," Nik said. "I didn't think anyone was — Tiernan?"

Tiernan moved into the light from the back door, water up to his chest.

"Nik?" he asked, swimming over to the edge.

"What are you doing?" Nik asked, surprised to find him here. He hadn't bothered to message him again thinking he'd probably be too distracted to reply. He would have been. "Training?"

"No." Tiernan shook his head. "No, no. Coach would kill me. I'm supposed to be relaxing."

"In the pool, where you are all day?" Nik asked. He hesitated a second, glancing back at the door, but no one had noticed them out there, so he sat down on the concrete near the edge of the pool.

Tiernan pulled himself out of the water, dripping as he sat next to Nik. He wasn't wearing his usual competition shorts. Instead, he had on regular swim trunks — blue with palm trees on them.

"It's the only place I don't have to think about everything."

"Are you worried?" Nik asked at length, brushing his fingers over the water.

"I wish people would stop asking me that," Tiernan said, wiping away some water on his face.

Nik grimaced. "Sorry, I shouldn't — "

Tiernan shook his head. "It's just, I'm usually not worried until they ask me that." He smiled easily and pushed his hair to the side where it stuck. "But if you want an answer, yeah, I'm worried."

Nik frowned, watching Tiernan swish his feet in the water. "But you're the best swimmer in the country."

Tiernan shrugged, making a face. "It doesn't mean as much as you think. Every meet's different. I could be first today and last tomorrow."

"Must be a lot of pressure," Nik muttered. He may not have understood sports, but he understood pressure.

Tiernan smiled. "Yeah." He didn't elaborate and Nik didn't expect him to. He shook away whatever shadow had settled over them with a nudge to Nik's side. "How are you enjoying Florida?"

"It's fucking awful," Nik said, shaking his head while Tiernan grinned. "I almost miss Arizona. I can't believe I said that."

"It's a dry heat," Tiernan said, quoting everyone Nik had ever met in Arizona. "Why don't you take a dip? It's nice in there."

"I can't really swim," Nik admitted, frowning at the look he got in return, surprise and confusion.

"You can't swim?"

"Well, I mean, I wouldn't drown if you threw me in," Nik clarified, feeling stupid. "But I can't *really* swim."

"You never had lessons or anything?"

"Didn't have money," he muttered. He hadn't done a lot of things other kids had. In the summers when they had taken swimming lessons, he'd hid out at the library so he wouldn't be home when his mom got there or so that Andre wouldn't find him and toss him in a dumpster.

Tiernan was silent for a moment, looking thoughtful. Nik hoped he wasn't thinking how sad his childhood must have been. He didn't need pity.

"I'll teach you," he said eventually, decisively, and Nik laughed.

"No," he said, shaking his head. "I'm fine."

Tiernan tilted his head to the side. "You're covering the Olympic swim competition. You should know how to swim, at least a few strokes. I'm a good teacher, I promise."

"I don't have a swim suit," he pointed out, gesturing at his clothes.

"Strip," Tiernan said simply then grinned.

"I don't think — "

"Nik," Tiernan interrupted him, leaning into him. "Just one stroke."

Nik couldn't tell if that was a come-on or if he was serious. Either way, he huffed and stood up, pulling off his shirt and unbuttoning his jeans.

Tiernan slid back into the water, floating back a few feet as Nik balled up his jeans and tossed them onto a plastic lounge chair.

Tiernan smirked. "This isn't *just* an excuse to get you down to your underwear."

Nik had wanted to learn how to swim, back in elementary school when kids would talk about it school, in their 'what I did over summer break' reports. As he'd gotten older, he'd learned how to doggy paddle and float, and that was all he could learn at a public pool.

He lowered himself into the pool carefully. It was much deeper than he'd expected. Tiernan was standing, but then, he was taller than Nik. Nik held to the edge uneasily. He couldn't remember the last time he'd actually swum in a pool.

"Hey," Tiernan said, taking Nik's hand from the edge and keeping a hold of it as he led them to shallower water. "You're not gonna drown. I promise."

Nik hated feeling like this, like he wasn't in control, but he forced himself to nod. He felt better once his feet could touch the bottom.

"You know how to float, right?" Tiernan asked, and Nik shot him a look.

"Yes, I know how to float."

"Just checking. It's really the first thing they teach you, mostly for safety reasons. Can't drown if you're floating."

"When did you first learn?" Nik asked as Tiernan guided him onto his back. He felt out of his element, his feet off the ground, water enveloping his body. Tiernan's hands kept a light but firm touch against his back, helping him stay up.

"I was five. I grew up in Vegas. Pools everywhere, so my parents put me in lessons early. Then it turned out I was good at it, so I joined the swim team in high school."

Water rushed up to Nik's ears and he fought the urge to flip back upright.

"Alright, I'm gonna teach you the backstroke," Tiernan told him. "It's really easy. You kick with your feet. Small kicks, and you move your arms backwards kind of like a windmill."

"This feels stupid," Nik said as he tried it, but he moved through the water, surprising himself. Tiernan drifted alongside him.

"Feels stupid but it's a good stroke to know 'cause when you're tired, you can just float. Good in case you get swept into the ocean."

"Why would I get swept into the ocean?" Nik asked, trying a few more strokes. It was a lot easier than he'd expected.

Tiernan shrugged, stopping Nik before he could hit the wall behind him. Nik let his body drift downward. They were in the deep end again, but he could keep himself afloat, treading water.

"I don't know; that's just what they tell you."

"Is this what you always wanted to do?" Nik asked as he propped himself up against the ledge. Tiernan moved beside him. It was cooler in the water, he admitted, where he couldn't feel the sweat. Water lapped at the edge of the pool, making a soft sound.

"I never really thought about it," Tiernan admitted. His face was partially in shadow, the light blocked by Nik's head. "It was the one thing I was better at than my sister. It was something I could win, something my parents were proud of. I guess I just got lucky and found something I liked."

"Would you do it again if you had a choice?"

Tiernan licked his lips and smiled. "I would do it again and again and again until somebody stopped me."

"Even though your family isn't here?"

Tiernan's eyebrows furrowed and he took a deep breath. Nik frowned. Maybe he'd stepped over the line of what was acceptable for two people who'd slept together a few times.

"It's not about them. Sure, it'd be nice if they showed up, and maybe they will. Maybe they'll come to the Olympics if I make it this time. I disappointed them last time, but I don't plan on doing it again."

Nik shouldn't have brought it up. He looked away from Tiernan, back towards the hotel. From here, he could see the window into the gym. Most of the guys had left now, leaving an eerily empty room filled with exercise equipment.

"Does your family support your photography career?" Tiernan asked, splashing Nik lightly to get his attention.

Nik wiped the water off his face as he shook his head. "Not really. My brother says I shouldn't go to school for something I could learn in a book."

"Well, you don't have to go to school for it. Lots of people don't."

"I want to go to school," Nik said, maybe too aggressively. He couldn't help it. "I don't care how much it costs or if it's pointless for this profession. I want a degree."

"Has anybody else gotten one?"

Nik shook his head and didn't respond. He'd be the first, not that anyone in his family found that impressive. Andre and Seth said it was a waste of time and money and that he should just join the construction businesses like them. Nik wasn't the type to walk around with a tool belt and hammers and other tools he didn't know the name or purpose of. Rae was the only one who'd told him to go, who'd given him the push he really needed to apply.

He looked up at the touch of Tiernan's hand to his jaw.

"Then you should get yours. Prove them all wrong."

"Is that what you're doing?"

Tiernan shrugged. "I'm proving it to myself too." He had drifted closer somehow without Nik noticing. His entire face was in shadow now, but Nik could still make out his features. He saw the slight quirk to his lips, almost a smile. It made something nervous, excited, flutter deep in Nik's chest.

"I hope you make it tomorrow," Nik said after a second, feeling the way the water rippled as Tiernan moved closer.

"Me too," Tiernan agreed, leaning in and kissing Nik.

His skin tasted like chlorine, but Nik was more focused on the slow slide of Tiernan's lips against his, tongue darting across his bottom lip, gently opening up his mouth and licking inside. Tiernan's hand on his jaw kept him from floating back involuntarily at the push of Tiernan's body against his. It wasn't a leading kiss, not hinting at more for once. Something stirred in Nik's stomach, something unfamiliar but not necessarily bad.

He breathed out slowly when Tiernan pulled away, licking his lips slowly and meeting his gaze. Nik almost didn't want him to go. It was a strange thought, unbidden, but he didn't hate it. It was nice to talk to someone who didn't judge, someone who listened, who could relate.

"I have to get to bed," Tiernan said after a beat. "Big day tomorrow."

"And the day after that," Nik replied. "And the day after that."

Tiernan smiled and nodded, drifting toward the ladder on the side of the pool. "The life of a swimmer."

Nik followed him out of the pool, grabbing a fluffy white towel from a pile on a nearby table. It wasn't as humid now that he was all wet.

"I'll see you at the pool," Tiernan said as he left, swinging the towel over his shoulders and leaving Nik to grab his clothes from the chair and tie the towel around his waist. Okay, so Florida wasn't so terrible, as long as Tiernan was there. Smiling to himself, he grabbed his shoes and headed for the door. Maybe he'd sleep better tonight.

Chapter 12:
Favoritism

Tiernan stretched, blocking out the sound of the crowd in the stands. He'd already made the finals in the hundred meter backstroke, but he wasn't thinking about the backstroke now. He wasn't worried about the backstroke. Now, it was time to focus on the butterfly and making sure his time was under fifty-two, as close to fifty-one seconds as humanly possible.

"Good luck, Pace. You're gonna need it."

Tiernan looked up as Dylan sauntered past. Dylan winked obviously as he took his spot on the block.

"Hey." Coach was there, forcing Tiernan to turn from where he was seriously considering punching Dylan in the face. "Ignore him. He's not your competition. You are his."

Tiernan nodded, focusing on Coach. It didn't matter if Dylan was the highest-rated in the butterfly, if his odds were better than Tiernan's. Dylan didn't matter. He took a deep breath, forcing the nerves out of his body. The feeling never changed, no matter how many times he swam these events. No matter how prepared he felt, he could never shake the tingle in his fingers, the clench in his stomach as he faced the pool.

"You're gonna be fine," Coach told him with a firm hand on his shoulder. "Watch your kick-offs, use every inch of your body."

Tiernan rolled his shoulders to get rid of any tension. He needed to be loose, to take full advantage of his height. He could do this.

Climbing onto the block, he didn't let the nerves overtake him. He ignored Dylan a few rows down, focusing on the water, the stillness of it in the moment. It wouldn't last long, but he'd be the one disrupting it, forcing it to move with him.

"On your mark," came the announcement, and Tiernan could sense everyone down the line tense in anticipation. On the next command, they took their positions, feet slotting against the starting block.

This was his chance to prove everyone wrong about him, all those spiteful articles that dug up his past and questioned if he could do it this time. This was his time.

On the gun, the tension released with a snap as he dove into the water. Even though Tiernan had goggles, swimming was more about feel. He knew how many strokes it took to get from one end to the other. He knew how far his dives took him, and he let his body take over.

He couldn't hear the crowd as he crashed through the water, hitting the other side and pushing back off. It wasn't important what everyone else was doing. All that mattered was that he got to the mark first.

His arms propelled him forward, powerful strokes as he crossed the pool, towards the mark. It was these moments when he stopped thinking, stopped worrying, and just let his body take over. All the training, all the conditioning only worked if he trusted in it, like the very first time he'd realized he could do this.

His first swim meet seemed so long ago as he glided through the water; the screams of the crowd lost to the rush of water in his ears. He'd been so nervous then, a bouncing ball of energy, skinny and bony and too eager to please everyone. He'd won that first match, a moment of pure exhilaration he hadn't quite managed to replicate in the last four years. He hit the water and stretched out his hands, slapping the X on the side of the pool. Spitting out water, he surfaced, panting for breath and searching out the screen showing the results.

A number two appeared over his lane, the replay showing beneath it.

Hands gripped his shoulders, shaking him in the water as he stared. Fuck, he couldn't believe it. Second place. That was good enough to go to Paris.

His head felt light as the guy in the next row shook his hand. It was a surreal dream he found himself in as he climbed out of the pool and people surrounded him to congratulate him. It was different than any other meet he'd ever swam in. This one meant so much more.

Coach finally appeared as other guys disappeared. He had a smile on his face — probably the first one Tiernan had seen.

"Good job, Pace. But don't get complacent. You've got two more events to qualify for."

Tiernan smiled anyway. Coach always had an eye to the future.

"Guess I'll see you in Paris, Pace," Dylan said as he passed. He didn't look particularly happy about it.

"Guess you will, Hoffman," he replied easily, glad when Dylan left. "God, he's such a dick."

Coach ignored him, handing him a towel. "Your next focus is backstroke. You're in for one event. Now let's better your odds of a medal."

Tiernan was all for that. It was officially official. Tiernan Pace was going to the 2024 Olympics.

Tiernan wasn't sure what he'd expected when he'd called his parents, but more than the distracted "Congratulations" that he got.

"Did you hear me?" he asked, pulling back the curtains at the window. His hotel overlooked Orlando which, despite what tourist brochures said, looked like any other big city from this viewpoint. He couldn't even see the beach from here.

"Hmm? Oh yes, honey," his mother said, sounding far away. "I'm just at a fitting with your sister for her dress. You should see how beautiful it is."

Tiernan would see her dress in a few weeks. He didn't care about her dress — mermaid cut, she'd told him, with a beaded top and a golden sash around the middle, more information than he'd wanted.

"But were you paying attention?" Sometimes it still felt like he was ten years old, showing off a stunt on his bike for his dad, but he was too distracted with Ella modeling a new dress.

"Yes, Tiernan," she said with a bit of a sigh, as though he was being annoying. "You're going to the Olympics. That's fantastic. Your father will be very pleased to hear it."

Pleased. Not happy, or excited. Tiernan frowned, turning from the window. His bag was half-packed, even though he had another day and one more final to swim. If he placed top two in freestyle, he'd be going for all three events.

"So are you coming?" he asked over the background noise of Ella saying something.

"Well," his mother said, and the knot in Tiernan's stomach tightened at the word. "Oh, that color is beautiful on you, Ella — I don't know, honey. It is very close to the wedding, and short notice."

Tiernan didn't point out that they'd known about this for months if not years.

"Ella will be there." Maybe he could use that as an angle. They loved Ella.

"Yes, but we don't want to intrude on her honeymoon."

"You wouldn't be," Tiernan pointed out. "You wouldn't be going to see *her.*"

They'd used to come to every meet back in high school. They'd used to cheer for him and buy him ice cream afterwards. Now, they wouldn't come to the biggest competition of his life. After he'd come out, they'd stopped paying for things. They'd stopped coming to his college meets, as though swimming had somehow turned him gay. He supposed it could be worse; they could not talk to him at all. Sometimes he thought it might be better that way. At least he wouldn't have to suffer through pretending their relationship was fine, trying to ignore the gay away.

On occasion, Ella acted as the buffer between them, even siding with Tiernan in rare moments, but she enjoyed the attention she got as the 'good child' too much to really push as hard as she could. It wasn't her responsibility anyway, but it was nice to have support once in a while.

"We'll have to look into it," his mom said. "It's expensive to fly to Europe, and we're paying for Ella's wedding, you know."

Yes, Tiernan knew. He'd spent the last four years relying on sponsorships to get by, and so far, it had worked out all right, but it could have been so much worse.

"Ella's not your only kid, Mom," he said before he could stop himself. He shouldn't have said it. It wouldn't get him anywhere.

"I am aware of that, Tiernan," she replied, a hard note to her voice that she rarely used. "I expect we'll see you at the wedding."

Tiernan sighed. It was pointless even to try. "Yes, I'll be there because Ella asked me to come, and because it's important to her." Just like the Olympics were important to him, but no one else seemed to care.

"Then I will see you at the wedding," she said and Tiernan flopped down in a chair by the window. There was no winning here.

"I'll try not to disappoint you this time," he replied, hanging up before she could respond. He rubbed his face and groaned. Why couldn't they just be happy for him? They'd spend thousands of dollars on a wedding, but not to come see him swim at the biggest sporting event in the world, the biggest accomplishment of his life.

It wasn't worth dwelling on, he told himself. He only had one more event to go, but no matter what, he was on the Olympic team. Coach would tell him to focus, that it wasn't worth letting anyone get in his head, and he was right. It didn't matter whether or not his parents came to the Olympics. He'd win with or without them. He'd already proven that he could do it. Now he just had to do it again.

Reaching for the remote, he turned on the television. He didn't care what Coach said. He was going to relax tonight by watching some stupid home-buying show and yelling at the homeowners when they complained about paint colors.

"You're not like I expected," Tiernan said thoughtfully, drawing a finger over the dark red mark he'd left on Nik's collarbone. The skin was still warm to the touch, and Nik raised an eyebrow in response to his statement.

"What do you mean?"

Tiernan rolled on top of Nik. The hotel's bed sheets weren't as soft as his, but they'd do. It was his last night in Florida before he headed back to Arizona for more training. Harder training, Coach said, since he was an Olympian now. He'd qualified in all his events — three chances to win a medal. It still didn't feel quite real, but he guessed once he got down to training, it would be all he thought about.

Nik's skin was soft and warm, body melding to his as he settled on top of him, sinking against his thighs. He wasn't hard, not yet, but he could get there again, especially with the way Nik shifted under him and brought his hands to rest on his thighs. His touch was easy, familiar, comfortable.

Leaning in, he breathed in against Nik's skin, pressing soft, slow kisses to his neck, enjoying the way Nik tilted back for him. Nik would probably let him do anything. The thought made his cock twitch, eager to go again.

"You're far more aggressive than your demeanor led me to believe," he murmured, sliding his tongue down Nik's collarbone. Nik's hand slid to the back of his head, tangling in his hair and tugging him up.

"This is the only time I get what I want," he replied, drawing Tiernan's mouth to his and kissing him deeply.

Arousal stirred deep inside Tiernan, warmth rising on his skin as blood pounded in his cock.

He had never really analyzed what had drawn him to Nik. He supposed it had to do with his dark, brooding look that was, in all honesty, a cover for the adorable puppy dog he was. He reminded Tiernan of a baby bird, a baby bird who was actually a full-grown eagle with talons ready to claw anyone who got in the way.

He liked how focused Nik was when he did his photography, how he went into some kind of professional mode and wasn't the awkward college kid doing an internship. When Nik knew what he was doing, it was beautiful. Like right now, when Nik pulled him closer, fingers digging into the back of Tiernan's neck and a groan escaped his lips.

"Tell me what you want," Tiernan panted, pulling back from Nik and grinding his hips down into Nik's half-hard prick. He watched Nik bite his lip and hiss out a breath.

Nik's fingers dug into the back of his neck and he kissed him again, harder than before but shorter, too short.

Tiernan groaned, hands pressing to Nik's sides, holding him steady as he ground down, their hips meeting in a glorious moment of friction that sent a jolt through his cock. He'd already fucked Nik once since he'd knocked on his hotel door that afternoon, but he could do it again. Fuck, he could do it a million times, if it meant Nik panting into his mouth when he came, grabbing at his hips to pull him in tighter, whining his name into the silent hotel room. He couldn't remember the last time he'd wanted to do that with someone, *really* wanted to.

Tiernan figured he deserved a reward. He hadn't seen much of Nik this week at all, and he hadn't had a single drink. He'd resolved to give up alcohol until after the Olympics were over; one less temptation to fuck it all up. Nik wasn't that kind of distraction, though. Nik was something else he hadn't quite figured out, but he liked it.

"What do you want, Nik?" Tiernan asked again, biting at Nik's shoulder, drawing out a gasp, returning to his mouth for a biting kiss, slick and wet and sharp. "Tell me."

"God," Nik groaned, pressing his face to Tiernan's neck as their hips met again, cocks rubbing together, too rough, too hot. "I wanna fuck you."

Chapter 13:
Something New

The request took Tiernan a little by surprise, the words Nik breathed into his neck, but he supposed he'd never asked. They hadn't really talked about it. They hadn't talked about anything, really.

Nik seemed to sense his hesitation and he pulled back from his neck, mouth pursing as he watched him, as though Tiernan might say no.

Tiernan gazed at Nik, over the downturn to the corners of his mouth, the crease in his brow, uncertainty etched in his features. He let the request wash over him, the way Nik had said it, full of desire that made Tiernan even harder if possible.

"Okay," Tiernan said after a second, pressing a kiss to Nik's shoulder. "Okay."

"Are you — "

"Yeah, I'm sure." He kissed away the momentary unease that crossed Nik's face, shifting them around so that Nik was on top. It was a different position but one he'd been in before.

Nik didn't hesitate after that, and Tiernan was glad. He didn't want it to be a thing between them, his momentary hesitation that didn't mean anything. When he was with Nik, he didn't have to think about competition, and that was how he liked it. He got the feeling the next couple weeks were going to be a whirlwind, so he'd better enjoy this while he could.

"I haven't done this in a while," he said as Nik rolled on a condom and popped the lid off the lube.

"Neither have I," Nik replied, eyes darting to his, almost as if embarrassed.

Tiernan didn't mention it, reaching down and stroking his cock once. There was no need to be embarrassed, not when it was Tiernan splayed on his back, fully on display, open and vulnerable. He was completely hard, just watching Nik touching himself, sliding his hand down his cock, squeezing it lightly like a promise of things to come.

Tiernan was definitely not as flexible as some of the gymnasts he shared a campus with, but Nik smoothed his legs up, knees bent as he slid in against him. Tiernan felt the warmth of Nik's body against his and he shivered in anticipation.

Nik's finger pushed in first, slick with lube, opening him up. Tiernan couldn't say he was used to this. His whole body seemed to tighten, tensing with each movement, but Nik moved slowly, slower than he would have let Tiernan get away with. The second finger joined the first, and Tiernan let out a huff as his body stretched. It had been a while, and the last time, it hadn't been very good. The guy had been drunk, or maybe Tiernan had been drunk, or maybe both. Either way, he'd been left with a throbbing ass and no release.

It wouldn't be like that this time, he could tell, if only from the way Nik rocked his fingers in, adding a third until Tiernan was stretched open and he panted for breath, hands tight on the back of Nik's thighs, tugging at him almost insistently.

"Fuck, Nik," he gasped as Nik's fingers pushed inside him, crooking at just the right spot where tingles ran up his spine. "Your fingers are — I could fuck myself on your fingers, come with you inside me, fuck, *God.*"

Words spilled from his mouth, heedless like they always did during sex. He'd tried to control it before, with other people who hadn't found it so appealing, but he'd found he wasn't good at that. Nik didn't seem to mind. Nik groaned at his words and pushed his fingers in deeper until Tiernan was clawing at the sheets, so close to coming, too close.

He was about to demand Nik do something more when the fingers disappeared. He felt suddenly empty, wide open and waiting, but the heat of Nik's body returned, and his cock, *fuck,* his cock was bigger than Tiernan had considered. Sure, he'd seen it, touched it, jerked Nik off in the locker room, but he hadn't thought about it inside him until this very moment.

E.E. Grey

For a minute, he wasn't sure he could take it, even with three fingers. Shutting his eyes, he bit down the noise threatening to escape, unsure, too eager to risk stopping Nik anyway.

The first press of Nik's cock against him drew out a soft whine, a sharp gasp at the pressure on his ass, the stretch that burned across his skin as Nik pushed inside. "Fuck, fuck, fuck," he cursed, breathless, forcing his eyes open, watching Nik.

Nik had his hands on Tiernan's legs, steadying himself as he slid inside, pausing every other inch until they were pressed against each other, heat radiating around them, warding off the chill of the air conditioner. For a second, Nik didn't move, as though he was absorbing the moment, drinking it all in. Tiernan could make out a sheen of sweat on his skin, and he wanted to lick it off, but it was too far away. All he could feel was Nik inside him, hard and hot. His own cock lay heavy against his stomach, neglected for the moment.

Pulling back slowly, Nik slid inside with short, quick movements, the rhythm not quite smooth at first, that made Tiernan moan and grab for his slim hips. Tiernan didn't do this a lot, mostly because people never asked, but also partly because he didn't offer. It wasn't always good this way, but he could get used to it with Nik. The way Nik built up his speed, listening for cues — the hitch of Tiernan's breath when Nik hit the spot that made his toes curl and heat shoot up his spine — adjusting to the rhythm of Tiernan's hips pushing up against him. Yeah, he could get used to this.

"Oh God, your cock," Tiernan moaned, hands twisted in the sheets, halfway lost to the feeling of Nik inside him, the friction of their bodies. "Fuck, Nik — "

He didn't finish his sentence before Nik was there, mouth pressed to his in a breathless, sloppy kiss, more tongue than anything, a hand on the back of his head, the other gripping his thigh to keep from losing his balance as he thrust inside him.

"Nikos," Nik said with a gasp as he pushed in deeper.

Tiernan was practically gone, but he managed a breathless, "What?" in response, fingers running over Nik's hairline, damp with sweat.

"Call me Nikos," Nik repeated, panting, hips snapping into Tiernan's as they both groaned.

Tiernan didn't ask why, only took the cue he was given, running his hands down Nik's back, tracing his shoulder blades, pressing his

96

face to Nik's shoulder as he murmured, "Fuck, Nikos, yeah, please I need to come, please. *Nikos.*"

He felt Nik come without so much as a word — the stutter of his hips coupled with a sharp breath exhaled against his temple. Tiernan was about ready to explode, his cock jumping in his hand when he touched it, aching and heavy, hot as he stroked it, Nik still inside him, Nik pressed against him, quickly unraveling as he came down.

"Shit," he cursed, his stomach tightening as he came, squeezing his cock as he groaned and let his head hit the pillow.

Nik pulled out carefully, and Tiernan winced at the feeling. He would definitely be sore tomorrow, but not in a bad way. Nik unwound beside him, like a cat in a sunny patch, spreading out on the bed next to Tiernan.

Tiernan felt tired, tired and sated and happy. He barely wanted to open his eyes, but he forced himself to, turning to Nik. Nik had his eyes closed like he might go to sleep, but when Tiernan smoothed a hand over his stomach, he opened his eyes.

"Nikos?" Tiernan asked curiously. He'd never questioned that Nik was short for something, but he'd thought it was Nicholas. "Should I call you that now?"

Nik shook his head. "No, no. Just call me Nik." Tiernan raised an eyebrow. That couldn't be the end of the story, but he didn't want to push it. After all, he wasn't even sure what they were, let alone what kinds of questions he could get away with. Nik looked away. "I just wanted to hear you say it."

Tiernan smiled. A baby bird. He pushed Nik's sweaty hair from his eyes, tracing down to his temple. Nik met his gaze, unsure this time, like the first time they'd met.

"I'll call you whatever you want, *Nikos,*" he said, pressing a kiss to his lips. He grabbed a towel from the floor and took a minute to clean up before settling back on the bed with Nik beside him.

For a long minute, the only sounds were their breathing, masked by the air conditioner in the corner. The air was cold against the sweat on his skin and he pulled Nik in tighter, pleased when Nik didn't protest or pull away.

"Why Chicago?" Tiernan asked as they lay there, uncovered, bodies pressed together. Nik frowned up at him, eyebrows furrowed. "Why'd you choose Chicago? New York has great art schools." Tiernan had never been to New York City, but everything pop culture told him was that it was a great place. All his friends who went raved about the pizza and art museums. Tiernan could go for the pizza. Art museums, not so much.

"It was far away," Nik muttered, rolling onto his back. The water stain hadn't changed as Tiernan glanced up at it.

"From your family?"

Nik sighed like he was tired now. "From everything. I don't know. It was new, different but the same. Plus they have a great program and they gave me a scholarship. Going to school in New York wouldn't have been cheap no matter what. If I'm going to put myself in debt, it might as well be somewhere I like."

"You don't like New York?" Tiernan couldn't really blame him for leaving home. He hadn't chosen to stay in Las Vegas, and everyone told him all the time how amazing it was. He hadn't grown up on the Strip; the rest of Vegas was just like every other town.

"Parts of it, but not the parts you see every day. Not the parts you have to live in."

Reaching down, Tiernan pulled up the thin top sheet to ward off the cold air permeating the room. Nik grabbed his underwear off the floor and slid them back on, but he didn't get up and get any further dressed. Tiernan smiled to himself.

"So after you use my photos to make you a famous photographer, what are you gonna do?"

"Go back to school."

Tiernan smiled, brushing a hand through Nik's hair, and Nik's eyes flicked to his. They were a dark hazel, almost brown except for the flicks of gold around the irises. "I mean after that. You want to keep doing sports photography?"

"I actually never wanted to do sports photography," Nik admitted, gazing at Tiernan, and Tiernan felt something warm glow under his skin, not arousal or desire, but something softer. He couldn't quite explain it, but he knew it had to do with how Nik wasn't rushing off, wasn't making an excuse to leave. Nik stayed there, arm brushing against his in the quiet of the room.

"I should be insulted," he murmured against Nik's temple, and he could almost feel Nik smile.

"I want to be a photojournalist, you know, tell stories through my photos, travel, be a part of the world in some way. I don't want to just sit in a studio and takes pictures of models."

It was a lofty ambition, Tiernan thought. "That doesn't sound easy."

"It's not." Nik turned onto his side to face Tiernan, their noses practically touching. "What are you going to do? After?"

Tiernan leaned into him, letting their mouths touch, soft and brief. "I haven't really thought about it."

"Not at all?"

Tiernan had thought about it, to tell the truth, but he didn't like to. He'd heard lots of horror stories of athletes retiring and not knowing what to do with themselves. Sure, he had a degree but what use would it be without any experience? He couldn't just go out and get a job based on the number of medals he'd won. "If I'm lucky, I'll make it to my mid-thirties before I have to retire, unless I choose to do it earlier, or I get injured or something."

"But then what?"

"I don't know. Maybe I'll become a coach or a model or I'll write a book about my Olympic experience and become a best-seller. Everyone loves stories about sex, scandal, and sports."

Nik's forehead pressed to Tiernan's and Tiernan let his hand fall to Nik's waist, a gentle touch that made him think of scented candles and bubble baths and all those things he normally didn't bother with when it came to guys.

"I hate to think what that foreshadows."

"Maybe it's a retelling," he murmured into Nik's skin, lips trailing down his cheek. "And the ending will be filled with success and no scandal."

"So you already know the ending?"

"No," Tiernan admitted, tilting Nik's mouth towards his, running his thumb over Nik's bottom lip. He liked it like this, like nothing else existed outside of this room. It was just the two of them, for just a moment. "But I figure I can write it any way I want."

Nik didn't reply and kissed him back when Tiernan leaned in.

Tomorrow it was back to training, Tiernan thought as Nik pulled him closer, but tonight, it was just this.

Chapter 14:
Through The Lens

Nik couldn't believe it, but he was actually glad to be back in Arizona, somewhere where yes, it was a thousand degrees outside, but he didn't drip sweat the moment he stepped out of his apartment in the morning. He called that an upside.

The coffee pot was full, probably courtesy of Brooke, when he poured himself a cup in the break room. He didn't even jump when Brooke popped in behind him.

"You're back!" she said excitedly. "How were Trials? It's so cool you got to go. I wish I had your internship." She reached for the coffee pot and poured herself a cup as well.

Nik smiled at her enthusiasm. "It was pretty great," he admitted. Between Marion's praise and Tiernan making it to the Olympics, he almost felt as if everything going on at home didn't matter. He hadn't heard from Rae in a few days, and he hadn't called her for fear of Andre yelling, or more bad news. There always seemed to be bad news. "How are things with David?"

Brooke dumped three sugars into her mug and deflated at the question, sighing at the swirling mess in her cup. "Still nothing. Do I need to wear a sign on my shirt that says, 'Ask me out, you idiot'?"

"Maybe." Nik was definitely not an expert on the subject.

"Maybe he's gay," she said after a second. "I mean, it didn't seem like it, but sometimes, you can't tell." She turned to him, eyes bright. "You should ask him out."

"What?" Nik choked on his coffee. He didn't even know David. They barely shared eye contact at work and Nik had never gotten any sort of vibe from him.

"If he says yes, then we'll know for sure."

"If he says yes, I'll have to go out with him," Nik pointed out. He had no intention of dating someone from the office, especially for some theory. "What if he says no?"

Brooke paused, frowning. "That wouldn't answer the question either."

"I think there's an easy solution here," Nik said, glad they'd bypassed the Nik asking David out scenario. The thought of going out with someone who wasn't Tiernan did funny things to his stomach, not that he and Tiernan were dating. They weren't. They were just... hanging out in a stress-free environment.

"I know, I know, I know," she said, turning her coffee cup around. "But what if he says no?"

"Why would he?" Nik had been here before, with Rae. Rae hardly ever asked him for advice concerning guys, mostly because Nik never had any advice, but she told him all her problems anyway.

Brooke reminded him of Rae, just a tiny bit, and it wasn't just their similar noses. Brooke came off as super confident, running around the office like she was going to own the place some day, but when it came to dating, she was just as clueless as everyone else. It made Nik feel a little better about his own uncertainty about Tiernan.

"I'm not smart enough," she said, listing off her fingers. "I don't go to a fancy school — he goes to Berkeley, you know. I'm — "

"You are smart enough," Nik interrupted. "And you're pretty and nice, and anyone who doesn't want to go out with you is stupid."

She smiled after a second. "Thanks. I needed that." She took a fortifying breath. "You're right. I should just ask him out. I'm gonna ask him out."

"Good," Nik said, and he meant it. She bit her lip, looking like she was steeling herself.

"I am," she said again, setting down her mug and straightening up. "I'm gonna do it. I am."

"Okay," Nik agreed as she headed for the door, but she cringed back as she reached it.

"But if he says no, we're going to eat all the ice cream, right? Ooh! We could watch the first Asbury series movie!"

"Of course." The only cure to a broken heart, according to Rae, was ice cream and movies. He actually had learned something, during all those years with a sister. It was nice to help Brooke. It was almost like being with Rae again, though Rae could read his thoughts without him even having to speak, half the time. He missed her.

"Okay," she said firmly. "Here I go."

"Good luck," Nik told her as she disappeared, but she didn't need it. Grabbing his coffee, he headed for the conference room.

Jennifer was already there and looked up as he entered.

"Well, you survived your first plane trip," she said as he slid into his seat across the conference table. She'd commandeered it for their meeting, though Nik wouldn't call it much of a meeting, since it was just the two of them, like always. "And your first Olympic trials. How'd you like it?"

"It was different," he said, thinking of the frenzy of the crowds, the excitement electric in the air. "I've never seen anything like that."

"That was only a taste," she assured him, spreading out her notebooks and calendars. "We've got three weeks to the Olympics. In that time, we need to stick close to Pace. This is a critical time in his training, so we can't get in the way."

Nik nodded, watching her scribble something down. She had notebook after notebook of notes, the same way that Nik's hard drive was stuffed full of photographs. He didn't plan on getting in Tiernan's way, not when he knew how important this was to him. The Olympics were what this internship was to Nik, and he wasn't going to let anything get in his way either.

"Marion seemed pretty impressed," Jennifer said, laying out her calendar and shooting Nik a knowing glance. "That's not bad for an intern."

Nik had tried not to think about what Marion had said for the past few days. He didn't want to get his hopes up too high, but when Jennifer said it, he couldn't help the momentary inflation in his chest.

"You think she meant it?"

"Of course she did," Jennifer said easily, waving away his uncertainty. "You've been doing a great job. Better than any other photographer I've worked with. Most are so self-involved and focused on sleeping with the models. You're there to do a job, you know, now worry about how much ass you can get."

Nik nodded and didn't say anything. He hadn't intended to sleep with Tiernan, which wasn't much of a consolation when she talked about how self-involved photographers were. Nik knew plenty of people back at school who claimed to be all about the art of photography but mostly used it to pick up girls. He couldn't say he hadn't used it as a come-on before, but that wasn't why he wanted to be a photographer.

He hoped Jennifer didn't think he was in this just to sleep with Tiernan, because he wasn't. It was just an unexpected perk.

"The Olympics editor does want me to do some out pieces, though, while we're here," Jennifer said, flipping through her notebook. "I've already set up the photo shoot with Dylan..." She checked her notes. "Hoffman. He placed first in the butterfly and uses the Center's facilities to train as well, so we're going to pop in, do a little interview. Normal stuff."

Nik hadn't heard of Dylan Hoffman, but he didn't like the idea of doing a story on someone other than Tiernan. He couldn't choose his subjects, he reminded himself. A real photographer did what the story required. Unless he was freelancing, he didn't always get to choose what he shot. Maybe once he worked his way up the food chain.

"You think he'll medal?" he asked, remembering Tiernan's face when he'd placed second. He'd looked so happy, in shock as though he hadn't quite believed he could do it. He hoped this Dylan person wouldn't take that away from him.

Jennifer checked the time on her phone and grimaced, gathering her things and shoving them into her bag. "Probably. Come on, we're gonna be late."

She ushered Nik out of the conference room, giving him no time to contemplate the consequences of her answer.

Dylan was *not* like Tiernan, Nik decided the minute they set up the shot. He didn't move as easily, stiff and bulky, his eyes unnervingly following Nik as Nik tried to direct him. Jennifer stood off to the side, arms crossed as she watched them.

The sun was in the right spot, but they would lose the light if Dylan didn't stop looking like Frankenstein.

"Could you just step over by the pool," Nik said, gesturing toward the silver ladder that glinted in the sunlight. Dylan walked clunkily, flat-footed, his chest muscled and bulging. "Okay..." It wasn't a great shot, but there wasn't much to work with.

"You know, I've seen you," Dylan said as Nik crouched to test the angle.

"Excuse me?"

They were outside, the sun beating down on the back of his neck. He was starting to sweat now, though they'd barely started.

"Trailing around Pace," Dylan said, eyes on Nik, dark and intent.

"We're doing a series on him," he replied, not liking the way Dylan watched him. "Turn to your left a little and lower your hand. Relax your shoulders." Whatever he said didn't seem to help, but he couldn't make a model out of a mole.

"She's doing a series on him." Dylan nodded at Jennifer, who was on her phone now, a hand to her ear to block them out. "You're taking pictures of his ass and calling it art."

Nik lowered the camera slowly. "Why do you care?" He hadn't told anyone about him and Tiernan and whatever it was they were doing. He wasn't really sure; he just knew that he felt good when he was with Tiernan, something he didn't say very often.

"Because he doesn't deserve it," Dylan replied, squinting against the sun. He was bulkier than Tiernan, shoulders broad, but he wasn't as tall. He definitely wasn't as attractive with a large nose and crooked teeth when he smiled. "He lucked his way into first place. After trials four years ago, he shouldn't have even kept swimming. He was washed up then. Now he's got you eating out of his hand when you should be focusing on me. I'm the next gold medalist at this Center."

"So you want me to take pictures of your ass instead?" Nik asked, pressing his lips together. So far, he wasn't impressed by what he saw. Tiernan was far more deserving than this asshole.

"It's pretty nice, don't you think?" Dylan asked, turning around and flipping down the waist of his suit slightly. Nik looked away, changing a setting on his camera instead. He wasn't interested in Dylan's ass.

"Let's just get this shoot over with," he suggested, glancing at the sun. It was setting too fast for his liking, but he couldn't get Dylan to shut up long enough to get a good shot. He wasn't sure Dylan was capable of a good shot.

"When you get tired of a second-rate swimmer, hit me up," Dylan said with a flat smile. "I'll give your photos some sizzle."

"I don't think I need advice on photography, thanks," Nik deadpanned, taking another shot, but it was just the same as all the ones before. His phone vibrated in his pocket with a text, but Nik ignored it. Probably Andre with some other new guilt-trip, to get him to come home. It wasn't going to work.

Dylan scowled finally, as though just getting Nik's disinterest. "Pace doesn't deserve to be profiled; he slept his way to the top, you know."

"We're losing the light," Nik said sharply, turning to Jennifer, who was watching him. She didn't say anything. "I think we got it."

They had nothing, but Nik wasn't going to stay here any longer with a self-involved jerk who was only interested in putting down Tiernan and showing off his (mediocre, in Nik's opinion) ass.

As he packed up his equipment, Dylan watched him intently.

"Don't go thinking you're special 'cause Pace fucks you," he said as Nik kept his gaze on his bag, trying not to listen. This guy clearly had a problem. "He fucks everyone."

Nik looked up sharply, snapping his camera case shut. "Apparently he hasn't fucked you or you wouldn't have such a stick up your ass."

It wasn't professional, but Nik wasn't going to be talked to like that, not from Dylan, not from anyone.

"Nik," came Jennifer's warning voice from behind him. "Let's wrap this up?"

"Coming," he muttered, a pit settling in his stomach as he turned from Dylan. He shouldn't have snapped, but it was hard to keep it together when Dylan was clearly goading him. He should be a silent photographer, like nature photographers. They blended into the background. That was the kind Nik wanted to be. Insulting the subject wasn't the best idea.

Jennifer didn't speak as they headed for the car. Unease gnawed at Nik's stomach until he couldn't take it, pausing at the door to the car, heat emanating in a wave as he opened it.

"Jennifer, I'm sorry, I shouldn't have — "

"You don't have to apologize to me," she interrupted him. "That guy was an asshole."

Nik let out a relieved breath, but she didn't get in the car.

"But he's also your job, and sometimes there are gonna be people like that and you have to deal with them. You have to be professional."

"I know," he said quickly, the pit coming back. He'd already fucked up twice on that account — sleeping with Tiernan and now snapping at Dylan. "I didn't mean — I shouldn't have — "

Jennifer shook her head. "We all have our breaking points. I remember my first year, I interviewed this famous musician. I was so excited to meet him, but he was so awful to me. He was rude and acted like I didn't know anything, kept calling me 'sweetie' and 'honey.' I wanted to cry and punch him in the face all at once."

"What did you do?" Nik asked, watching her twist her lips as she sighed.

"I went home and threw my phone at the wall. Not the smartest thing I've ever done, but it was better than throwing it at him. Then I got the recording of the interview off the cloud and wrote a scathing article. My editor loved it."

"So it wasn't all bad?" Nik wasn't sure there was a way he could repeat that with a photograph, and he definitely was not going to throw his camera at the wall because of some asshole. He did feel a little better, though, as she smiled.

"That sexist old man taught me that not everyone was going to be nice and if I wanted a story, I couldn't be afraid to hold back. You're young, but it's better to learn now that you can't please everyone so you might as well please yourself."

She slid in the car, finally, and Nik followed. That was one thing he'd figured out already, though it was harder than he'd expected.

"Speaking of pleasing yourself," she said as they pulled out of the lot. Nik turned the AC down, willing it to cool down. She glanced at him with a knowing look and he purposefully stared out the window as his heart thudded in his chest. "Tiernan?"

Fuck. Another professional failing. He shoved a hand through his hair and didn't reply. So far, he wasn't doing too well keeping his promises to himself.

"It's not..." He didn't know what it wasn't, exactly. He hadn't thought enough about what he was doing with Tiernan; that it wasn't really just sex, not anymore, though he didn't know what else it could be. "I didn't..."

Jennifer didn't seem to need him to finish his thought — he couldn't if he'd wanted to. She simply nodded knowingly as they drove.

"I don't think you're one of those guys who uses your work to get ass," she said, "but don't you dare turn into one either." She glanced at him, and Nik was sure he was about to get chewed out. He winced internally, already hearing the reprimands. He should have known better. He shouldn't get involved with subjects. It was only going to end badly because most things in his life did. You'd think he would learn. "You're still a little naive, kid," she said, nudging him in the side. "I like it. Don't lose that."

She wasn't yelling at him. That was... new. He almost didn't know what to do. He wasn't used to getting off the hook. In his life, someone always had to be responsible. There always had to be someone to blame, and that person was usually him, for one reason or another. It was strange that Jennifer just dropped it, like he hadn't done anything wrong.

He didn't ask why — if he'd learned anything in his twenty years of life, it was don't look a gift horse in the mouth. But he didn't know what to make of it as they merged onto the freeway. As they drove, he allowed himself a smile as he stared out the window at the beige buildings whipping past. Maybe he hadn't screwed it up by sleeping with Tiernan. Maybe he'd made the right decision this time. Maybe.

Chapter 15:
Runs In The Family

Nik glanced around Brooke's room, the walls not elegantly decorated as he'd expected them to be. They looked more like Nik's room at home, except instead of magazine pages and bands plastered on the walls, there were world leaders, well-known judges, senators. All women. What weren't covered in pictures of women were shelves crammed with books, figurines from popular novels, a wand in a box displayed on a shelf. The walls behind were painted a light shade of pink and her bed was piled high with too many pillows. It was weird being in a room with a girl who wasn't Rae.

"Are you sure this is a good idea?" he asked as Brooke flipped open her laptop. She moved to the bed, sitting next to him. Her mom hadn't said anything when Nik had arrived except to offer him a drink and remind Brooke to feed the dog. Andre had always wanted to know where Nik was, what he was doing, with who, as if Nik had anything to do with anyone but Rae. Just another way to control him.

"Of course it is," she said, pulling up his website. "All press is good press, especially when it comes to developing your career. I write a feature on you, it gets picked up by some big website, and we both benefit." She sounded wistful, and Nik wasn't going to turn down the opportunity to get his name out there.

As she typed, Nik looked around the room again. It was twice the size of his bedroom in New York, but stuffed with way more than Nik could fit in his whole apartment. Brooke had an old flat-screen TV and a desk with a plush chair pushed up to it. It was covered in clothes at the moment. Her mattress was twice the size of Nik's, and had a real bed frame. Nik had always slept on a mattress on the floor.

A fluffy white dog trundled inside, sitting on Nik's foot and panting up at him until he patted its head.

"There's a lot of women on your walls," he said, and she glanced up.

"They're my idols," she said simply. "There's nothing better than a strong, smart, confident woman. I want to be like that."

"I think you are like that." He immediately thought of Rae when she said it. Rae was the strongest woman he knew. He couldn't exactly count his mother in that category.

She smiled. "Thanks. I think you are too."

"A strong, confident woman?"

She laughed, pulling up a new document. "Strong and confident. Brave. Smart. Like Grace Asbury or Harry Potter."

"Katniss Everdeen."

"Jon Snow."

"Elizabeth Bennett."

"Mr. Knightley."

"We're getting off the subject," Nik said with a smile. It was so easy to fall into conversation with Brooke, to forget about the rest of the day, about Dylan.

"I just want to make a difference, is all," she said with a shrug.

Nik nodded. "Me too." He didn't want to just photograph celebrities. He wanted to tell stories, get out into the world and make a difference. He and Brooke weren't so different.

"Then let's get started," she said eagerly, pulling up her blog.

Nik couldn't help smiling at the excitement that ran through him at the idea. It wasn't anything big, just a feature on her blog, but she got a lot of hits. He'd checked it out, and it was a pretty thorough and professional website. Not just current events but art, sports, and a bit of celebrity gossip, which obviously got the most views.

Nik's phone vibrated with a text as Brooke talked about picking a theme for the feature. Tiernan's name appeared on the screen and Nik's heart contracted slightly. He hadn't texted Tiernan after the interview with Dylan — he'd been too preoccupied with what Dylan had said, then he'd forgotten about all of it between Jennifer and Brooke.

Come over later? the text read with an inappropriate emoji that Nik hid from Brooke as he typed his response and put the phone away.

"So theme or no theme?" Brooke asked, skimming through his photos. "I'm thinking no. Better to show a range of skill, don't you think?"

"Sounds good," Nik agreed, but he was preoccupied with thoughts of Tiernan as she debated the merits of themes.

"When you invited me over, I didn't think it meant sitting on the couch watching trial videos."

He'd thought, when Tiernan had texted, that he wouldn't have spent the first half hour watching other swimmers under foreign-language voiceovers. A part of him didn't mind, leaning against Tiernan's shoulder, breathing in the persistent scent of chlorine that always seemed to linger in his hair. Tiernan was warm, his skin smooth and soft, and he hadn't protested when Nik had propped his chin over his shoulder.

Nik leaned away from Tiernan's shoulder with a sigh, sinking into the couch. The leather stuck to his arms, the AC not cool enough in his opinion.

"Sorry," Tiernan said, sounding distracted. His thumb hovered to pause the video but he didn't yet. "Coach wants me to go over other qualifiers."

"Won't that freak you out?"

Tiernan shrugged, and Nik brushed a hand against his forehead, sweeping his hair back. There were tiny lines under Tiernan's eyes that he didn't remember being there before.

"It's good to know the times to beat, and who knows, maybe I'll pick up a trick or two."

Nik pressed his face back to Tiernan's shoulder, eyeing the video as it ended. The guy on there had finished his butterfly in fifty-one seconds flat. Tiernan said nothing about the time, though, turning off the tablet and setting it on the table.

He couldn't imagine that knowing what he was up against would help. It would just have made him more nervous, but he wasn't Tiernan. Tiernan didn't seem to worry about things like that.

Tiernan shook his head as he slumped down on the couch. He seemed more tired than Nik had seen him before. It was strange, just being here together. All the other times, they'd be halfway to naked by now or already done, but Nik couldn't deny the flutter in his chest when Tiernan's hand moved to his thigh, resting there lightly. It wasn't an invitation or a question, just a gesture.

Swallowing down the way his heart sped up, Nik hesitated.

"I met Dylan today," he said at length, listening to Tiernan's heartbeat, feeling the warmth of Tiernan's hand through his jeans.

He felt more than heard Tiernan's short laugh. "How was that?"

Nik probably shouldn't have said anything, but self-preservation had never been his strong suit. "He said you slept your way to the top."

Tiernan scoffed, but his hand tightened briefly over Nik's thigh. "If only that were possible."

"He said…" Nik stopped himself. Why was he even bringing it up? It didn't matter. They weren't dating or anything that it would affect him. He grimaced to himself at the thought that he even cared, but he couldn't get Dylan's words out of his head.

"What?" Tiernan asked, frowning as he turned to him. Nik was forced to sit up and he bit his lip. He shouldn't have said anything.

"He said you fuck everyone."

"Everyone like you?" Tiernan asked, watching Nik.

Nik shook his head. "He was just doing it to be an asshole." He shouldn't have brought it up, but not knowing was chewing a hole in his chest.

Tiernan sat back on the couch, drawing his hand from Nik's leg and moving to his own, tapping his shorts with his fingers.

"He wasn't wrong," Tiernan said finally, and Nik looked over sharply. He couldn't mean… "I've slept with a lot of people."

Nik frowned. He hadn't meant to dredge up Tiernan's past.

"We don't have to do this," he said quickly. "I didn't — I just — I don't know why I brought it up. I really don't need to know."

Tiernan nodded slowly. "I'm not embarrassed," he said finally. "I was young, stupid, horny. Just like any other guy. If you're asking because you're worried, I'm not sleeping with anyone else."

"I'm not worried," Nik scoffed. There was nothing to worry about. "You can do whatever you want."

"I know what I want to do," Tiernan said simply, and his hand slid back to Nik's thigh, gliding up his inseam towards his cock.

"Yeah?" Nik asked, but he swallowed as Tiernan leaned in and his hand crept higher. He didn't want to be just a distraction for Tiernan. He wasn't going to be the reason Tiernan failed.

Tiernan's hand slid over his dick, pressing down on his jeans as Nik bit back a noise. Leaning in, he nuzzled Nik's neck, pressing a kiss to his jaw as his hand massaged Nik's cock through his clothes.

"I'm not fucking anyone else," he murmured, mouth trailing over Nik's jaw and Nik shivered at the hot breath on his skin. "And you're not one of those guys I used to hide behind last time."

"What were you hiding from?" Nik asked, closing his eyes and sucking in a breath as Tiernan's hand rubbed against his cock, the friction too rough against his jeans.

Tiernan's tongue slid down the tendon in his neck. He paused to pull back the neck of Nik's shirt, scraping his teeth against his skin, sucking as Nik cursed under his breath and struggled to stay focused. It would be too fucking easy to let Tiernan get away with this, with his hand on Nik's prick, his mouth hot against his skin. It was unlucky that Tiernan knew just the way to shift himself so he was pressed up against Nik's side, a heavy warmth taking over him in a way that made Nik forget what he was doing.

Tiernan never replied, reaching for Nik's button. He got it open one-handed and slid his fingers teasingly over the bare skin underneath.

Nik's stomach jumped, his cock hardening in anticipation. He was exposed like this, the blinds still open to the pool beyond, his legs spread wide and Tiernan half on top of him, teasing his way over his skin.

Nik didn't know what Tiernan had been hiding from last time. It could have been a million things, but now wasn't the time to push it, not with Tiernan's hands pulling his shirt up, mouth landing on his stomach and sucking until Nik arched into him with a breathless sigh.

"Are you gonna touch me or should I do it myself?" Nik ground out finally, pushing Tiernan's head back so he could see his face, see the way his green eyes darkened. It sent a thrill through Nik's body, too eager for this, but he didn't fucking care.

"Just wanna make sure you know what you're doing," Tiernan replied, running his thumb under Nik's lower lip and arching an eyebrow.

Nik's heart rate slowed for a second as he stared at Tiernan. He didn't know what the fuck he was doing. He didn't most days, especially when it came to guys. Most of the guys he slept with didn't care about his life or his family. They didn't ask and he didn't offer. It wasn't like guys were his priority. Mostly, he spent his time worrying about paying for school, not who he was sleeping with.

Tiernan leaned in and kissed him, long and slow, fanning the flutter in Nik's chest. *Fuck*, he really didn't know what he was doing. He lifted his hands to Tiernan's face, keeping him close, licking into Tiernan's mouth. If he was kissing Tiernan, he didn't have to answer any questions. He didn't want to think about how easily this could be explained, if he accepted that Dylan was just messing with his mind, if Tiernan really did like him more than just an occasional hook-up.

"I don't fuck around anymore," Tiernan murmured when Nik had to pull away to breathe, panting against his mouth, biting his lip as Tiernan's hand *finally* slid under his waistband and wrapped around his cock. "And I don't fuck just anyone."

Nik's fingers tightened over the back of Tiernan's neck as Tiernan stroked him, slow and steady at first. He should have been trying to come up with a response, but he couldn't think. He could only groan as Tiernan's thumb brushed over the head of his prick, slick with pre-come.

This wasn't where Nik was supposed to be. He was supposed to be in his apartment, editing photos and adding shit to his resume so when he graduated, he could get a good job and pay back those thousands of dollars worth of student loans before he died. He shouldn't have been moaning into Tiernan's neck, straining not to come, not yet, with Tiernan's fist tight around his cock, jerking him off in his jeans.

But he was, he was here, gripping Tiernan's thigh, hips pushing up into his hand, his heart racing, blood pounding in his ears. And he fucking wanted to be here. He may not have known what he was doing, but he was glad he was doing it.

"Shit," he cursed as Tiernan's hand moved faster, his prick throbbing in his grip. He tried to shift, but there was nowhere to go, pushing against Tiernan.

"Yeah," Tiernan muttered against his temple, pressing barely-there kisses to his skin, mouthing down his jaw, hot and open-mouthed kisses littering his neck. "Come for me, Nik, come on, I want to feel you."

Groaning, Nik's hips pushed up into Tiernan's grip, the twist of his wrist that made Nik whimper as he came, heat coursing through him, toes curling into the carpet.

His eyes drifted closed as Tiernan pulled his hand out, reaching for a box of tissues on the floor. He could just go to sleep right then, but he had to get back to his apartment. There was work to do in the morning. Still, he didn't move, not until he felt the shift of the couch, Tiernan's body close to his.

Opening his eyes, he glanced at Tiernan. Tiernan's eyes were on his tablet, like he was thinking about those other swimmers again.

"I should get going," he said finally, adjusting his jeans and frowning at the wet spot on the front.

"Hey," Tiernan said as Nik stood, zipping up his jeans and slipping his shoes back on. "I don't know what I'm doing either."

Nik smiled after a second, grabbing his jacket off the couch. "I'll see you later."

"Don't listen to Dylan, okay? He hates not getting all the glory."

"I won't," Nik assured him, pulling open the door. "Goodnight."

"Goodnight," Tiernan called after him as he shut the door, "*Nikos.*"

Nik smiled to himself as the door latched. No matter what Dylan said, Nik was glad Tiernan was fucking him. Swinging on his jacket, he headed down the stairs to the parking lot. He was in such a good mood that when his phone pinged with a text, he simply ignored it and kept on walking. Whatever it was could wait until later.

The text was from Andre. Nik sighed as he unlocked his apartment, frowning at the words on the screen. He'd thought Andre had given up texting after their fight, but apparently not.

Instead of replying to Andre's profanity-laden message about responsibility, Nik opened up Rae's message thread instead.

Tell Andre to fuck off will you, he wrote. He didn't expect a reply — it was almost one AM in New York, but Rae's reply came almost immediately.

Tell him yourself.

Nik flopped down on the couch and scowled. He had already told Andre that, but Andre never listened. Andre was the oldest so what he said went no matter what anyone else wanted.

He never listens.

Runs in the family, came Rae's reply.

It was hard to read tone in text, but Nik frowned at her words. Something seemed off, though he couldn't pinpoint what.

Everything okay? he wrote, watching for the bubble indicating she was writing to pop up. It never came. She didn't reply.

Despite the clawing in his chest, the voice deep inside telling him to let it go, not to open up that can of worms, Nik pressed the call button on Rae's name and waited, listening to the ring tone.

The phone rang and rang until it went to voicemail.

"Hey, you've reached Rae. Leave a message or I won't call you back."

Nik hung up but the clawing in his chest didn't subside. She always answered his calls. She was the only one who did. He didn't like it.

She never texted back even though Nik waited, staying up, editing some photos to take his mind off the silent phone, but when he checked it before bed, there was still nothing. Unease settled deep in his stomach as he pulled the covers up. Something was wrong, but, he thought as he lay in the dark, maybe he had lost his right to ask what.

Chapter 16:
Booze And Boys

Dylan was the last person Tiernan wanted to see when he stepped inside the lounge to grab a drink before training, but there he was, blocking the vending machine with his bulky frame. It was bad enough that they shared training facilities, that he had to see Dylan every day and be reminded that he didn't swim the best butterfly in the country, but Dylan had to go out of his way to try to turn Nik against him.

"It's not rocket science," he said finally while Dylan stared at the choices in the machine.

Dylan turned slowly, still blocking the machine, as if deliberately trying to be as annoying as possible. On reflection, he probably was. Dylan had always been a little standoffish around him, threatened, Coach would have said, by Tiernan's talent. Tiernan never thought of himself as threatening — he disliked the term in general. Competitive was a better way of putting it, but that wasn't how Dylan acted.

"Jealous you're not the only one getting press treatment?" Dylan asked instead of responding to his barb. "Your little photographer friend couldn't stop staring at me the other day."

"What'd you tell him?" Tiernan asked, though he knew perfectly well. Nik had haltingly brought it up, the question of his past, if Nik was just another fuck to keep himself distracted.

"The truth," Dylan replied with a sneer, punching in a number on the machine finally. "If he's going to let you near him, he should know what he really is. Just another fuck."

"What the fuck do you care what he is?" Tiernan asked, crossing his arms and frowning at Dylan. "Unless you want me to fuck you too."

Dylan glowered, grabbing his drink as it clunked into the chute. "I wouldn't let you touch me with a ten foot pole. We all know where your ass has been."

"For all your talk, you don't come off very straight," Tiernan pointed out. "Maybe all this anger is just repressed homosexuality."

"Fuck you," Dylan spat. "You're so full of yourself, Pace, and that's why you screwed up last time. You're not God's gift to swimming and not everyone has to like you."

"I never said they did," Tiernan replied coolly. "But Nik's none of your business, and what we do is between us."

"Just trying to warn the kid." Dylan shrugged as though he really did have Nik's best interests at heart, but Tiernan knew he was full of shit. Dylan couldn't care less about Nik. He just wanted to fuck with Tiernan.

"There's nothing to warn him about." Tiernan knew, he *knew* he shouldn't rise to Dylan's bait. He shouldn't have even started this conversation, but here he was. He never learned.

"It's a good strategy," Dylan said, bypassing Tiernan for the door. "When you don't even medal, at least you'll have someone to blame."

Dylan left before Tiernan could muster up the response he wanted, glaring after him. Nik was not an excuse. Tiernan knew what excuses were — they were going out to clubs until three in the morning the night before competitions, letting guys suck him off, nameless, faceless guys in alleyways, in the back of his car, in bathrooms. Excuses were blowing off practice to sleep off a hangover. Nik wasn't any of that.

Nik was something he looked forward to after practice. He wasn't a nameless fuck in a club bathroom.

Turning from the door, Tiernan pushed a hand through his hair and sighed. He shouldn't let Dylan get to him. Dylan wanted him distracted so he could steal a gold medal out from under him. Tiernan may have messed up last time, but he wasn't going to do it again. He'd already passed trials. Now he just needed to place at the Olympics and he sure as hell wasn't going to let Dylan get in his way.

—◻—◻—◻—

"Where's your head, Pace?" Coach stared down at him, one hand on his whistle, thick eyebrows contracted, looking like one big caterpillar crawling across his face.

Tiernan wiped water out of his eyes and shook his head. "Here?"

Coach knocked painfully on his head. "Apparently not. That was the worst butterfly I've seen you do. Keep swimming like that and you'll give the medal away.

Tiernan hauled himself out of the pool, dripping all over the concrete as he stood up. "Sorry, Coach. Got a lot on my mind."

Coach didn't look sympathetic, crossing his arms over his chest. His mouth twisted to the side, and Tiernan sometimes wished he didn't have an ex-Marine coach who didn't take shit excuses. Tiernan wasn't sure what was wrong with him. This was his big chance and he couldn't even swim a decent time.

"Olympics are a big deal," Coach said, scribbling Tiernan's time down on his chart. "Anxiety, excitement, nerves. It's all normal."

"So what do I do?" Tiernan asked. He hadn't made it this far last time. He didn't know what he was supposed to be doing aside from training. Jennifer's interview sessions had become shorter, more clipped, like she was waiting for him to actually do something impressive she could put on the blog. There was only so much someone could write about the anticipation of competition.

"Focus," Coach said simply. "Push everything else out. This competition is about you and you alone. It's not about your family, your friends, your fans. Let yourself get caught up in that shit, and you get lost."

It was easy for him to say, Tiernan thought with a frown. He didn't have a nagging Bridezilla sister to deal with or Nik and his adorable scowl to greet him.

"So I give everything up until after the Olympics?" He didn't think that was possible. His sister would murder him, and Nik — he didn't want to give Nik up.

"I didn't say that," Coach replied shortly. Coach wasn't usually one to give Tiernan advice outside of swimming and this was probably why, Tiernan figured. He wasn't very good at it. Tiernan preferred him giving gruff critiques about competition rather than commenting on his life. "Life is all about balance, Pace. You work hard in here, you can do what you want out there." He gestured toward the doors.

Coach was right. Tiernan was letting the pressure get to him, and he knew what happened when he did that. This wasn't going to be a repeat of last time. Things were different. He was different.

He nodded finally. "Sorry, Coach. I'll work harder."

Coach nodded as well. "Get up on that block. We're running it again."

Tiernan climbed onto the block and got into position. When he was in here, he was focused on swimming his best. When he was out those doors, though, he could focus on whatever he wanted, and he wanted to focus on Nik.

A locker door slammed as Tiernan entered the locker room. Praying it wasn't Dylan, he stuck his head around the corner.

"Sam," he said, and Sam looked up from where he stood at the lockers, his stuffed full duffle bag at his feet. "I didn't see you out there. What are you doing?"

"Packing up," Sam replied with a sad smile.

Tiernan frowned, confused. "Where are you going?"

"Home." Sam grabbed his bag, and it occurred to Tiernan that he hadn't heard anything about Sam's times at trials. Guilt gnawed at his stomach. "Get out of this infernal heat."

Tiernan stared, stomach sinking as he watched Sam shut the locker. "Shit, man, you're leaving me?"

Sam shook his head. "You don't need me around. You're gonna kill those Olympics."

Tiernan's stomach curled in on itself as Sam hooked his bag over his shoulder. He hadn't even bothered to text Sam after trials, to see how he'd done. Some friend he was. He'd been so wrapped up in making it to the Olympics, too focused on himself. That was what you were supposed to do, Coach would have said, but Sam was his best friend at the Center. He should have asked.

"Hey, wait," he said as Sam passed him for the door. "You can't leave without a send-off drink. Let me change real quick and we'll go out." Sam hesitated and Tiernan put on his best serious expression. "Come on. I owe you that much."

"One drink," Sam allowed with a small smile. "Not like it matters now."

Tiernan rinsed off quickly and threw on a shirt and shorts, meeting Sam out front. His shirt stuck to his damp skin as they headed for the parking lot.

"I'm sorry, man," Tiernan said as they wandered down the concrete path, past the gym. "I didn't even ask how it went."

Sam shrugged. "Don't sweat it. You were too busy qualifying, which is what you should have been doing. What I should have been doing."

Tiernan didn't want to ask it, but he had to. They always had to ask. "What happened?"

Sam shook his head inconsequentially. "Nothing really. I'm just not as good as everyone else."

"Bullshit," Tiernan corrected him. "You're one of the better swimmers here."

"But not in Florida." Sam didn't seem outwardly angry or upset, just disappointed, which made Tiernan more annoyed than anything.

"You're not giving up, though," he said. "You're just taking a break, right?"

Sam glanced at him and shouldered his bag. "I don't know. I just need to not be here for a while."

Tiernan fell silent, watching across the way as a couple people emerged from the gym. Gymnasts, he guessed, by their build. He recognized one, the blond guy. He'd seen him before, watching training sometimes. They'd never spoken but Coach had mentioned some of the gymnasts here had made the Olympic team. Tiernan wondered if that guy had.

Glancing at Sam, Tiernan just hoped he wouldn't give up swimming completely. After last trials, that was all Tiernan had wanted to do — crawl into a hole and forget that he'd ever tried to be anything. He'd thought briefly about getting a job, a real job. He had gone to college after all. It had only been because of the swim scholarship and free training, but still.

"Fuck, I can't believe you're leaving me here with Dylan," he said as they reached the parking lot and headed towards his car.

"You'll be fine," Sam assured him with a small smile. "Just keep reminding him he's second best."

Tiernan laughed, tossing his bag in the backseat and Sam did the same. "I'm sure that'll help," he said, sliding inside. Sam merely laughed and shut the door.

"So what happened with the reporter?" Sam asked over the noise of conversation, glasses clinking, the sound system pumping out some old rock music from before Tiernan was born.

"Nothing new coming out," he said, taking a sip of his soda. So far, he'd kept his resolution to give up alcohol. "She's been doing some spotlights on other people."

"Dylan?"

Tiernan sighed. He wasn't jealous of Dylan's turn in the spotlight — he would gladly have given some of his to Sam. Sam deserved it. Dylan, on the other hand... It just went to his head and made him more of an asshole than usual.

Sam didn't push it, and Tiernan appreciated that. Dylan was the last person he wanted to think about.

"What about the photographer?"

"What about him?" What about him indeed. Tiernan smiled at just the thought of Nik, the camera permanently glued to his hand, the appraising way he seemed to look at Tiernan, as though he wasn't always sure what Tiernan was doing. He wanted to wrap Nik up in a big, fluffy blanket and never let go. He didn't even grimace at how fucking cheesy that was.

Sam shot him a knowing look. "I don't even say his name and you light up like a Christmas tree."

"Fuck off," Tiernan said good-naturedly. It was true.

Sam didn't smile. "I just don't want this to be like last time."

"This is completely different than last time." Last time, Tiernan hadn't even known their names. Last time, he'd been way more interested in partying than training. Last time, he'd rejected his parents' rejection of him the only way he knew how — booze and boys.

Sam paused, eyeing his drink then glanced at Tiernan. "You like him."

Tiernan shoved a hand through his hair and smiled at Sam. "Yeah." He hadn't spent a lot of time thinking about his feelings for Nik — feelings got in the way of training — but he wasn't the type to ignore how he felt. Balance, Coach had said. It was all about balance. He liked the balance he felt with Nik.

Sam lifted his glass. "To you, then," he said, "winning a medal and finding someone who can tolerate you."

Tiernan shook his head. "And to you for not giving up. I expect to see you back here next season."

Sam didn't disagree as they clinked the glasses together. Tiernan emptied his glass and set it on the table with a clink. Sam was right, Tiernan had found someone who could tolerate him, and he intended to keep that someone as best he knew how.

Chapter 17:
Rattlesnake Cove

Nik hadn't actually thought anywhere in Phoenix could be pretty, at least in a non-landscaped, rock garden and cacti kind of way. He supposed it had to do with the fact that he'd been there over a month, and had never bothered to go anywhere other than the office and the Center, all in populated areas.

"You're telling me there's an actual lake out here?" he asked doubtfully, peering out the window at the scraggly landscape surrounding the car. The narrow road wound past low mountains, scattered with a wild thrall of barrel cactus, Saguaros, yucca and aloe plants, and something Tiernan said was a Jumping Cholla and warned him to stay far away from. Nik didn't need telling twice, with the angry-looking balls of spikes hanging off the cactus.

Tiernan smiled and rolled down the window, hot air rushing in and clashing with the air conditioning. "Phoenix actually has several lakes, believe it or not. Bartlett is my favorite, though."

They'd been driving for almost an hour already, and Nik wasn't sure how he'd been talked into this. Maybe because Tiernan woke him up at six AM on a Saturday and he hadn't been fully aware of what he was agreeing to, or maybe because the thought of getting out of the city for a day, to photograph something other than pools and city lights was too appealing to resist. Since he'd been there, the only things he'd photographed had been Tiernan — not that he was complaining. He could easily spend hours admiring Tiernan's body, the way it caught the light when wet, but those were for work. They weren't photos he would post on his website, photos that really said something.

E.E. Grey

Turning from the window, Nik watched Tiernan. The air conditioning ruffled his hair and Nik couldn't see his eyes behind his sunglasses. They were out here, alone, spending a whole day together. It made a part of Nik nervous, the realization that this wasn't just fucking. He didn't know when that had happened.

He'd never had a real boyfriend, in the typical way everyone expected people to date. There had been a few hookups in college, but never anyone he'd wanted to call Rae and tell her about. Rae was his measuring stick. He told her everything, or he used to, so if it wasn't important enough to tell her, it wasn't important.

He hadn't told her about Tiernan, he thought, turning his gaze back out the window. It would just be another nail in the coffin to Rae, that he was doing so well away from home, without her and the responsibility of Mom.

What struck him most was that he *wanted* to tell her about Tiernan. He wanted her thoughts on what all this meant — spending days together at a lake, that night in the pool at Trials. She would know what he was supposed to do afterwards, after sex. He'd never been good at that, but Rae always seemed to have an answer.

Every time he thought about calling or texting, just *asking*, he stopped himself. They'd spend five minutes on Nik, then another ten on everything else at home and Nik would hang up feeling guilty and angry. He didn't want to feel that way, so he didn't call. Avoidance was what Rae would have called it if he'd bothered to tell her.

The car turned down a narrowly-paved road, past a sign that read, "Rattlesnake Cove."

"'Rattlesnake Cove,'" Nik said, staring out at the ground around the car. He didn't see any snakes. "That's reassuring."

Tiernan smiled and patted his leg as they drove downhill and a glittering blue lake came into view as they rounded a corner.

The water dazzled a bright blue, reflecting the cloudless sky, and a short sandy beach swept down to the water. On the other side, peaked mountains (hills, Nik allowed) rose up, dotted with scrub bushes and cacti. Tiernan pulled into the small parking lot, up to a little row of shaded picnic tables, and turned off the car.

Nik shielded his eyes as he got out of the car. Tiernan went around to the back and pulled out a cooler and a backpack.

124

"I brought sunscreen," he said, rounding the car to Nik's side and giving him a playful nudge. "Not sure your skin has ever seen the sun. Don't want you to burst into flames."

Nik had heard it all before, so he just rolled his eyes and followed Tiernan down to the beach. The sand burned his feet where it got around his shoes and the sun beat down on them, cheerfully bright.

"How do you stand it?" Nik asked as Tiernan pulled out two towels from his bag and laid them on the sand.

"Stand what?"

"No clouds." He gestured upwards. He could swear he'd only seen clouds once or twice since coming there. "It's weird."

Tiernan shrugged. "It's the desert. Come here and take off your shirt or you'll get heatstroke."

Nik sat down on the towel, fiddling with his camera as Tiernan pulled out the sunscreen and began lathering it on. Nik had been prudent and worn a t-shirt today, had left his jacket in the apartment. He wasn't sold on this lake swimming thing, since his swimming abilities amounted to doggy paddling and one very short backstroke lesson. He'd rather wander around in the desert and take some photos. His camera bag sat on the sand next to him, baking under the sun.

"You're gonna document this moment, right?" Tiernan asked, handing him the sunscreen and tugging at his shirt until Nik let him pull it off. It was different than when Tiernan pulled it off before sex. This was simple, an easy gesture not meant to lead to anything else, comfortable. He liked the way Tiernan's fingertips grazed over his stomach, up his ribcage as he skimmed the shirt off. "You not wearing all black?"

"I wear other colors," Nik protested, flipping open the sunscreen and putting it on. Even with his Greek genes, he still burned like a red-headed kid in the sun. He obviously hadn't gotten the good genes.

"White, grey," Tiernan allowed, pulling out his phone. "Let's take a selfie."

"Selfie?" Nik asked, shooting him a disapproving look at which Tiernan laughed.

"Okay, so it's not as distinguished as your photography, but we're still young enough to get away with the narcissism of our generation. Come here." Leaning over, Tiernan slid his arm around

Nik and pressed a kiss to his cheek as the camera clicked. "Besides, selfies are just another art of self-expression. And cheaper than oil paintings."

"You're not going to post that online, are you?" Nik asked apprehensively. If Rae ever saw it, he'd never live down not telling her first.

"I've learned my lesson about posting shit like this online," Tiernan assured him. "Once it's out there, you can't take it back. Press goes crazy for dating rumors."

Nik wasn't sure what to say to that. Were they dating? Is that what this was? "Yeah," he said instead, checking his phone as Tiernan texted him the photo. "Jennifer would be really upset if someone else got a scoop before her."

"So you haven't told her then?" Tiernan asked, spreading out on the towel. Where Nik's skin was naturally darker, Tiernan's was tanned by the sun to match. He wasn't wearing the usual skin-tight swim shorts today but looser trunks that left quite a bit more to the imagination than usual.

"What's to tell?" Nik said, chancing a quick glance at Tiernan. He hadn't told anyone what they were doing. He wasn't sure what they were doing anymore. Maybe it had never been clear.

Tiernan shrugged after a minute, eyes on the lake, and Nik couldn't see his expression behind his sunglasses.

"That you think I'm hot and can't keep your hands off me," he said simply then grinned, leaning over to kiss Nik soundly. "Come on. I'll teach you another stroke."

Nik couldn't help smiling as Tiernan rose and held out a hand. "A swim stroke, you mean?"

"Either's good."

It was the first Saturday in a long time Nik hadn't spent home alone and he let himself laugh as Tiernan splashed into the water ahead of him. He couldn't remember the last time he'd had just let go. School was all about studying and making sure he could afford to pay his tuition. Any free time he had outside of school and work, he spent doing photography, but that was mostly a solo act. He had friends at school, but they were all broke like him, so a Saturday night was usually spent watching a movie or playing Mario Cart in a dorm room that smelled like socks.

"You coming?" Tiernan called back to the shore, up to his waist in the water already.

Kicking off his shoes, Nik stepped into the water and smiled at the way it lapped at his feet, a gentle invitation.

"Yeah," he said and waded in.

It was entirely cliché, Nik thought as he straddled Tiernan's hips, camera poised to capture Tiernan's face and his chest against the bright towel underneath him. Like some sappy romantic movie that Rae always wanted to watch.

"You're not going to put these on the magazine's blog, right?" Tiernan asked, though Nik wasn't sure Tiernan would completely mind the thought of people ogling his body.

"These are just for me," he replied, ignoring the cheeky arch to Tiernan's eyebrow, the smirk at the corner of his mouth.

"I bet they are," he said but he didn't stop Nik from taking another photo.

Leaning back, Nik adjusted the settings on the camera. The sun was too bright — it wasn't really the right time for photos, but part of his job was to work with whatever light he had. He paused as he felt Tiernan's hands slide to his thighs, but kept working.

Taking photographs was a lot of work, a lot of thought had to be put into every shot, much more than Nik had ever imagined when he'd gotten his first camera, an old camera phone with no service. Every new thing he learned, he filed away like treasure in a chest.

"Have you ever had one?" Tiernan asked as Nik tested the shot. He wanted to capture the shadow now that the sun had moved into the west.

"One what?" He focused the lens on Tiernan's eyes, stormy green, speckled with blue and gold at this resolution. He rose up on his knees to get the leverage, snapping a few shots of Tiernan's open expression, relaxed with a hint of a smile.

"A boyfriend."

Nik lowered the camera for a second but shook his head. "Not really." That was probably why he had no idea what the fuck he was doing with Tiernan. "Have you?"

"A few, but nothing serious."

"So what are you supposed to do with a boyfriend?" Nik asked after a second, partially curious, partially nervous at the way this was going.

Tiernan smiled, shading his eyes. "Stupid stuff. Make the other watch your favorite movie, order too much take-out, admit your stupid obsession with 00s TV shows, sleep in on the weekends, hang out downtown for no reason at all."

"Isn't that what you would do with any friend?" Not that Nik would know. His friends in Chicago were all art students who spent their time working on pieces or else figuring out a way to get drunk on ten dollars.

"But with a boyfriend, you get to do all those things and have sex. It's like friendship but better."

The way Tiernan described it, it sounded perfect. Relaxed, not demanding, a nice way to spend time. Movies always made it seem so dramatic. Nik was beginning to realize he hadn't had much exposure to real life things.

"What about friends with benefits?"

"Never works." Tiernan shook his head, pushing himself up when it became apparent Nik wasn't taking any more photos. Nik scooted back to let him sit up, fiddling with the camera. "Either you fuck and you aren't friends or you just go for it."

Nik could feel his heart beating faster at the implication. They were definitely more than just fucking at this point or he wouldn't be here, at this lake, with Tiernan, laughing and having fun.

"So…" he said at length, unsure what to do, tensing slightly, eyebrows furrowed. Did that mean they were more than friends?

"So," Tiernan echoed, pushing back Nik's hair, almost dry now. "What's your favorite movie?"

It was that simple. To go from nothing to something. It didn't hit him like a shock, like a panicked moment in which he scrambled to figure out what to do. Instead it was a wave of something warm and soft, drawing him into Tiernan like that was what Tiernan had meant to do all along.

His body un-tensed and he sat back on the towel. "Moonrise Kingdom," he said at last, and at Tiernan's confused frown, he shook his head. "It's this weird old movie. One day when I was eight, I didn't want to go home after school so I snuck into this theater."

"Bad boy," Tiernan teased, dropping down his sunglasses.

"It was one of those pretentious independent theaters, you know? And they were playing this movie. For an eight year old, it was a pretty weird movie, but it was kinda nice. It's set in, like, the 60s and these two kids run away on an island to be together, but they're only ten so, you know, nothing happens. I don't know. I just liked it."

Nik remembered sitting in the theater, enthralled with the cinematography, watching these kids his age take matters into their own hands. He'd gone home and looked up all the gifs and pictures he could find from the movie and hoarded them away, like his own little picture show of beautiful camera shots. Up to that point, he hadn't realized movies could be so beautiful.

"We should watch it," Tiernan said, sliding an arm around Nik's shoulders.

"Okay," he agreed, letting himself lean into Tiernan. It was that easy. "So what's your favorite movie?"

"Terminator," Tiernan said, and Nik scoffed.

"Liar."

"Okay, fine, it's totally She's The Man," Tiernan admitted, elbowing Nik when he couldn't help laughing. "What? I told you I had a thing for 00s. My sister used to watch it all the time. Plus I was in love with Channing Tatum before I even knew what gay was."

"We can watch that too," Nik assured him, smiling at the happy flutter in his stomach as Tiernan pressed a kiss to his shoulder.

"You try to get through it without being jealous of Amanda Bynes."

"I'll try."

Tiernan arched an eyebrow. "You're a sarcastic little shit, you know?" Nik frowned, but Tiernan leaned into him, kissing him softly. "I like it."

Nik rolled his eyes this time but kissed Tiernan back. It was the first time anyone had said it when it wasn't meant as an insult.

"I'm glad you like it," he said when Tiernan moved back.

"I like you," Tiernan said simply, and Nik smiled. That was the first time anyone had ever said that to him before either.

Chapter 18:
Something Old

Nik smiled to himself as he flipped through the photos on the camera, the one of Tiernan standing in the lake, backlit by the sun. It cast a golden glow around his body. The one of Tiernan staring up at him like he'd be content to do that forever.

Dating. Nik had never really dated anyone. In high school, he'd been far too weird to even consider dating anyone. Of the two of them, Rae had been the one who dated. She was pretty and sweet, but tough. Guys flocked to her. Andre and Seth scared them away when they could. They merely teased Nik about his pathetic dating life; that he couldn't even get a guy to go out with him. Guys had lower standards, they said, which should have made it easier.

He paused on the photo of Tiernan lying on the sand, an arm flung over his eyes, a knee in the air. It looked like something out of an old movie. Nik smiled at the photo. Arizona was starting to grow on him, and so was Tiernan.

He had to tell Rae. Normally, he would have told her after the second time they'd fucked, not that he'd understood anything then. He wanted to tell her about the stupid feeling he got in his stomach when Tiernan smiled at him. He wanted to tell her about Tiernan's ability to make life's problems go away, to make him feel like he wasn't totally alone.

He was going to call her; he was going to tell her. She'd be happy for him. Steeling himself, Nik grabbed the phone. He shouldn't have been nervous to call, but lately he was nervous every time he called home.

"Nik?" Rae answered the phone finally, and Nik sat up, frowning. Something was wrong.

"Hey," he said, pressing the phone to his ear. He couldn't say what it was — maybe it was a twin thing like Tiernan had asked — but something was definitely off.

He heard her sniff, a short exhale into the receiver. "Long time no call," she said, her voice overly perky, the way she did when she was pretending everything was fine. Nik had heard it a thousand times growing up. "I should be insulted."

"Rae," he said, not buying into her act for a second. He knew her better than he knew himself. "What's going on?"

"Nothing. God, Nik, you call once in two months and just assume something's wrong?"

Nik wasn't fooled. Leaning forward on his knees, he shifted the phone to his other ear. He could hear her breathing, hear his own heartbeat, unease rising in his throat. He didn't say anything, waiting. He just had to wait her out.

She huffed a minute later. "It's nothing," she said again, the perkiness gone. "It's, it's stupid, I..." She hesitated and Nik's stomach tightened.

"Is everything okay?" He asked though he wasn't sure he wanted to know, especially when she sniffed again, like she'd been crying, like he'd interrupted her crying.

"God, Nik," she said finally, her voice breaking, and Nik's heart plummeted. "You don't understand, you're not here."

Nik didn't have anything to say as he listened to her voice shake. His stomach lurched, churning with guilt. So much for a light, easy conversation. He put his head down, closing his eyes as he sat in his apartment far away from her. This was his fault.

"I'm just so tired," she said, her voice thick, a sob escaping "It's been so hard. You're gone and Mom's worse, and Andre..."

"Andre what?" Nik asked, lifting his head. His mind flew to all the times Andre had locked them in their room so they wouldn't get in the way, the time he and Seth had left them behind at the park when they were five. His heart fluttered in his chest, above the nausea churning in his stomach.

"He's just stressed. We're all stressed."

Nik wanted to say something to make it better, but he didn't have anything to say. She was right — he wasn't there. He'd run as far away as he possibly could, and he hadn't regretted it until this very moment.

131

She let out a shaky breath as if trying to pull herself together. "I wish you were home."

Nik felt a swoop of guilt. He had never felt bad about getting away from Andre and their mom, but he'd left Rae all alone to deal with the things he'd run away from. His hands shook as he switched ears, like he was there beside her, unsure what to do. He'd never comforted anyone in his life, and Rae had been the only one to ever comfort him. She'd always been the strongest of the two, the one who could handle staying when he couldn't.

"I can't," he said quietly, his stomach clenching with guilt as she sniffed again.

"I know," she said, sounding more like herself. It didn't help the twist he felt deep down, squeezing his lungs, a lump rising in his throat. An hour ago, just an hour ago, nothing had been wrong. Everything had been great. Now it wasn't again. Nik couldn't remember the last time he'd seen her cry. "Your internship. Your life. I wish I had — " She stopped herself. "I get it."

"You could come with me," he said, though he knew it was hopeless to offer, his stomach sinking even as he said it. "You could move to Chicago, get away from Andre and everything else."

There was a pause, but Nik knew what her answer would be.

"I'm not like you, Nik," she said with a sigh. "I can't just *leave* everything. They need me."

"But you want to." Nik knew she wanted to. They'd used to talk about it, about getting away after high school, moving somewhere far from New York City, where they could have their own place and do whatever they wanted. "And you could. Come stay with me. You could get a job or go to school or something. You don't owe Andre anything."

"He took care of us, Nik," she reminded him, as if he needed reminding. "We wouldn't have made it without him."

"He ignored us," Nik replied sharply. "The only reason he wants me there now is so I can pay for shit and take care of Mom so he doesn't have to."

"What do you think I'm doing?" Rae demanded, her voice rising an octave. "*I'm* doing it because no one else is. I have to sit with her every day when she's in pain, when she wants to drink and I have to stop her, when the doctor says they can't find a donor match."

Nik's stomach twisted as she spoke, guilt welling up deep inside him.

"Rae, I — "

"I don't want to hear it," she interrupted him. "It's hard enough knowing you are out there, having a life, hanging around hot swimmer guys, and I'm... I'm stuck here. So I don't want to hear that you're sorry." She sighed, and Nik rubbed his forehead as the guilt gnawed at his insides. "Tell me something better, tell me some good news, Nik."

He didn't know what to say. He should say something to reassure her, but he couldn't. She didn't want to hear it anyway. He was a terrible brother.

"Nik?" she asked when the silence stretched too long. "Is everything okay?"

"Fine," he muttered, wiping away the wetness at the corner of his eye.

"So any good news?" she asked, and Nik curled up onto the couch. "Please just tell me something good."

Nik thought about Tiernan, the way Tiernan smiled at him, the way Tiernan brushed his fingers over his jaw and kissed him. He thought about Marion's offer to help him, Jennifer's words of confidence in his abilities.

He couldn't tell her any of that. It was bad enough that he'd left but it was worse that he was enjoying himself.

"My apartment has a pool," he said lamely, but he knew she wasn't fooled.

"Take a swim for me," she said, though, not pushing for a real answer. She must have been really tired if she didn't insist on an answer. Normally, she wouldn't have let him get off that easy. It wasn't a good sign.

"Rae," he started, but she cut him off with a noise.

"I should get to bed," she said. Nik glanced at the clock. It was past midnight in New York. She sighed. "I miss you."

Pushing down the sick feeling in his stomach, he rubbed a hand over his jeans. "I miss you too."

He hung up a minute later, tossing the phone on the couch and pressing his hands to his face, sucking in a deep breath to quell the nauseous feeling in his stomach. He blinked back the wetness in his eyes, wiping it away as he cursed to himself.

Life couldn't go smoothly. Everything was so fucked up, and he didn't know how to fix it. He couldn't go home and give up everything he'd worked so hard for, not for Andre or his mom. For Rae, though, he would, Rae who needed him whether she said it or not.

He couldn't decide this right now. It was late and he was tired. No good decisions were ever made late at night. Pushing himself up from the couch, he headed for the bedroom. Maybe things would be clearer in the morning. At least, he hoped so.

Things weren't clearer in the morning, and Nik slogged through a morning of editing photos, bolstered only by the coffee at his elbow and Tiernan's face on the screen. He'd never talked to Tiernan about his family, not really. When he was with Tiernan, he didn't have to think about it. He liked that.

At work, though, he had no distraction from the guilt mounting in his stomach. Rae was as strong as anyone he knew, but if she was breaking, something was really wrong. He couldn't just go on pretending it wasn't.

"You look tired," Brooke said when she stopped by his desk later in the morning. She looked the opposite of tired, bright-eyed and bushy-tailed.

"Thanks," he muttered, taking a sip of his long-cold coffee. Disgusting.

"I didn't mean like that," she said, leaning against the desk next to his. "You wanna get some lunch? It's stuffy in here today."

Nik had more photos to edit. With the Olympics coming up, Jennifer was pushing out an update every day. When they weren't about Tiernan, they were about Dylan, speculating on their chances or an in-depth look at their lives. Nik hadn't read any of the articles, except to check for his name underneath the photos. He still got a warm glow every time he saw it.

Nik could use some air, though, and he saved what he was working on. "Yeah, I could use a break."

Brooke fell into step with him as they headed for the door. On the way, they passed David, who was talking to one of the managers. His eyes followed them out and Nik turned to Brooke.

"Did you ever ask him out?"

"David?" She perked up, swinging around to look, but the door had already shut. She had her hair up in a ponytail today, and it whipped around her shoulder. She smirked. "I did. Aren't you proud of me?"

"I'm guessing he said yes," Nik said, judging by her smile.

"He did. Turns out he really was just shy."

They walked down the hall to the elevator and took it to the first floor. Last night, Nik had felt exactly like Brooke did, excited to tell anyone about Tiernan, but the reminder of why he didn't flooded back, and he felt the same sense of dread overtake him.

"So what about you?" Brooke asked as they stepped out onto the sidewalk. Nik could swear he saw the haze of heat rising from the pavement. "Is there somebody special at home?"

The only one special there was Rae. "No," he said, thinking of Tiernan. He was probably training right now, probably not thinking of Nik. He could tell Brooke about Tiernan. Jennifer already knew, so what harm could it do? Maybe she might even have advice on how to date someone. "Well, sort of."

"Sort of," she echoed interestedly, turning them down the street. Nik wasn't sure how he hadn't melted yet. "Tell me."

Nik hesitated. The only person he'd ever really talked to about guys was Rae, and usually only to listen to her complaining about them. He rarely told people about his dating, or well, non-dating, life.

"There's a guy," he said slowly. "I've been kind of seeing him for a couple months."

"Kind-of like hooking-up, or kind-of like dating?"

"Both." Nik wasn't sure. "I think we're dating now."

"You sound unsure," she said as they reached a restaurant and she held open the door for him. A gust of cold air met them and they paused at the host's stand.

"I've never, I've never done it before," Nik admitted, pushing past the hesitation. Talking to Brooke was like talking to Rae, except there was no looming threat of their brothers bursting in. It was nice to just talk to someone. He talked to Tiernan, but he didn't want to drag Tiernan into his problems. Tiernan had his own things to worry about; he didn't need Nik's stupid life too.

"Oh," Brooke said knowingly as the host led them to a table and left them with menus. "So it's *new* new." She unrolled her napkin and placed it on her lap. "How is it?"

"I like him," he offered.

"That's a good start."

Nik fiddled with his fork. "But we don't really know each other that well."

"That's the point of dating," Brooke said, opening her menu. "To get to know them."

Certain things, Nik knew about Tiernan. He knew he was smart, determined, focused. He knew he had a sister and an unsupportive family, just like Nik. He knew Tiernan would do whatever he had to succeed. He knew how Tiernan liked to snuggle up to him after sex, liked to stay in physical contact — a hand, a knee, a pair of lips against skin. He knew Tiernan pushed his hair back when he's nervous, though he'd thought at first it was to show off. Maybe he knew more than he'd thought.

"I posted the feature this morning," Brooke said when Nik didn't offer anything else about Tiernan.

"Yeah?" He felt suddenly anxious as she nodded at her menu.

"It's got two hundred hits already." She beamed across the table at him, and the anxiety eased in his chest, replaced by disbelief.

"Really?"

"People like it," she said. "They like 'discovering' new artists, like they found you first. Maybe if we're lucky, it'll get picked up. Wouldn't that be amazing?"

"Amazing," Nik echoed, but as she went on about her plans for the website, Nik couldn't help thinking of Rae, sitting all alone in the apartment with no one for company but a dying woman and three brothers who used her as a caretaker. Nik felt guilty for the way things were going for him. It was ridiculous, he told himself firmly as the waiter returned to take their orders. There was absolutely no reason he couldn't be happy about the good things in his life. He owed himself that much.

Still, he couldn't shake the gnawing in his stomach as he placed his order and listened to Brooke talk excitedly about the future.

Chapter 19:
Wedding Bell Blues

After a grueling practice session, Tiernan wasn't sure he felt as prepared as Coach wanted him to be, as he wanted to be. He'd been practicing almost non-stop the past few weeks, but he wasn't sure it was making any difference, except for the ache in his arms as he hefted his swim bag over his shoulder and turned from his locker. He was pretty sure Coach was trying to kill him, or else make him the best swimmer he could be. Same difference.

As he left the locker room, he wished Sam was there. Sam would have some self-deprecating remark to make Tiernan feel better, some crack about Tiernan not needing to win any more medals.

"Leave some for the rest of us," Sam would have said, but Sam was gone. Tiernan couldn't exactly go to Dylan about his worries. He shoved the anxiety pushing at his chest down deep; now wasn't the time to let doubts take over. If he did, he'd let himself lose.

Outside, the sun was just setting, casting a golden hue over the Center's campus. Tiernan meandered down the cement path towards the parking lot, taking his time. He didn't have anywhere particular to be and he was judiciously avoiding looking at the text Ella had sent about rehearsal dinners and gift etiquette. How many gifts did he have to give? Wasn't one enough?

Tiernan kicked a rock off the path. It bounced into a barrel cactus. Life would have been so much simpler if he was an only child. Of course, if that were the case, there would be no one to take the attention off of his failures. Ella didn't have any failures, at least according to their parents.

He wasn't looking where he was going, which was probably why his shoulder plowed into someone coming the opposite direction on the path.

"Shit, sorry," he said as his bag dropped to the concrete and he heard the thump of another bag. Turning, he found a guy about his age, with dirty blond hair, reaching for his bag on the ground. "Hey, I know you."

The guy straightened up, frowning slightly as he took in Tiernan. It was that gymnast he saw around sometimes.

"You watch my practices."

The guy's eyebrows went up. "Excuse me?"

"I've seen you," Tiernan said. "In the stands."

"Oh," the guy said finally, shaking his head. "I just go there to think sometimes."

Tiernan paused. It was probably presumptuous to ask but he was curious. "Are you the one who made the Olympic team?"

"Me and Trayce, yeah." The guy nodded.

Tiernan grabbed his bag off the ground and took the guy in. He was quieter than Tiernan would expect a gymnast to be.

He didn't know why he asked it. He shouldn't have, but Tiernan had never been known for his tact. Maybe it was something about the way the guy hesitated, like he was waiting for Tiernan to say something, like he needed someone to talk to.

"You nervous about the Olympics?"

For a moment, the guy only frowned, a small crease in his forehead. It was a personal thing to tell a stranger. Tiernan half expected him to say 'no' and walk away, but finally the guy shrugged.

"Yeah."

"Me too," Tiernan agreed, meeting the guy's eyes and smiling. There was no point in lying about it.

"I'm late to meet my friend," the guy said finally, pointing vaguely past Tiernan, toward the dorms.

Tiernan stepped aside. "I'm Tiernan, by the way."

The guy paused then jerked his head. "Auden."

"Good luck," Tiernan said as Auden took a step towards the dorms.

Auden paused a minute. "You too."

Tiernan watched him go for a minute then turned away. He had never spent much time getting to know any of the gymnasts at the Center, but he'd seen Auden around the past couple years. Him and that blond girl who sometimes sat with him in the bleachers.

His phone vibrated in his pocket as he headed toward the parking lot. He pulled it out, groaning at Ella's name.

"Yeah?" he answered, pulling out his keys and unlocking his car.

"Are you coming to the rehearsal dinner or not, Tiernan?" she asked without any proper greeting, but Tiernan wasn't surprised.

"Why? I'm not in the wedding."

"It's tradition," she said, and he could practically see her rolling her eyes. "Why do you have to make everything so difficult?"

Tiernan ignored her. "I can't come on Friday. I have training. I'm flying up Saturday morning. Besides, don't you think it's a better idea that I don't get drunk at the rehearsal dinner and spend your wedding hung over?"

"As long as you don't paw the groomsmen," she muttered. "Who are you bringing?"

Tiernan grimaced as he turned on the car and cranked up the air conditioning. "Bringing?"

"Your date," she said, exasperated. "I need a name for the place card."

"Just put 'Plus One,'" he said. He hadn't really thought about the date part. The wedding was in, like, four days. Who was he supposed to find now? Maybe Auden's blond friend.

"Tiernan," she said in that warning tone he hated. "You better be bringing someone appropriate or Mom and Dad are going to kill you. *I'm* going to kill you. For once, just do what you're told. Follow directions. Be responsible."

Tiernan rolled his eyes, leaning back in his seat and eyeing a tumbleweed that blew in front of his car. "I don't need a lecture on responsibility."

"I'm not sure about that," she said. "Just do it, okay? Don't make this a thing with Mom and Dad and your sexuality. Just bring a date. And don't hit on any waiters."

"I gotta go, Ella," he said, cutting her off. How many times did he have to hear this? How long until people started trusting him to follow directions? He wasn't a kid. He wasn't the irresponsible asshole he had been four years ago.

"Do the right thing, Tiernan," she implored before he hung up on her.

"Fuck," he muttered. God, didn't anyone have any faith in him? Was he destined to be the disappointment forever? He didn't even think a gold medal would change his family's opinion of him.

Shaking himself, he tried to put it out of his mind. He'd find a date, a fucking picture-perfect date to please his family, just like they wanted. Maybe they'd just give up and accept who he was. He scoffed to himself as he pulled out of the lot. That was a fucking joke.

Tiernan still didn't have a date. What he did have was Nik spread out on his bed, deliciously flushed as he traced the lines of his muscles with his tongue. The wedding was in three days, and Ella was going to murder him, but he didn't care as he slid up Nik's body, running his hands over Nik's hips, up to his chest. Nik groaned.

"I like you like this," he murmured against Nik's skin, breathing in the scent of his shampoo.

"Like what?" Nik asked, a hand tangled in his hair, urging him up to his mouth.

"Relaxed," Tiernan said as he kissed Nik slowly.

He should have been calling every girl he knew, begging someone to attend a wedding five hours away, sending them into a panic as they tried to find an outfit for a wedding in less than two days. Instead, he had his hand sliding to Nik's cock, stopped by Nik's hand on his wrist, pushing it away.

"What — " he started to ask as Nik followed the shove of his wrist by pushing his whole body over, onto his back. He wasn't complaining as Nik straddled him without answering his question, his gaze dark and intent.

A thrill ran through Tiernan as he lay trapped beneath Nik's weight, under his heated gaze, tense with anticipation. He let his eyes travel lazily down Nik's body, the trim lines of his hips, his olive skin tanned, but not from the sun. He wasn't like other guys Tiernan had been with, but he didn't want to compare. There was something about Nik that made Tiernan forget about all those other guys before, focusing solely on him.

"You should be relaxed too," Nik said, licking his lips as he shimmied down, pushing Tiernan's legs apart.

"Oh, fuck," he breathed as he felt Nik's tongue slide along his balls, his hand pushing his cock out of the way, wrapped around the hot skin, a firm but soft grip.

Closing his eyes, he lost himself to the feeling of Nik's mouth, the easy way he went down on him, sucking his balls into his mouth, pulling away with a pop and bathing his cock instead. *Shit*, he wouldn't last long with the way Nik was moving.

Looking down, he met Nik's eyes as Nik slid his mouth over his cock, hot and wet and slick in a way that made his toes curl, his stomach clenching in deep desire. Nik never broke eye contact, sucking hard, his tongue flicking over the head of Tiernan's prick.

Nik was fucking good at this, Tiernan decided as he let his head fall back. He only paused briefly to catch his breath, so enthusiastic that Tiernan found it hard to believe that outside the bedroom, he was the kind of guy who kept his head down, the quiet kid in the back of the room. This was always how he would think of him — a guy who didn't wait for what he wanted. He just took it.

"*Nik*," he breathed, reaching for Nik, hand landing on his shoulder, but it didn't sway Nik from taking him in deeper, a hand wrapped around the base of his prick, squeezing gently, urging him not to come, not yet.

Tiernan groaned, fingers digging into Nik's shoulder, his cock straining in his grip, under the warm slide of his mouth. He wasn't going to last much longer.

Nik pulled his mouth away abruptly, hand stroking him fast and hard in a way that made Tiernan curse out loud.

"Jesus Christ," he ground out as he came, stomach clenching, heat stealing over his body as Nik's hand stroked, smooth and easy.

Nik's mouth slid back over his cock a second later, sucking and licking away any remnants of his release as Tiernan panted for breath. Come painted Nik's face when he pulled back, and Tiernan's thumb swiped over his jaw, wiping it away. Nik didn't seem bothered, breathing heavier, leaning into his touch.

"Fuck," Tiernan breathed as Nik crawled back up, lying down beside him. "You're really good at that."

141

Nik smiled and didn't reply. Scooting over, Tiernan draped an arm over Nik, pressing a kiss to his chin. After the last few days, he needed this. He needed to just be here, relaxed, with Nik in his bed.

"What do you do?" Nik asked when the silence descended on them, broken only by the tick of a clock in the living room, too loud. "When you're not training?"

Tiernan gazed at Nik, the sheen of sweat on his brow, his breathing still quickened. "Training doesn't really leave a lot of free time, but I like to cook. I took a class once. I can make four different kinds of bread."

Nik smiled and something unexpected bloomed in Tiernan's chest at the sight, a surge of affection. "Impressive."

"I watch really trashy TV," Tiernan admitted. "Like terrible reality TV that's not reality. People buying houses with outrageous expectations, cooking competition shows. I especially like the cooking shows where everyone gets yelled at."

Nik laughed but frowned at him. "Why?"

He shrugged, brushing Nik's hair back, out of his eyes. "Makes me feel better that other professionals get yelled at too, and makes me glad my life is not televised."

"It practically is," Nik pointed out. "The interviews, the meets."

"Yeah, but they're not following me around with a camera shoved in my face, capturing every time I do something stupid. How would they ever decide what to air?" Part of being a professional athlete was living under a spotlight, which Tiernan knew came with the job. He'd liked it back when it got him hook-ups and free drinks, but he'd long since learned it was better to stay on the fringes of the spotlight.

"You don't do that many stupid things," Nik murmured, and Tiernan smiled, settling in next to him and listening to him breathe for a moment.

"I used to," he allowed. "But I'm working on it." It was so easy to just lay here with no responsibilities, to ignore the fact that he was leaving for the Olympics in just over a week, and he still had so much to do. "Hey," he said after a minute as a thought occurred to him. "You wanna come to a wedding?"

Nik moved back slightly, enough to frown, eyebrows raised. "What?"

Ella was going to murder him, but Tiernan didn't care. She'd be too busy getting married to even notice, and he didn't want to suffer through an entire wedding with some random girl he'd begged at the last minute.

"My sister's getting married on Saturday and I have to bring a date," he said, propping himself up on his elbow so he could look at Nik better.

Nik still had on his frown, as though it was a suspicious proposition. "That's pretty short notice."

Tiernan shrugged, but Nik was right. He should have found a date weeks ago, but he'd been so busy. "I'm not asking just 'cause it's in two days and I don't have a date," he said, brushing Nik's hair aside, gaze flicking down his face. Nik's pouty lips were pressed together uneasily, like Tiernan was doing this because he was desperate. "I want you to come."

It was true. He'd have a much better time with Nik than with someone else, someone who might make his parents happy. At this point, he didn't give a fuck what they wanted.

"Have you ever been to Vegas?" Tiernan asked with a grin, but Nik hesitated, apprehensive now.

"I can't afford — "

"Don't worry about it," Tiernan interrupted. There was a good reason he had sponsors; they paid for things like plane tickets. "Just come with me." He soothed away the creases in Nik's forehead. "Help me make this wedding bearable."

It was a lot to ask, he realized, since it wasn't just a wedding. It was his sister's wedding and probably meeting his parents and "going away" for the weekend, which people always seemed to think was some kind of relationship marker. He didn't care.

"You really want me to go to your sister's wedding?" Nik asked, sounding doubtful.

"I really do," Tiernan replied. He couldn't think of anyone else he'd rather suffer through this weekend with. At least with Nik, he wouldn't have to pretend to be having a good time. They could spend ten minutes at the reception, make his brotherly toast, then slip out and spend the rest of the time in a hotel room all to themselves.

Nik's frown disappeared as he smiled softly, leaning into Tiernan's hand cupping his jaw. "I don't have anything to wear."

Tiernan laughed, leaning in to kiss Nik slowly, soundly. "We'll find you something."

His heart swelled excitedly as Nik kissed him and they fell back on the bed. Fuck Ella and fuck his parents for telling him how to live his life. He could bring whoever he wanted, and he wanted Nik.

Chapter 20:
Lavender And Cream

Nik had never gone *away* with a guy before. Hell, he'd barely ever been *away* anywhere with anyone. The last time he remembered going anywhere was a class trip to the Jersey Shore in fifth grade. He'd somehow scraped together enough money carrying people's groceries to pay for him and Rae to go. He'd gotten sunburned on that trip.

Las Vegas was different than he'd imagined, less glitzy and more just like Phoenix. Tiernan had pointed out the Strip as they flew in, but they hadn't passed it in the car.

"Are we going to your parents' house?" he asked, peering out the window at the houses they passed; identical to those they'd left behind in Phoenix, all beige adobe houses with rock lawns and an odd cactus or two.

Tiernan shook his head as they took a turn down an identical street. "I don't think I could survive a whole weekend under their roof."

Nik smiled. "Your parents sound worse than my brothers."

Tiernan shot him a smile and pushed his hair back. "They're really not that bad, some times. It's just gonna be crazy and they're probably pissed that I didn't come for the rehearsal dinner yesterday."

The way Tiernan talked about it, coming home was a chore, the wedding was a chore. Nik understood that. He had a voicemail on his phone from Andre that he hadn't been able to bring himself to listen to. No doubt it would be a tirade on his irresponsibility. He didn't need to hear that when he was supposed to be focusing on this trip, on the fact that he was here with Tiernan, alone, for a whole weekend. It was a big deal.

"I'm gonna meet your parents," Nik said slowly as the thought dawned on him. He'd never met parents before. As a kid, most parents had pulled their kids away from him with warnings of unkempt children from the wrong side of town. Half of New York was the 'wrong side' so he didn't really see how it mattered.

"Yeah." Tiernan glanced at him, as though it wasn't surprising at all.

"I," he said, frowning as his heart rate beat faster, nervous now. "I've never met parents."

"They'll be too busy fussing over Ella to even notice," Tiernan assured him. "Are you worried they won't like you? Who wouldn't like you? You're adorable."

Nik took offense to the adorable comment. He'd tried very hard not to look *adorable* throughout his life. Maybe if he got a tattoo on his face. It was just the fact that he was short that made people say that. Short and skinny and mussed all the time.

"Don't tell anyone else I'm adorable."

Tiernan laughed. "You're totally hardcore," he said instead. "You wear black in Arizona and take pictures of woodpeckers. Both kinds."

"I've never taken a picture of your dick," Nik said, but he felt better, more relaxed as Tiernan joked. He'd never felt this relaxed with anyone that wasn't Rae. Usually it took months before he was comfortable with friends or teachers or bosses. Sometimes, he never was.

"Not even your own?"

Nik shook his head. "Never." He didn't have anyone to send them to, so what was the point? There was little skill in taking out your cock and taking a picture.

"Then I must teach you the subtle art of dick pics," Tiernan said, completely serious, as they turned into a hotel parking lot. It wasn't like the Strip hotels, glitzy and glamorous. It was just a normal boring chain hotel. Tiernan turned off the car and turned to Nik. "Great for sexting, which might be the only thing that keeps me sane during the Olympics."

146

Nik shook his head but smiled to himself as Tiernan climbed out of the car. If Nik had his way, sexting wasn't the only thing he'd see of Tiernan during the Olympics.

"We have a couple hours before the wedding," Tiernan said as he grabbed bags out of the trunk. "Plenty of time for you to help me perfect lighting and composition."

Tiernan pressed a quick kiss to his lips with a mischievous quirk to his eyebrow. Nik didn't argue, grabbing his bag and following Tiernan, suppressing his smile as the lobby doors slid open automatically.

Nik wasn't sure what he'd expected from a Vegas wedding. A chapel in a casino? The priest dressed as Elvis? It certainly wasn't this.

A lush golf course spread out past the parking lot, with picture-perfect palm trees and gentle slopes down to sand pits and man-made lakes. The thick, heavy wooden doors to the Country Club were thrown wide open, a sign for the Pace-Avery wedding placed out front and wrapped with trailing white flowers.

Tiernan's hand on his back guided him inside, and Nik tried not to fidget in the suit jacket Tiernan had gotten him. He'd opted for black jeans and the one button down shirt he owned. Tiernan had loaned him a tie and tied it for him with expert fingers. Nik hadn't exactly been expecting a wedding when he'd packed for the summer. Even back home, he only owned one suit jacket, which he used for art shows and job interviews.

Nik could feel his heart beating faster as they entered the Club, air conditioning smacking him in the face, for which he was glad. It was boiling outside. He didn't know anyone they passed, though a lot of them seemed to know Tiernan and greeted him like old friends. He didn't know why he was nervous. Anxious, Rae would have said. *You have anxiety issues, Nik.* Like Nik wasn't fully aware.

"Why don't you find a seat," Tiernan said as they reached the lavishly decorated room where the wedding was to take place. "I gotta find my parents. Prove I came." He said it jokingly, but he frowned at the end. "I'll be right back." He pressed a kiss to Nik's cheek, then he was gone.

Fully alone now, Nik stood at the entrance to the room. There was no indication if he was supposed to pick a side, and he didn't know who was whose guest. A girl in a violet dress handed him a program as he stepped inside.

"Who are you with?" she asked with a bright smile.

"Um, E-Ella?" he said nervously.

"To the left," she said, directing him with her whole hand.

Nik stared at the rows of chairs. Normally, he would have picked a seat at the very back, but this wasn't his event. Tiernan would probably be expected to be near the front. He didn't know who anyone was and avoided making eye contact as he sat down.

Edging past strangers, Nik picked a seat in the middle, more towards the front than he would have liked. Sitting down, he crumpled the program between his fingers and kept his eye on the door for Tiernan. His tie was too tight and he tugged at it, taking a breath.

He felt like everyone was watching him, though no one was. Tapping his foot, he kept craning back to the door, but Tiernan didn't appear. The rest of the room filled quickly, people talking excitedly, girls comparing dresses. The color scheme seemed to be violet and cream, as far as Nik could tell from the random girls he caught sight of, all in the same violet dress.

"Hey."

A voice at his elbow made Nik jump, but he let out a relieved breath as he saw Tiernan.

"Hey."

"Come on. There are seats at the front for us."

Nik wanted to say no, but he couldn't. It wasn't his wedding. Instead, he followed Tiernan down the row and up to the front where an older couple was already seated, looking like they were going to church. Tiernan's parents, Nik guessed from the man's hair, similar in color except for the gray streaks, and the woman's small nose and green eyes that matched Tiernan's exactly.

The woman's mouth pursed together when she saw Nik and she looked at her husband instead as Tiernan paused before them.

"Mom, Dad, this is Nik," he introduced them.

"Hello," his dad said curtly while his mother said nothing.

"Er, hi," Nik said, but Tiernan nudged him along, down to the next seat. As they sat down, Nik glanced over, but Tiernan's mother appeared to be whispering furiously into his dad's ear. "Is something wrong?" he asked Tiernan.

Tiernan's face, usually bright and sunny, seemed tight and lined for a moment, but he shook his head and smiled. "Absolutely nothing."

Nik wasn't sure he believed him. He felt a chill in the way Tiernan's mom glanced his way, reminiscent of the way Andre looked at him as though he were a stain on the family. Tiernan slid an arm around his shoulders. His dad got up and went to the back as Nik watched.

"Is your sister nervous?" he asked instead of drawing more attention to the way Tiernan's mom shot him a frown. He would have thought Tiernan's parents didn't mind that Tiernan was gay. Tiernan had never said otherwise.

The room towered over them, a domed ceiling with translucent glass panels to let in the light. Each row of chairs was tied with more purple flowers. The whole thing was so elaborate, so *expensive* that it made Nik's chest hurt to think of how much of his tuition this wedding could have paid for. He tugged at his tie again, shrinking down in his seat. He couldn't help feeling out of place.

"She's being an even bigger bitch than usual, so I'd say she's terrified."

"Was she at least happy to see you?" Nik knew if he went home, at least Rae would be glad to see him. Andre would just put him to work after a long bout of yelling about how he should have been there sooner.

Tiernan shrugged. "In her way."

Nik opened his mouth to ask what that meant, but the music started then and he was forced to turn and watch the bridesmaids come up the aisle, a groomsman with each. He wondered why Tiernan wasn't a groomsman. He'd never asked.

The wedding march started and everyone rose, turning to the back. Nik had never been to a wedding before, had never seen a bride come out of the back, accompanied by Tiernan's father. The only thing Nik found himself thinking as he watched Ella step down the aisle was that despite how much this wedding probably cost, it really was beautiful.

Sunlight streamed into the reception hall through tall glass doors that stretched the entire span of the wall. They weren't open, due to

E.E. Grey

the fact that it was well over a hundred degrees outside, but with all the light, Nik felt like they might as well be outside. It was one of the most beautiful rooms he'd ever seen.

The tables were covered in cream tablecloths with purple flowers in clear vases on each, name places set delicately in each spot. Tiernan was momentarily corralled by yet more old friends to talk about the Olympics and his career. Nik lingered awkwardly by the wall, hoping no one would try to talk to him.

"Yeah, I leave in a week," Tiernan was saying, glancing at his water glass. Nik bet he wished it was alcohol right now, and he smiled to himself at the thought. "It's crazy. There's still so much to do."

A flurry of white caught Nik's eye and before he could blink, Tiernan's sister stood before him. She looked beautiful, her short blond hair pinned back with a purple flower under her veil. Her pure white dress flowed to the floor, backless and sparkling on the bodice. Nik didn't know anything about wedding dresses, but he thought hers was nice. She looked so much like Tiernan, Nik wasn't sure they weren't twins too.

Her smile didn't quite reach her eyes, though, when she faced him.

"You must be Nik," she said, voice gracious and smooth, like maybe she'd practiced it. She grabbed two glasses of champagne off a tray as it passed and handed one to him.

"Thanks," he said, taking the glass. "It was a beautiful wedding." Nik wasn't sure there was anything else to say about a wedding.

Ella smiled again, but still, it wasn't quite genuine. "So you're my brother's date?"

Nik nodded, clutching the champagne glass and trying not to look around for Tiernan. He couldn't help feeling uneasy at the way she cornered him. "Yeah."

It wasn't that Nik wasn't used to the looks, the whispers about how he was *different*. Gay. Andre had done his best to point it out his whole life. In Chicago, no one cared at school. It was an art school. Half of the student body was gay or bi or trans. Maybe he'd been lulled into a false sense of security being away from home so long, around people who couldn't care less about who he fucked, but that didn't seem to be the case as Ella's eyes rested on him.

"How long have you known him?"

"About a month." Nik shifted his weight under her gaze, not accusatory, but not welcoming either. Tiernan had said she was high-strung, but Nik had figured he was exaggerating.

Ella clinked her own glass with her brand new wedding ring. "Did Tiernan introduce you to our parents yet?"

Oh God, Nik hoped she wasn't about to do it again, so he took a quick gulp of the champagne, shocked at the sweetness he hadn't been expecting. "Y-yeah," he said quickly, praying she wouldn't try. "Sort of. Wedding, they were busy, you know."

He needed to stop talking, but her intimidating stare made his mouth keep moving until he clamped it shut.

For a long moment, Ella said nothing, eyes flicking over him as though trying to see what Tiernan saw in him. She didn't appear to find it as she snapped her gaze up and put on another brief smile.

"Great," she said, short and staccato. "Well, enjoy."

She swept away before Nik could wrap his head around what had just happened. How could someone so blond be so terrifying? Nik drained his glass as Tiernan came up beside him, lacing their fingers together. Nik thought he caught sight of Tiernan's mother frowning at them before hurrying in the opposite direction.

"Everything okay?" he asked, glancing around the room.

"Fine," Nik said, gazing after Ella. She was laughing with some other guests now, her smile genuinely happy this time.

"Remember the plan," Tiernan murmured in his ear as he steered him away from the wall. "A few minutes here. One abbreviated speech, then back to the hotel for a night of relaxation."

Nik nodded, but as they turned away, he thought he caught Ella's eyes on them, a twist to her lips that echoed the one her mother had had earlier. Nik didn't like it. He didn't like it at all.

Chapter 21:
Something Borrowed

Tiernan should have known that 'a few minutes' was wishful thinking when it came to his family. They'd never had a family holiday dinner that didn't last at least three hours, and they didn't even have any relatives nearby. Now, the whole hall was filled with relatives, people he had never met, people Ella had probably invited so she would get more gifts. As it were, the gift table was practically groaning under the presents piled on top.

Tiernan had shaken more hands and hugged more people tonight than he had in the last five years of his life.

So far, he'd avoided the disapproving glare of his mother, though he couldn't escape Ella's narrowed eyes whenever she passed.

Tiernan should have known this would be a lion's den. He should have known and he'd come anyway.

"Tiernan," Ella said in that voice she used when she didn't want to appear angry in front of other people — it was the same one their mother used. "May I borrow you?"

She tugged him away from the group of relatives who said they were distant cousins. He was all too glad to be rid of them, though he wasn't sure he wanted to hear what Ella had to say either.

She led him over to the buffet table and picked up a plate.

"Was I not clear?" she asked as they moved down the line. Tiernan popped an olive into his mouth.

"You're always clear, Ella," he replied, looking around for Nik, but he couldn't find him in the crowd. He hoped he wasn't lost somewhere in the Club.

"Because I'm almost a hundred percent sure that I specified who you should bring as a date."

"You didn't give me a name."

Ella turned to him, face stern, muscles tense. Her makeup was starting to wear slightly around the edges. "I didn't think I would have to hold your hand."

"Relax, Ella," he said, shaking his head. It wasn't worth fighting over. "It's almost over. Nik and I will leave, and everything will be fine."

"Fine," she repeated to the finger sandwiches. "It's not you who will have to listen to Mom and Dad argue over you for the rest of your life. You don't have to suffer through weekly dinners where they only talk about if you'll ever get over your 'phase,' if you'll stop sinning."

"Tell them it's none of their fucking business," Tiernan said, rolling his eyes. She was so dramatic.

"One day, Tiernan," she said with a sigh. "One day you couldn't make it about you and your lifestyle."

"Sorry my *lifestyle* is such an inconvenience to you," he replied, shaking his head. Everything was always about Ella. "But it is my life."

"And this is mine," she said, gesturing to the room. "I just wanted you to bring a normal date."

"Nik *is* a normal date."

"Not for Mom and Dad, and you know it." She shook her head like he didn't understand anything. Tiernan understood plenty. She was their perfect child. She always had been. Swimming had been the only thing to distinguish him, but he'd let them down. "Why do you always have to be so immature?"

"I just want to be who I am."

Ella set down her plate and glanced at the room behind them. Everyone seemed to be having a good time. Tiernan finally spotted Nik standing near the cake, looking trapped in a conversation with one of the bridesmaids. His eyes darted around as if looking for help.

"We know who you are. You don't have to rub it in their faces."

"Until they accept me, maybe I do." Tiernan felt anger bubbling up inside him. His parents had never tried to accept that he was gay. They insisted it was a phase, kept setting him up with friend's daughters, ignoring anything he said about guys, getting upset when he talked about dating.

"Fine, rub it all you want," she said, sounding angry now. "Just give me *one day.*"

"You get *every* day," Tiernan pointed out, but he didn't get to finish as someone started clinking glasses. It was time for the speeches.

Beside him, Ella took a deep breath and pasted on her smile as she left him by the food and headed to the center of the room with Michael.

Pinching his nose, Tiernan bit back his sigh. This was exactly why he hadn't wanted to come. That, and the fact that he was flying to France in less than a week. He didn't have time for this kind of stress.

The guests gathered into a crowd facing the front table. More champagne glasses had been passed out and everyone waited as the Maid of Honor stepped up to give her speech. Moving around the edge of the crowd, Tiernan sought out Nik. He still lingered by the cake but was thankfully alone this time.

"Where the hell were you?" Nik muttered. "That bridesmaid was about to eat me alive."

"Glad you're okay," Tiernan said despite Nik's glare.

"What happened to getting out of here?"

"Soon," Tiernan murmured as everyone raised their glasses and took a sip. It was the Best Man's turn next.

"Good, because I don't think your sister likes me very much."

"Ridiculous," Tiernan said despite the twisting in his stomach. He slipped an arm around his waist and pulled him closer.

Tiernan was beginning to think this had been a mistake, but it was too late now. He kept his grip firmly on Nik throughout most of the speeches until it was his turn. Ella hadn't said anything specific about a speech, but he figure it was sort of expected. After all, he wasn't in the wedding party. He had to say something.

Letting go of Nik, he stepped through the crowd as everyone drank to whatever the groomsman had said.

"Everyone, everyone," he said as he reached Ella. She was smiling but it got tighter when he reached her. He turned from her face. "I suppose it's my turn, the annoying little brother's turn."

A ripple of laughter went through the crowd. Tiernan had known most of these people since he was a kid, excepting the random relatives from the East Coast and Michael's friends and family.

"I've known Ella my whole life," he said with a charming smile in her direction. "She's been a sister, a friend, a secret-keeper — though not always a very good one. She's always been there... even when I didn't deserve it. To be honest, I don't think about marriage that much. I never really thought I'd get married, and not just because it's hard to pin a guy down."

Another bit of laughter. He could feel Ella tense beside him. In the front row, his parents said nothing but the grim looks on their faces was enough to annoy Tiernan.

"But Ella. Ella always wanted to get married. She used to make me play wedding with her Barbie dolls. I didn't get to pick the music then, either." He turned towards her and smiled. She was smiling, though it looked forced, worried. "When I was five, she was eight, she made me dress up in my Sunday best and marry my stuffed penguin. Not to worry, she married the polar bear. It was a beautiful double wedding."

The crowd chuckled, but Ella hadn't relaxed.

"Of course, Michael is a step-up from a polar bear, and Nik's a step-up from the penguin." He smiled at Nik through the crowd. A few people twisted to look. His parents didn't move. "I think, overall, we made good choices to leave the stuffed animals behind." He turned to Ella and raised his glass. "Ella, you'll always be my sister, but you'll never get to plan my wedding." More laughter. "To Ella and Michael. May they be as happy as I am."

Everyone clapped and took a sip of their champagne. The music kicked back on a second later as the crowd dispersed, a few coming forward to congratulate Ella and Michael.

Tiernan tipped his glass to Ella as he stepped away. She shouldn't have been worried. He may have been immature, but he wasn't cruel. She could have this day and every day after.

"Not a bad speech," Nik said as Tiernan reached him through the crowd. "Almost heartfelt."

Tiernan raised an eyebrow. "I am a great sibling."

"You're better than mine at any rate," Nik admitted. Tiernan heard his phone ping with a text. His phone was filled with never-ending pings of texts, it seemed. "I can't imagine any of my brothers giving a toast like that if I ever get married. I don't know if I'd even invite them."

155

"Sisters are different," Tiernan said. Half the guests were dancing now and Ella was back to smiling with Michael. She did seem happy to be married, which Tiernan could be glad for. Everything he'd said had been true. She'd always wanted this.

"Did you mean what you said?" Nik asked after a minute as they stood admiring the cake. It was a ridiculous confection, five layers tall of white frosting and purple glaze, cream flowers carved delicately into sugar and placed strategically.

"Yes," Tiernan said. "I did marry a penguin. Please don't hold it against me."

Nik smiled softly, and it made Tiernan's heart swell. He couldn't believe he could be so sappy. Four years ago, he would have said that feeling this way about a guy was impossible, a lie made up by TV and movies.

"That you're happy."

Tiernan pulled Nik closer and leaned into his forehead. "Completely. Four years ago at this time, I'd been drowning my disappointments in tequila. I didn't leave my apartment for a week. I wasn't sure I'd ever get back to normal, let alone going to the Olympics with an *adorable* photographer at my side."

"Call me adorable one more time," Nik warned, but he was smiling.

"Come on," Tiernan said, pulling away and taking Nik's hand. "Let's get out of here."

They almost made it out. Tiernan could see the front door, but he was brought to an abrupt stop by his father's voice behind him.

"Tiernan."

So close. Nik glanced back first so Tiernan had to turn. His parents stood behind him, united in their disappointment.

"Meant to say goodbye," he said quickly, avoiding the glare on his mother's face, though it wasn't directed at him. "We're heading back to the hotel. I'll see you... later."

"Not one step," his mother said as he tried to turn.

Resigned, he met her gaze. He hadn't wanted this fight. Or maybe he had. Beside him, Nik's frown seemed permanently etched on his face.

"What?" he asked finally. From here, he could still hear the music from the hall, the tinkle of glasses and toasts and cheers.

"Just what did you think you were doing?" his father asked, and Tiernan sized him up for a minute. His dad had always been the more rational of the two, but now, his face echoed his mother's, tight and stern. Her mouth, so much smaller than either Tiernan's or Ella's, was pressed together in a thin line.

"I don't know what you mean." He knew *exactly* what they meant, as if it wasn't clear enough from the way his mom shifted and glared at Nik beside him.

His mom broke first, gesturing sharply at him and Nik. "How *dare* you bring... *him*... here. After we specifically *told* you — "

"Told me that I can't choose my own dates?" Tiernan interrupted. "That I can't bring who I want to a celebration? That I have to be straight when I come here?"

He felt Nik shift but didn't look at him. This wasn't about Nik. It was about his parent's antiquated thinking. It was 2024 for fuck's sake. Gay marriage had been legal for ten years. There were TV shows on mainstream cable about gay people. Not every movie was a tragic story about coming out.

"You have no respect," his mother hissed, crossing her arms tightly. "You flaunt your *lifestyle* — "

There was that word again. It rifled Tiernan, rubbed him the wrong way.

"I'm not who you want me to be," he said firmly, looking between her and his dad, who frowned deeply. "I never have been and I never will be. But you can't control me. I'm twenty-three. I'm not a kid that you can ground because I did something you don't like. You already cut me off. You don't come to my meets. You act like I don't exist. What more is there?"

"Maybe if you showed more responsibility," his mom said, a shadow darkening her face, but Tiernan couldn't listen to this lecture again. She glared at his reaction, the scoff. "If you wanted to hurt us, you didn't have to bring some... *person* to Ella's wedding. You humiliated her and us! You've never grown up, Tiernan."

"You've never grown up," he retorted, a flush racing over his skin, his hands curled into fists at his side. "No one cares who I date. No one except you."

His mom drew herself up, though she was still quite a few inches shorter than him. She lifted her chin, and he could see the flush on her cheeks even through the makeup.

"Congratulations, honey," she said stiffly. "You've made your point. You've humiliated us and ruined your sister's wedding day. I hope you two are happy together." She spit the word 'happy' like it was on fire. Spinning, she marched back into the hall, his dad close behind her.

Groaning, Tiernan rubbed his face. *Fuck.* That wasn't how he'd wanted the day to go. Why couldn't they just accept who he was?

Turning to Nik, he shook his head. "Welcome to my family."

Nik didn't say anything, staring at him, eyes narrowed, and he turned without a word, stalking towards the exit.

"Nik? Nik!" Tiernan stared after him, confusion rolling over him, but a sigh made him look back.

Ella stood in the doorway to the hall. On Tiernan's frown, she shook her head simply, her mouth flat. Tiernan didn't have time to deal with her. He went after Nik instead.

Chapter 22:
Something Blue

Nik slammed the hotel door shut, which didn't really work since it was a hotel door and physically incapable of slamming. Instead, it swung far too slowly closed, too slow to shut Tiernan out. Nik wanted Tiernan out. He didn't want to have to face him right now, but they'd driven back to the hotel together. They were sharing this room.

"Nik," Tiernan said, catching the door and shoving it open with his shoulder. "What the hell is wrong?"

Nik wrenched off his tie, throwing it on the bed. His face felt red, flushed, angry, like the blood coursing through his body, heart pounding against his ribcage.

"Is that what I am to you?" he asked, searching Tiernan's face. Tiernan only looked confused, too put-together in his suit, too poised whereas Nik felt like he was struggling to keep up.

"What?" Tiernan asked, shaking his head. The door finally clicked shut behind him.

"Is that why you brought me?" Nik's hands were shaking, in anger and something else. Humiliation? Embarrassment? Fuck, he didn't know. He just knew that when Tiernan's mom had given him that *look*, that look of disgust, like he was a blight on their family, it had made him want to crawl into a hole and die. It made him think, for even just a moment, that he'd be better off home with his own ugly family. At least they had a reason to dislike him. "To prove some fucking point?"

"No," Tiernan said quickly, taking a step forward, but Nik stepped back. A lump rose in his throat. Could he have been so stupid to think that someone like Tiernan would actually want him? Tiernan was a world champion swimmer and Nik was an intern.

"So you didn't wait until the last minute to ask me to come then parade me in front of your friends and family, who didn't want me there? Why am I even here?"

"Because I want you here," Tiernan said, voice sincere, but Nik couldn't believe him.

"No, you wanted to get back at your parents. You used me." Nik felt sick, shaking as he sat on the edge of the bed, champagne threatening to come back up. It was too stuffy in the room, choking him, but he wasn't going to cross the room to turn on the AC, not past Tiernan.

"That's insane," Tiernan said, running both hands through his hair in frustration.

"Tell me you didn't bring me to piss them off," Nik said sharply, facing Tiernan and staring straight into his annoyingly green eyes, eyes he would have gladly stared into forever just a few hours ago, but now he could barely stand a few seconds.

Tiernan swallowed and blinked, hesitating.

"I knew it," Nik said, shaking his head and swallowing down the lump. "I fucking knew it. How could I be so stupid? I'm just a distraction for you. Just like last Olympics. And when you lose, you're going to blame it on me."

Tiernan stared at him, and his fingers twitched, like he couldn't keep them still. "That's not true."

"So you're just sleeping with me because I take your picture? Because you're bored? Because I'm something to do?" Nik didn't want to know the truth. The truth was that Tiernan had used him to get back at his parents. That was all that mattered. He wasn't a thing. He was a person, not there to prove any point. "Why would you do this? I don't understand."

"Neither do they," Tiernan said, too loudly, gesturing out the door. "My parents think it's all some stupid phase and one day I'll just wake up and be straight and their problems will be over. But that's not what's gonna happen. They have to get it through their heads that I can't be what they want."

"And you had to use me to prove that point?" Nik stared at Tiernan, his chest seizing up when Tiernan looked away. He'd thought... It didn't matter now. It turned out Andre was right, as always. Nik would never get his happy ending. Something always went wrong. People always had ulterior motives. "Well, you did it. I don't think your parents will ever forget this. I definitely won't."

"What about you?" Tiernan asked and Nik frowned, eyeing him suspiciously.

"What about me?" He hadn't done anything to Tiernan.

"Aren't I just a distraction for you?"

"What are you talking about?"

"You never talk about your family," Tiernan pointed out, voice rising. "And someone's texting you all the time but you never even look at it. Can you really say I'm not just a distraction for you?"

"You don't get to turn this around," Nik snapped, panic rising in his chest at Tiernan's words. "You don't get to be a giant asshole, then blame me for not wanting to talk about my shitty family. They're my problem and I didn't want to drag you into it."

He shook his head, glaring at Tiernan. Tiernan wasn't a distraction. He was someone Nik had liked, maybe even something more, but not anymore. He'd been fooling himself.

"Nik, wait," Tiernan said as Nik reached for the door, sounding desperate now. Nik's heart thudded, blood rushing in his ears, and he hated himself for hesitating, hoping. "Just let me e — "

"Explain?" Nik tore off the jacket Tiernan had bought him. He threw it at Tiernan, hitting his chest forcefully. "No need. I should have known better." He wrenched the door open, biting back the tears springing to the corners of his eyes. "Good luck in the Olympics."

The door didn't slam behind him, and Nik was already halfway down the hall when it clicked shut. Tiernan didn't come after him this time. Standing in front of the elevator, he pressed the heels of his hands to his eyes, forcing any wetness out.

"Fuck," he muttered to himself, taking a shaky breath, forcing himself to calm down. *It's fine*, he told himself. *It's fine. It's fine. It's fine.*

The elevator dinged and he stepped inside, the anxiety in his chest deflating slightly as he kept up his mantra. His mind felt fuzzy, confused, tired.

He'd thought Tiernan actually cared, that he wasn't just some distraction from competition. He should have known better. After everything he'd been through in life, he should have seen it coming, but he'd let his guard down.

In the lobby, he asked the front desk girl to call a cab and sat on the ugly red couch until it came, pressing his hands together and willing himself to be calm, not to think about Tiernan or else he might have a panic attack. He'd only had one once before, right before high school graduation. He hadn't even known what it was, just that he couldn't breathe for a few minutes, the whole world pressing down around him. He never wanted to experience that again.

When the cab arrived, Nik pulled himself together enough to slide in and buckle his seatbelt.

"Where to?" the guy asked and Nik took a breath, turning to the window.

"Airport."

The cab pulled away from the hotel, and Nik firmly didn't look up as he left Tiernan behind.

"You look terrible."

Nik lifted his eyes from the screen to face Jennifer. She plopped a cup of coffee on his tiny desk and took the chair next to his.

He felt terrible.

It was a combination of being hung over and not sleeping well. He hadn't heard from Tiernan since the wedding, not that he'd expected or wanted to, but he'd figured, maybe, he might call. He hadn't, though. Tiernan hadn't done anything. *Good riddance*, Nik thought, though it hurt to think it.

"What's on the agenda today?" he asked instead of acknowledging her statement.

"Lucky for you and the hangover I suspect you have," she said knowingly, "this week is just prep work. We fly out for Paris on Thursday then it's Olympic coverage! Exciting!"

Nik hummed, but he was sure he didn't sound too excited. He dreaded having to see Tiernan again, to face him and remember how he hadn't argued, hadn't assured him that it had been some stupid mistake. Because it hadn't been a stupid mistake. He sighed and rubbed his eyes.

"What's going on here?" Jennifer asked, gesturing at him and the way he was slumped in his chair. "What's wrong with you?"

"Nothing. I just don't feel good."

She frowned but didn't comment. "Okay, well, Tiernan and the other swimmers will all be arriving on Friday, though they can't get into the training center until Saturday. The actual Olympics start the next Friday, but we need to be there all through training for the magazine. Lucky you, it means three whole weeks in Paris."

Nik should have been excited, but he just felt nauseous. How had this all gotten so fucked up?

Jennifer leaned in closer to him, and he grimaced away. "Are you sure you're okay? You don't look good."

"Bad weekend," he muttered, taking the coffee she'd set on his desk and taking a sip. It didn't really help to settle his stomach.

She frowned, seemingly unconvinced. "Buck up," she said instead, and swiveled back on her chair. "We've got to get through the next couple days before we get to have fun."

"Yeah," he muttered, though he didn't think any of this would be fun anymore. Any hope he'd had of a great summer had gone out the window. Now, he only hoped he could get through the rest of it without any more terrible news.

Jennifer left him alone with one more concerned glance over her shoulder. At last he was alone, but he didn't feel much better as the office bustled with activity and he sunk onto his desk with a long-suffering sigh. He just wanted it all to stop, but life didn't work that way. It should work that way. Forcing himself to open his eyes, he sat up and went back to editing his last photos of Dylan. At least Dylan wasn't Tiernan.

Mom's dying.

Nik hadn't thought this week could get worse, but he was wrong. He was so, so wrong.

For a long minute, he stared at his phone, at the two words typed there, like staring might change them. They hadn't changed since he'd gotten the text five minutes ago. Two words that changed everything.

She'd been dying for months. This wasn't news. She'd had cancer for months. It felt different, though. Why would Rae have sent it? He wanted to ignore it. He wanted to delete the message, pretend he'd never received it.

Instead, he pressed the call button and listened to the ringer, hearing the silence as Rae picked up.

"That's not very funny, Rae," he said, turning from the balcony and stepping inside. Even after dark, Phoenix just never cooled down.

"I'm not laughing."

She wasn't crying either, not this time, but her tone was sharp, to the point. It pierced Nik's skin, stinging in a way Nik hadn't felt in years.

Sinking onto the couch, he leaned forward, elbows on his knees. "What do you mean she's dying?" he asked calmly, forcing himself to be calm. He didn't know how much more bad news he could take before he just imploded.

Rae huffed into the phone, a short breath that put Nik on edge. "I mean there's no donor matches. She's been getting worse for months. The doctors think she only has a few weeks."

"A few..." Nik closed his eyes. He'd known it was serious. Cancer was always serious, but he hadn't thought that this would actually happen. He never wanted her to die. "What am I supposed to do?"

Rae's scoff, cold and angry, prickled at his skin. "What are *you* supposed to do? I don't know what *I'm* supposed to do, and I'm the one here. I'm the one taking care of her, putting my life on hold so you can go off and *become* something. Don't ask me what you're supposed to do."

Nik opened his mouth, but he couldn't say anything. She'd never snapped at him like that before, but she had every right. He'd left, and what had he accomplished? A few photographs on a magazine blog and a guy who'd used him as petty revenge on his parents. He sighed at his knees; Rae had fallen silent as well.

He couldn't let her do this all on her own. Sure, she had Andre and Seth and Dan, but what good were they? They'd never helped when it came to the difficult stuff. They made sure there was food and clothes that didn't look as if they picked them out of a dumpster, but they'd shrugged off everything else, everything that Nik had needed growing up. He and Rae had been left to fend for themselves, and now Nik had left Rae all alone.

"Rae," he said, but she cut him off this time.

"I don't want to hear it," she firmly. "I don't want to hear that you can't come home because your life is just so fucking great right now. Why don't you go enjoy Paris, surrounded by swimmers and press, and everyone else that's gonna make your life better. I'll be here, doing what I have to do for *our* family. You can just fuck right off, Nik."

She hung up before Nik could say anything and he stared at the phone as it fell to his lap. He couldn't move, rooted to the couch, his heart clawing at his throat, trying to escape.

She was right. He'd been so caught up in his own life that he'd stopped caring about hers, so determined to get away that he hadn't thought about what he was leaving behind. He didn't deserve her understanding.

He'd fucked up. He'd fucked up everything.

His phone rang, catching him off-guard, and he jumped, fumbling to look at the screen.

Tiernan.

His heart, which had been clawing its way out of his body, now sunk like a rock. Tiernan hadn't called or texted since the wedding. Nik didn't answer it, listening to the phone ring until it went to voicemail. He had nothing to say to Tiernan. He couldn't even think about Tiernan right now. His mom was dying. Even after all the years she'd spent ignoring him, drinking her life away while he struggled to get by, she was still his mom.

A sob choked him unexpectedly and the phone dropped to the floor with a clunk as he leaned forward, head in his hands. Everything was screwed up. He was supposed to leave for Paris in two days. He was supposed to be finished packing what little he'd brought since they wouldn't be back to Phoenix after the Olympics. After the Olympics, athletes went home, and his internship would be over. He'd go back to Chicago and get ready for school.

He couldn't think about the internship, the Olympics, Tiernan. Right now, he could only think of Rae and how much he'd let her down. How much he'd let everyone down.

Chapter 23:
Quelle Surprise

"It's Nik. Leave a message."

Tiernan sighed as his call went to voicemail for what had to be the hundredth time that week. Nik was obviously avoiding him, still angry about the stupid wedding and Tiernan's stupid parents.

He hung up and sat back on the bus, staring unseeingly out the window. He couldn't even enjoy the scenery flashing past, the Eiffel Tower peeking between buildings. Paris was supposedly one of the most beautiful cities in the world, and all Tiernan saw was Nik's hurt expression as he'd left Tiernan at the hotel.

"Who you calling? Girlfriend?"

Tiernan looked over at Josh, one of the other guys on the US swim team. Josh grinned at Tiernan as though they shared some kind of inside joke. The last thing Tiernan wanted to do was bond with his teammates, but there was a protocol to follow. Pasting on a smile, Tiernan opened his mouth to respond.

"Please," Dylan scoffed from the seat behind him, leering out the window. "Pace couldn't get it up with a girl if he tried."

"Fuck off," Tiernan replied without thinking, his fake smile falling as quickly as he'd put it on.

"What's the matter?" Dylan asked, hooking his elbows over the back of the seat and leaning in too close for comfort. "Spat with the boyfriend? He finally figure it out?"

"If you don't get away from me right now," Tiernan said slowly, calmly, much calmer than he felt, "I'm going to break your fucking arm."

"Touchy." Dylan sat back. "That kid's smarter than I thought."

Tiernan wasn't in the mood to spar with Dylan. He hadn't been in the mood to do much of anything lately, which scared him more than anything. It was probably a good thing that Coach had had him working his ass off every day. When he was training, he didn't have to think about how much of a colossal fuck-up he had made of his life.

He couldn't train all the time, though, and when he wasn't up to his ears in butterflies and backstrokes and freestyles, he couldn't erase the wedding from his memory. How he'd just *stood* there and said nothing, didn't defend himself or really explain anything. He'd just let Nik think that he didn't care, that it had all been some petty revenge scheme.

He should have stopped Nik and… fuck, he didn't know. He hadn't known what to do then, and he still didn't. Maybe he had, subconsciously, brought Nik to piss off his parents. They couldn't pretend forever. But he'd never meant to hurt Nik. Nik was the only good thing in his life, aside from swimming. Nik was the only one who actually believed he had a shot, aside from his coach, but he paid Coach.

He should have said *something* to stop him from leaving.

Instead, he had let Nik leave. Nik had stormed out of the hotel room and never came back. Nik didn't answer his calls or texts. Tiernan hadn't had it in him to ask Jennifer if she knew anything, when she'd called to set up a quick interview once they got to Paris. That would have seemed desperate. Then again, he was desperate.

You were such an idiot, he told himself as the bus rolled through the streets of Paris, past the Arc de Triomphe on its way towards the Seine, crossing over and heading for the southern end where the Olympic Stadium was. *You didn't even fight.*

He'd just been caught off-guard by Nik's accusations, the thought that he would *use* Nik like that. He supposed Nik had a point. He'd used other guys like that, the distractions, the ones he'd thrown himself at after the last Olympic trials. He'd been younger, stupider, and desperate to please his parents then, unable to in the way they wanted.

He still couldn't, but he didn't care now. It didn't matter what they thought of Nik, or why he'd brought him to the wedding.

167

He hadn't talked to Ella either. She was probably just as angry as his parents. He dreaded the phone call that would inevitably come after she got back from her honeymoon.

Leaning against the window, he sighed to himself. If Coach had been there, he would have knocked him on the head and told him to stop letting himself be distracted. Thinking about how much he'd fucked up with Nik wasn't going to help him win. It wasn't going to get him that gold medal he'd wanted since high school.

Knowing it didn't stop him, though, and Tiernan closed his eyes to the chatter going on around him. He was jetlagged as it was, the early morning sun shining through the window, but thoughts of Nik weighing on him tired him out even further. He wondered how Nik was faring with such a long plane ride. Maybe he'd taken a sleeping pill to get through it. Coach had said no sleeping pills. They fucked up your brain, and Coach wanted him sharp right away.

"We're nearing the stadium," came the voice of the Olympic official from a speaker above Tiernan's head. "Once there, everyone will be checked in and shown their rooms. A map will be included, as well as important phone numbers. Please remember that you are guests here, and to behave as such."

A cheer went up from the people on the bus. Guys ribbed each other and the women smiled knowingly. Tiernan didn't feel much excitement, and sunk into his seat instead.

A night's sleep didn't revive much of Tiernan's excitement. It didn't help that his roommate, Josh from the bus, woke up bright-eyed and bushy-tailed, raring to go.

"I can't believe we're finally here," he said as he pulled out clothes, dropping the ones he rejected unceremoniously on the floor. Tiernan eyed him, looking past his broad shoulders to the boyish glint of excitement in his dark eyes. He couldn't have been more than eighteen. At eighteen, Tiernan had been overly confident in his abilities, so sure he was going to become an Olympic champion, riding high on his first time away from home.

"Yeah," Tiernan said, dragging himself out of bed and grabbing a towel from his bag. He needed a shower to wash all the plane grime off him. He wasn't over-confident anymore, and he'd learned that freedom still had its restrictions.

"This is my girlfriend," Josh said, seeming not to see the cues Tiernan gave, turning from Josh, silently rummaging through his bag. Josh shoved his phone in front of Tiernan and Tiernan blinked at the dark-haired girl on the screen. He probably should have said something like, 'pretty,' but Josh didn't seem to need him to. He took back the phone and sighed dopily at it. "She's coming to watch. I'm so excited. Is your family coming? Your, uh, boyfriend?"

Tiernan slung the towel over his shoulder as the pit in his stomach grew. "He'll be here," he said, though it was without Josh's enthusiasm. He doubted very much that Nik wanted to see him, though he was sure to be with Jennifer. Tiernan would probably have to suffer through quite a few angry silences before he could get Nik alone and *try* to explain what the hell had happened at the wedding. If Nik would even listen.

He didn't really blame Nik. Tiernan hadn't come off very well, and he hadn't been very nice about Nik's family either. He cursed to himself and ruffled his hair. He'd be lucky if Nik ever looked at him again.

"My parents got tickets to the finals," Josh said, sounding anxious now. "Hopefully I'll make it that far."

Normally, Tiernan would have reassured Josh that he would, that Josh was the only thing standing in his way. But he slipped on a pair of flip-flops instead, and opened the door. Between the situation with Nik and his own worries, he didn't have it in him to reassure a stranger. He felt as if he'd lost all the excitement he'd once had for this.

"I have an interview in, like, an hour. I'm gonna get ready."

Josh turned to him, still distracted by his girlfriend's photo. "Good luck!"

Tiernan would have to see Nik in an hour, a thought that made his stomach twist uncomfortably. He still didn't know what he was going to say, if Nik would even care — Nik had been so hurt, so disappointed by Tiernan. Even disappointing his parents hadn't felt as bad as when Nik had accused him of using him. If Tiernan couldn't get past this, if Nik refused to listen, hated him forever, Tiernan wasn't sure he could handle that.

Tiernan shut the door on Josh's bright expression, his unbridled enthusiasm. He didn't need luck; he needed a miracle.

"How's the jetlag?" Jennifer asked from across the table. They were in the press lounge, a small room decorated with team USA colors, various podiums, interview areas, and space for cameramen set up, but it was mostly empty at the moment. Most of the athletes got right to training, and Tiernan had strict instructions to cut the interview short at half an hour and get to the pool. What time wasn't filled with training was taken up shooting promos or doing interviews with every journalist in the country.

Tiernan took a sip of coffee and forced himself to stop looking around for Nik. He hadn't been there when he'd walked in, and ten minutes had already passed. No Nik. The bundle of nerves in his chest was worse than it was before competitions.

"Not too bad," he said. He had to be on for the press, for Jennifer. He didn't want anyone catching wind of how out-of-sorts he felt and spinning some story about how he hadn't changed since last time. He wasn't going to give them an inch of weakness. The press were like rabid dogs when they got hold of a story. "Though the dorm room beds don't exactly make for a great night's sleep."

Was Nik so angry that he refused to even come to the interviews anymore? Tiernan would never get him alone, would never be able to say how sorry he was for doing something so stupid. He had been so stupid to think his parents would change, that they might just accept who he was. They never would, and instead, he'd let Nik get hurt in the process.

Jennifer smiled. Her phone sat between them, recording every word. "I bet. Hard to sleep when you're so excited too, right? This is your redemption, for all intents and purposes."

Redemption. Not a word Tiernan would have used, but it fit. "I guess, yeah. My chance to do it right this time."

"Any word on the competition? What's your take?"

"Haven't seen much yet," he said, though he had seen all their qualifying tapes. "We'll see when I get to the pool. But it doesn't really matter. It isn't about their times. It's about mine."

The door opened and Tiernan's head swiveled to it, but it wasn't Nik. Just some girl with a press badge. She ignored them completely. Tiernan's heart sunk. What if he never saw Nik? He'd never be able to explain.

"Speaking of, I have to get back before Coach kills me."

Jennifer nodded, reaching over and switching off the recorder. "Right, lots of preparation to do."

Hesitating, Tiernan bit his lip. It was completely unprofessional to ask, but he was about ready to explode if he didn't find out. "So, uh, where's Nik?" He hoped he sounded casual and not desperate, though from the way Jennifer's eyebrows furrowed at the question, maybe he hadn't succeeded.

"He's not here," she said, frowning as she tucked her phone away.

"Went sightseeing?"

She shook her head, still looking at him as though she wasn't sure why he was asking. He didn't take it as a good sign, a knot growing in his chest. "He went home. Didn't he tell you?"

"Home?" Tiernan repeated as the word hit him. The knot tightened, sharp in his throat. "Like New York home? Why?"

Tiernan knew why and his heart plummeted at the thought. He couldn't believe Nik would give up everything, his chance to travel, his internship, because of something stupid Tiernan had done. He felt like complete shit. He'd ruined Nik's life.

Jennifer looked more sympathetic now. "His mom is sick. Cancer. I guess she's not doing well. I wish he were here too, but family comes first."

Tiernan didn't know what to say as he thought what a selfish prick he was to assume Nik had left because of him. He hadn't even known about his mom. He'd never bothered to really ask about Nik's family. Maybe Nik had been right. He had used Nik to distract himself from the pressure of trials, had used him as childish revenge on his parents. Tiernan felt like the world's biggest asshole. He didn't even deserve Nik's forgiveness.

"That's… that's…" He couldn't think of what it was, and Jennifer nodded.

"I know. But we'll get through the Olympics without him, I promise."

The Olympics, right. The reason he was here. Tiernan gave himself a shake, trying to rid himself of the guilt weighing him down, the sheer stupidity of his actions. It wasn't that he hadn't cared about Nik. That was perhaps what made it all so much worse. He hadn't thought he was using Nik. He'd felt a real connection there, and he'd been sure Nik had too.

"If you talk to him, tell him, tell him I'm sorry," he said, sliding off the stool and looking away from her questioning look. Nik obviously hadn't told her anything. He wasn't sure Nik had told anyone about him.

He was going to be late to meet Coach, so Tiernan left without another word to Jennifer. Nik wasn't even there. Nik had left town and Tiernan would probably never see him again. As he reached the pool, he resolved to leave his problems outside. Losing would only prove everyone right. He was determined to prove them wrong this time, and he was going to prove himself to Nik too.

Chapter 24:
Homecoming

Nik steeled himself as he stood in the grim hallway, dark but for a stark light between the doors. He heard a crash behind one door, but he was focused on the one in front of him. He couldn't hear anything behind it. Probably no one was even home. It was the middle of the day.

He didn't use his key. It felt wrong, like it wasn't really his apartment even though he'd spent most of his life there.

He couldn't put it off forever. Raising a hand, he forced himself to knock. The noise echoed, and for a long moment, nothing happened.

No one was home. They were all working, working to support each other, to help each other. A part of him was relieved when no one answered. He wasn't sure he was ready to face this. He hadn't really let himself think about it; if he thought about it too much, he'd talk himself out of it. He didn't want to see Andre or his mom.

The door swung open before he could retreat and pretend he'd never come. Standing in the doorway in a threadbare t-shirt and yoga pants, black hair pulled in a messy bun, was Rae. Her dark eyebrows contracted as she stared at him, a beat too long.

"Nik?" she said, as if she couldn't believe her eyes. "Nik!" Relief flooded her voice and Nik was enveloped in a tight hug, one he couldn't struggle out of and he didn't try.

Her hair smelled of something faintly tropical, and though she was as small as him, her presence surrounded him, warm and welcoming. A heavy weight settled over him as she hugged him; he hadn't realized how much he'd missed it, had missed her.

"Oh my God," she said as she finally let go of him, taking him in, from the plane-rumpled clothes to the suitcase sitting behind him. "You're here. You're — what are you doing here?"

"Coming home?" he said, uncertain. When he'd decided to come, to leave Phoenix and everything associated with it, it had seemed like the right thing, but the plane ride had given him time to rethink, to doubt. Had he really made the right choice? He could have been in France, covering the Olympics, a chance that he'd probably never get again. From the way Rae's eyes misted over, though, he thought maybe he had made the right choice to come home.

"Fuck," she said in between a smile and wiping at her eyes. "Get in here."

Nik grabbed his suitcase and rolled it in behind him. The television was on some terrible daytime TV show. The apartment was a mess, just like he'd left it. Dishes were piled in the sink, random clothes scattered on the couch and chairs. Rae didn't bother trying to clean up as they entered.

Nik dropped the bag by the couch and turned to Rae. "I see no one's learned how to clean since I left." He meant it to be a joke, but Rae didn't laugh. Instead, she looked pained now as he watched her, her eyes still wet. It unnerved Nik slightly. Rae wasn't the crier in the family.

"I didn't mean what I said," she said finally, and Nik's stomach clenched. "I was just mad and, I don't know. I'm glad you got to leave — "

Nick stopped her, shaking his head. "You were right. I was being selfish and hard-headed. I should have been here with you." He should have been. He never should have left when their mom got sick in the first place. He'd only been thinking about himself, like he always did, Andre would have said. Nik had always been more concerned with himself than other people.

Rae smiled and brushed away a tear. She hardly cried. She had never been the crier of the two of them, but it seemed like a lot of things had changed since he'd been away.

"I probably would have done the same thing." She said it, but Nik knew it wasn't true. Rae had always cared more. She never would have abandoned their family when they needed her. She frowned. "What about the internship?"

Nik moved to the couch. He was exhausted after the plane ride. He wasn't sure he would have survived going all the way to Paris. He'd probably never get there now. He'd given up his chance to travel, to see the Olympic games up close. The only good thing about it was that he didn't have to see Tiernan every day, and be reminded how Tiernan had only used him for his own gain.

"I talked to the editor. She said I could finish out in their New York office." He'd still get the credit, get the work experience, but it wouldn't be the same. He'd been lucky Marion had understood.

Jennifer had just stared at him when he told her, like he had to be joking. *"What about Paris? What about Tiernan?"*

Nik hadn't told her what had happened. He'd only said his mom was sick. He didn't want to admit that he'd made such a mistake with Tiernan; that he was exactly what Jennifer had told him not to be. He wasn't proud of how things had ended. He still hadn't talked to Tiernan. He didn't want to hear some lame excuse about how Nik was wrong, how Nik had misunderstood.

Rae sat down next to him, shifting a jacket out of the way. Andre's jacket by the looks of things. Nik wasn't looking forward to that reunion. He doubted any of his brothers would be thrilled to have him home. He always just messed things up, in their opinion.

He shifted, a spring poking the back of his leg. They'd had the couch since before he was born. Hesitating, he didn't want to ask, but why had he come back otherwise? It hadn't been just to avoid facing Tiernan. "How's Mom?"

Rae's shoulders drooped and she swept a stray hair behind her ear. She wasn't wearing any makeup, eyes tired, lips pale. She even looked thinner than usual.

"Not great. She's been in the hospital for a week. The doctor's don't think…" She trailed off and shook her head.

Nik scooted closer and she instinctively leaned into him. They'd done this a million times before: when they were five and their mom came home drunk and smashed all the pictures of their dad; when they were eight and Andre punched a hole in the wall because Nik's teacher had called home to ask why he never ate lunch; when they were thirteen and Andre and their mom had a shouting match about whose responsibility they were.

175

"Maybe it'll be quick," he said because he couldn't think of what else to say. He wasn't good at comforting, and he couldn't deny the mixed feelings he had about all of this.

He could feel Rae's gaze on him. "I know you don't like her, but she's still our mom."

Nik stayed silent this time. He'd never known what to feel about his mom. There had been days, good days, when she'd tried to be like a real mom. But they'd gotten fewer and further between as time went on, and Andre had always blamed Nik for it. How could he have been expected to care when he was constantly punished for it? He'd never wished for her to die, but he'd wished for her to go away so he wouldn't have to feel so confused all the time.

"I'm glad you're here," Rae said as the silence stretched.

Nik wasn't sure he could say the same and mean it, but he put an arm around her shoulders anyway. He was glad she was glad at any rate.

"So when he gets here," Rae said, sounding like a coach, pacing in front of the couch. "Just don't say anything stupid."

"Great advice, thanks." Nik rolled his eyes, but Rae glared at him.

"I'm serious, Nik. Andre is beyond pissed at you. I mean, I can't even go a day without hearing what a selfish, pretentious, no-good son-of-a-bitch little shit you a — "

"I get the point." Nik had known this wouldn't be easy. He couldn't just pop home and expect everyone to welcome him with open arms. Andre would not happy to see him, despite all his threatening voicemails. Seth would probably ignore him if he was lucky. Dan... Dan might not totally hate him, but Nik couldn't be sure.

Rae sat down and smacked him upside the head. "My point is, you just got here. Don't make him regret it."

"He didn't do anyth — " Nik stopped himself and took a breath. This was the problem with Andre. Nik always wanted to argue with him. He couldn't help it. It was part of the problem of being fifteen years apart. Andre always treated him like a little kid, like he was still five years old and needed someone to walk him to school.

Rae's eyes widened, silently pleading. He knew he should try, for her sake. He'd come back for her sake, not Andre's. "Just don't do anything stupid," she implored him, a hand on his knee, squeezing too tightly.

"I'll try," he said, but it didn't seem to reassure her. She did release his knee, though, and the door opened at that moment.

Rae practically vaulted the couch to greet Andre, putting on a big smile that anyone could see right through.

"Andre! You're back." She bounced up on the balls of her feet and Nik's stomach curled into a ball at the sight of Andre. He loomed in the doorway, bigger and stronger than Nik had ever been, six feet tall with mussy brown hair and a small nose. Where Nik and Rae looked practically identical, Andre and their other siblings were big, muscular, and looked much more like their mother with her light brown hair and fair skin. "Guess who's here?" She said it brightly, like it was a good surprise, but Andre's eyes skimmed over the living room, suspicious, and they narrowed as they landed on Nik.

"You little asshole," he said, kicking the door shut behind him.

"Nice to see you too," Nik said, rising from the couch and standing his ground. He had to stay calm or he'd say something they'd both regret. He could feel the tension radiating off Rae as she stood there, shoulders tight.

"Finally decided to grace us with your presence, huh?" Andre asked, still glaring at Nik, like he was a bug on the bottom of his shoe. "Finally decided you care about your family?"

"Never said I didn't." Nik kept his sentences short, too short to insult anyone, he hoped. It was hard when Andre's glare practically burned a hole in his shirt. He came back for Rae, he kept reminding himself. Rae needed him here. She stood behind Andre, frowning at his back but not intervening yet. Nik didn't know what she'd expected. He didn't know what he'd expected.

He hadn't expected a big, warm welcome. He hadn't even expected a lukewarm welcome from Andre. Andre was always the first to point out Nik's mistakes, his shortcomings. Nik hadn't expected him to be pleased no matter how much he'd chided Nik for staying away.

"For fuck's sake, Andre." A voice interrupted the bitter silence and the door burst open again. "You could at least pretend to help."

Seth walked in, arms loaded with groceries. He stopped abruptly as his eyes swept over the scene. His mouth twisted and he shook his head. "The prodigal son returns."

Now all they needed was Dan to burst in with some snarky comment to complete the family reunion.

Rae moved over to Nik's side. Andre's eyes followed her, narrowing again.

"What happened to your perfect *internship*?" Andre asked, tossing around the word like it was diseased. "Couldn't make it in the real world so you came crawling back here?"

Nik couldn't help it despite Rae's hand closing around his arm. "Fuck you, Andre. I chose to come back."

He had chosen to leave. He could have been in Paris right now, taking photographs that would make his portfolio shine compared to the rest of the kids at school who spent their summers perfecting their Instagram looks. He could have been, but he wasn't. He was here, staring down his older brother.

"Nice to see you finally learned something," Andre spat. "Maybe now you can say thank you."

Nik frowned, anger rising in his chest. "For what?" *Thanks for ignoring me? Thanks for never helping me? Thanks for driving me away?*

Andre opened his mouth, but Rae stepped between them with a hard look. "Don't. Nik's back. That's all that matters. He came *home*."

Nik watched Andre seem to fight with himself, chest puffing out as he glared at Rae instead. Seth had set down the groceries and watched like a spectator at a boxing match, vaguely detached.

Rae had always been the one who could diffuse Andre's anger. Seth and Dan had never really bothered to help situations, only make them worse or ignore them completely. Nik remembered Andre yelling at Dan growing up, talks about irresponsibility, but Dan had never listened, and Seth never cared what Andre said. Nik always got the brunt of it.

"You're in my house now," Andre snapped finally instead of saying whatever choice words he likely had in his head, "but don't fucking act like you belong here." He unclenched his fists, and Nik's body vibrated with anger at his words, but he bit his tongue, hard.

"Stay out of my way," Andre growled at Nik and stalked into his room.

The door slammed shut and Rae's shoulders slumped.

"So glad I came back," Nik muttered, but he let out a breath. It hadn't been nearly as bad as it could have been. He wasn't sure how long he could stand to stay, though, at this rate. He was already dreaming of his apartment in Chicago where his family was far away, where everything was far away.

Seth made a noise by the counter. Nik had almost forgotten he was there.

"Got lucky, little bro," he drawled with that sharp smile of his that had never reassured Nick. "But I'd watch your step." He left the groceries on the counter and headed for his room.

Rae shook her head, putting away the groceries instead. Nik could feel a headache coming on. One day here. How many more would he have to survive?

"It's good to be home," he said sarcastically and she smiled, shoving a box of cereal into the cupboard.

"Isn't it?"

Chapter 25:
Religion of Avoidance

Nik was seriously rethinking this whole coming home thing, and he dug his heels in as Rae urged him towards the white door before him. The hallway smelled of cleaning products and sick people, sterile and cold.

"No," he said, stepping back from the door. "No, I can't."

He couldn't go in there. Going in there would mean he forgave her, and he wasn't ready to do that. He didn't think he could ever do that.

Rae tilted her head to the side. She looked a little better today, but maybe it was just the makeup she'd thrown on before herding him out the door and onto the subway. Even after two years away, falling into the routine of New York was easy.

"Yes, you can," she said confidently. "This is why you came."

"I came for you," Nik corrected her, swallowing down the lump rising in his throat as he stared at the door. She was in there, dying.

"And you can do this for me, right?"

Nik took another step backward, bumping into a cart in the hallway. It rattled, and he jumped. He shook his head.

"I don't think I can."

"Nik," she said, reaching for his arm, but he jerked it out of her way.

"No, I — " He huffed out a breath, curling his hands into fists to stop the shaking. He wasn't strong enough to walk in there, to see his mom, to watch her die. "I can't. Don't you get it? This is why I left."

Rae frowned and reached for him again. He let her this time and she led him over to a chair and sat down beside him. "I thought you left because of Andre."

Nik rubbed his legs, willing his heart to stop beating so fast. He hated feeling like this, like he wasn't in control of his own body. He didn't meet Rae's eyes, chewing on his bottom lip.

"That was part of it. But Andre, I mean, at least Andre was there. He might have been a giant asshole my whole life, but..." He swallowed around the lump again. It wasn't getting any smaller. "At least he didn't abandon us."

Nik remembered being six years old, waiting for his mom to pick him up from school, waiting two hours after until Andre finally showed up and dragged him home. He was ten, and on his birthday, Rae was the only one who remembered. His mom stumbled into the apartment after midnight and spilled a bottle of beer on the couch where he'd been trying to wait up for her. He was sixteen and he found her passed out in front of the apartment. She hadn't remembered the next morning.

"It wasn't her fault," Rae said quietly, but Nik shook his head, blinking back the tears forming.

"No, it was my fault. That's what everyone always said. If I hadn't come along, Dad would still be here. They'd be a happy family."

"That's not true," Rae said, and he heard the quiver in her voice. He determinedly didn't look at her, knowing it would only make it worse, the tight feeling in his chest. "They weren't happy before we were born. Dan told me they used to fight all the time. When she got pregnant — I don't know, it was just the last straw."

It didn't make Nik feel better, and he glanced at the door. He wasn't ready.

"I can't go in there," he said. "I can't."

Rae sighed, quietly, and her hand slipped from his arm. "Maybe tomorrow."

Nik wasn't so sure about that, but he could breathe again as he rose from the chair and headed for the exit. Maybe tomorrow everything would be better. Too bad his life didn't work like that.

A missed call from Tiernan. Nik frowned at the reminder on his phone. That made three calls this week alone. Tiernan shouldn't have had time to call him from the Olympics. He should have been training or finding some hot French guy to insult his parents with next.

Rae climbed onto the couch next to him, shoving a pile of laundry out of the way. She hadn't said anything else about the hospital, about the way he'd refused to go in. Andre would have said Nik was being a rude little shit, but he always said that.

Instead of bringing it up again, Rae reached for the remote and turned on the TV. They only got basic channels, and she flipped through for a minute, passing daytime Soaps and infomercials. Nik wasn't surprised when she settled on Olympic coverage. It was the best thing on, even if he didn't want to watch it. Opening ceremonies weren't until that night, but press coverage was in full-force. Flashes of the USA mens and womens' gymnastic teams rolled by and suddenly, Tiernan appeared on the screen.

"That's your guy, isn't it?" Rae asked, but Nik was too busy staring at the screen. A flash of anger followed by sadness hit him as he took in Tiernan's face, unchanged though his smile seemed a little too bright, as if he were forcing it.

"Tiernan," the reporter, a pretty brunette girl with long straight hair, said, "you're the top ranked swimmer in the United States. How would you put your chances at medaling in this year's Games?"

Tiernan leaned in to her as though they were sharing some secret, as though there wasn't a camera shoved in his face. "I don't know about odds. I'm just going to do my best and hopefully it will get me where I need to be."

He was charming, Nik would admit. Charming, and a liar. He scowled at the television and ignored Rae watching him instead of the interview.

The reporter laughed, tinkling like glass. "You've been getting a lot of press lately. I hope it hasn't gone to your head?"

Tiernan's smile fell slightly but he hitched it back up. "If anything, it's brought me back down lately."

Nik scoffed, rolling his eyes. Tiernan could charm a rock if he tried. He bet everyone in America was drooling over him right now.

"He's pretty hot," Rae said after a minute, watching Nik. Nik pulled his hoodie on tighter even though the humidity was through the roof. The air-conditioner blew feebly from the window. "Even you have to admit that."

"Yeah, yeah," he muttered. "He's hot. And an asshole."

"What, he wasn't nice to you? I mean, you were just an intern."

"He was nice," Nik said, frowning as the reporter asked about his diet and Tiernan laughed. "For a while."

Rae turned from the TV to face him, nose scrunched up in that way it did when she suspected he wasn't telling her everything. "What's going on? You're being weird."

This was it. Nik couldn't keep it from her anymore. He'd wanted to tell her before, before the whole wedding fiasco, but then he hadn't wanted to admit how fucked up everything had gotten. She'd think, well, she'd think he'd come back because of some stupid fight with a guy. A guy that didn't even matter!

Now, though, she watched him through narrowed eyes, searching his face for the secrets he was hiding.

"There's something I didn't tell you," he said, but he was interrupted as the door opened and Dan entered. He tossed his keys on the counter with a clatter and hardly noticed Nik as he breezed through the living room.

"Don't rot your brain with all that TV shit," he told Rae, grabbing a beer from the fridge and cracking it open. For a moment, he lingered in the kitchen, checking his phone and drinking his beer. Nik felt on edge, waiting for him to leave, to do something. He hadn't really talked with Dan yet, but Dan didn't seem to care. Dan had never really seemed to care what he did as long as he was out of the way. He always said he wasn't supposed to be the big brother. "Shit," Dan said to himself after a minute, taking a few gulps of beer quickly before grabbing his keys. The apartment door slammed shut behind him.

Ignoring was better than yelling, Nik had decided. If only Andre would do the same.

Rae turned back to Nik, expectant. Right. Tiernan.

"When I was in Arizona, Tiernan and I..."

"Tiernan and you?" Rae repeated curiously then her face lit up. "Wait, oh my God! You didn't." She was smiling, but Nik didn't echo it. Instead, he got up and went to the fridge, yanking it open. There wasn't much inside but a few beers, an old case of Coke, and some eggs. He grabbed a soda and turned to find Rae watching him eagerly from over the couch. "You so did."

"Yeah, we so did," Nik muttered, leaning against the counter. "And we so fucked it up too."

"What happened?"

Sighing, Nik came back to the couch and set the soda on the coffee table unopened. "He fucked it up, okay? Not me."

"I didn't say you did," she said, but Nik knew she'd been thinking it. Everyone always did.

He frowned. "I thought... I thought maybe it was real. Maybe he did actually like me, but he was using me."

"For what?" She sounded skeptical, like Tiernan would be crazy to do that. Nik wasn't so sure.

"I don't know. To piss off his parents, his sister, to get back at them for not supporting him."

Nik kept thinking of the wedding, the way Tiernan's mother had looked at him, how she wouldn't use his name, how she'd stormed away.

"It was fucking awful."

Rae tilted her head to the side sympathetically. "That sucks. But I can't believe you didn't tell me!"

Nik slumped on the couch. He felt bad enough already. "I don't know. I wanted to tell you. I just... didn't. I didn't want you to feel like I was bragging or, or that my life was so much better than yours. I don't know what's wrong with me."

"Lots of things," she assured him and he rolled his eyes. "But seriously, you could have told me. You're my best friend."

"Built-in," Nik replied. "It just happened so fast. One minute, I was happy and then we were at his sister's wedding and his parents were looking at me like I was dirt under their designer shoes."

"He took you to a wedding?"

"So?" Nik didn't see that it made any difference. It was a good a place as any to humiliate someone in front of friends and family.

"So you don't just ask anyone to a wedding," Rae pointed out, but Nik didn't see where she was going with this.

"If you need a date, you do. He asked, like, two days before."

"So he didn't plan it, then."

Nik frowned. "What are you saying?"

"Why would he take you to a wedding just to piss off his parents?"

"Because he's an asshole." Nik had come to that conclusion already. He'd as good as admitted it.

"But if he was planning it, don't you think he would have asked before?" Her eyebrows went up as though he should have understood. He didn't.

"No." He frowned. The television had switched to diving coverage instead. "Why would you bring someone you know your parents will hate to a wedding, unless you want to piss them off?"

"Because he liked you," she suggested. "Why else do you bring dates to weddings?"

"To get laid." Nik had no idea. He didn't go to weddings. This had been his first, and probably last. Nik glared as Rae opened her mouth again, probably to try to convince him that this had all been some big misunderstanding.

"Okay, sorry," she said, changing tact. "You're right. I don't know him or what happened. You just seemed kind of sad."

Nik huddled into the couch. He wasn't sad. He was angry. Disappointed. Confused because he still liked Tiernan.

"Well, it's over now and he can do whatever he wants with Parisian guys." No doubt, he was out fucking as many as he could, now that he didn't have to deal with Nik.

Rae was silent for a moment as the voiceover on TV talked about *determination* and *spirit.*

"Is that why you came home?" she asked after a minute, quiet, and Nik couldn't bring himself to look at her.

"No," he said, but when she didn't reply, he sighed. "Maybe a little. I didn't want to see him every day and just keep remembering. But Mom's sick, and you're here."

Rae fixed him with that look, that look that Nik hated. It was the look she'd given him when he told her he was moving to Chicago, that he wasn't coming home again. Somewhere between disappointed and annoyed.

"You're running away again," she said, so matter-of-factly, like it was something he did on a regular basis.

"What are you talking about?" He crossed his arms over his chest and sunk into the couch.

"You do this all the time, Nik," she said, not being at all sympathetic, as he'd hoped she'd be. "You ran away to Chicago when things where bad with Andre. You ran away to Phoenix when

Mom started getting worse. And now, you ran here, away from that guy. You always run away."

Nik stared, indignant. "I do not." He'd left because Andre was insufferable and he couldn't live his life like that. He hadn't come back because his mom didn't deserve his forgiveness. He'd come home because Rae needed him. He wasn't running away. "Don't think you can trick me with your psychology crap."

"It's not psychology," she said, annoyed. "It's the truth."

Nik didn't appreciate the accusation. He'd done whatever he had to get out of here, and she accused him of running.

"I'm not saying you made the wrong choice," she said in that forced calm voice she had. "You went to college and you almost escaped this family, but we're still your family. I'm just saying that sometimes, you have a tendency to avoid things that are hard."

"Avoidance is a religion in our family," he said, but the weight had settled on his chest. Why did she always have to be right? It was all that reading she did. Where Nik had drowned himself in fantasy, she'd opted for the more practical route of the human psyche. He sighed. "Maybe I did run away from here, but I had to. You know I had to."

"I know," she agreed. "Sometimes it's your only option. Staying in a bad situation never makes things better. What I'm trying to say is that maybe you didn't come home for all the right reasons."

Looking at her, Nik saw the doubt behind her eyes and the weight on his chest attempted to suffocate him. He was a terrible brother.

"I'm sorry, okay? I..." he said. "I want to be here; not for Andre or Mom or whoever else — for you. You're the only one who ever really cared about me, and I should have been here for you, and I am now. I want to be now."

For a moment, she didn't reply, watching him. His heart throbbed in his chest, stomach twisting into knots. He'd been so stupid, so selfish. He hadn't even come home for the right reasons, but he was going to make it up to her.

Rae shrugged finally. "I don't care why you came home. I'm just glad you're back."

Nik said nothing and watched the camera swooping over Paris with an ache in his chest.

Chapter 26:
Inevitability

On the one hand, Tiernan had made it through preliminaries in all his events. On the other, there were still semi-finals to do before he even had a chance at a medal.

Inevitable, the press kept saying. His win was inevitable. The more they said it, the less he believed it. But he couldn't let that doubt get to him, which was where he found himself before the Butterfly semi-final, shoving reporter's voices out of his head.

"There's nothing I can say that I haven't already," Coach said, ignoring the way Tiernan bounced on his toes, too nervous to stand still. "Just keep swimming."

Tiernan almost smiled. "Are you quoting a Disney movie at me?"

Coach arched an eyebrow, unimpressed. "Whatever's going on out there — " He gestured beyond the pool, beyond the bleachers filled with people who'd paid to see semi-finals. " — doesn't matter in here. In here, you're a swimmer and that's it."

Tiernan took a deep breath, tamping down the nervous flutter in his chest. He hadn't told Coach about Nik, about how much he'd screwed up, but Coach always seemed to know when he was distracted.

"And it was Pixar," Coach grunted as the Olympic official announced they were ready.

Tiernan smiled this time as he climbed onto the block. Stretching out his muscles, he determinedly didn't look down the row to where Dylan stood on his block. He'd so far managed to avoid Dylan, which was a good thing considering he wasn't sure he could restrain himself from hitting Dylan, if Dylan said one more thing about Nik.

Tiernan had called. He'd called and called, but Nik never picked up. He was beginning to think he should just give up. Nik obviously didn't want to talk to him, and he wasn't sure he deserved Nik's forgiveness even if he could get him to answer the phone.

Pushing Nik out of his head, Tiernan took his start position. If he let it get to him, he'd never get anywhere.

The start gun echoed around the room. The crowd screamed, and Tiernan hit the water.

It was like his brain went on auto-pilot, the seconds ticking by too fast to count as his body cut through the water. He could hear the rush of his own blood in his ears, feel the sharp breaths he took every time he broke the surface. The turn went smoothly, a fast kick-off and he was almost to the end.

His hand hit the edge of the pool and water slapped him as he pulled off his goggles, searching for the score screen.

Third place. High enough to get him into the finals.

"Yes!" He hit the water with his fist, a smile spreading over his face. His chest felt light as he climbed out of the pool, congratulated by other swimmers, though Dylan passed by without a word. Tiernan checked the screen again. Dylan was first.

He shook the annoyance away as he reached Coach, who handed him a towel.

"Good job," he said, gruff, but Tiernan thought he might have seen a glimmer of pride behind his eyes. "Backstroke semi-finals next. Don't even think about slipping away for any sightseeing crap."

Tiernan's days were planned out from the minute he got up to the minute he went to bed. There was no time for sightseeing. When he wasn't training, he was doing interviews or press parties, or he was just trying to relax and not think about the competition. Thinking about it too much made him nervous. He hated being nervous.

As Coach hustled him off to the locker rooms, Tiernan glanced up at the stands. People had begun filtering out, and there were fewer people than he would have expected, but it was only a semi-final. The only people who watched semi-finals were either family or they couldn't get tickets to a main event. The tickets were wildly expensive, after all.

He did a double-take as he caught sight of bright blond hair. Ella had always gotten highlights.

She stood in the stands, watching him silently. She didn't react when he found her.

"Coach, I just have to — " he said, nodding at the stands, but Coach frowned.

"We don't have time for any detours. Family can wait."

Tiernan glanced back at Ella, who hadn't moved. "Just five minutes, please."

Coach remained unimpressed, but he shook his head after a minute. "Five minutes then I want you dressed and ready for the next interview."

Tiernan slapped his shoulder in thanks and ducked away, down a hall and through a door that led to the outside hallway. He wasn't surprised to find Ella there, waiting.

He only had five minutes. He had to make this quick, but still he hesitated as they stood there. He hadn't spoken to her since the wedding.

"What are you doing here?" he asked finally.

She frowned, as though it was a stupid question. "I said I'd come."

"Yeah, but after what happened, I didn't really expect you to come." He hadn't expected anyone from the family to talk to him for a long time. His mom hadn't called yet, pretending nothing had happened, like she usually did.

She tilted her head to the side, hair brushing against a scarf that looked very Parisian.

"Do you really think so little of me?"

"No." Tiernan shook his head, but he paused. "I thought you'd be pissed."

"Because you ruined my wedding?"

Tiernan grimaced. That hadn't been his intention. It had been the last thing on his mind when he'd asked Nik to go with him. He hadn't meant to 'make a statement' or anything like that. It had all gotten so twisted around.

Ella sighed. "You didn't ruin my wedding. Mom and Dad were the only people upset. If anything, they ruined it by making such a big deal."

"But they wouldn't have if I hadn't — "

She held up a hand to stop him. Tiernan was big enough to admit when he'd made a mistake. He should have listened to Ella, just followed directions, not been so selfish to make her wedding about him.

"It's partially my fault," she admitted, and Tiernan stared. How was this her fault? "I should have just told Mom and Dad to go screw themselves when they insisted you bring a woman. I should have stood up for you and I didn't because I wanted everything to be perfect." She sighed, tucking her hair back, and Tiernan almost didn't believe he was hearing this. She'd been on his side at times, but she'd always liked getting their parent's attention. He never doubted that she cared about him, in that annoying way only siblings could do. "It was my wedding, and you're my brother, and I'm not ashamed of who you are. You know that, right?"

"Yeah," Tiernan said, but it was nice to hear it.

"Good," she said seriously. "I knew we were headed for trouble the minute I told you who to bring. But it's okay. I'm used to being upstaged by you."

Tiernan stared at her for a minute as her words sunk in. "Upstaged? When have I ever upstaged you? You're the favorite."

Ella had always been the favorite, since before he was born. She did everything first, and she did it better. Except swimming. He'd beat her there. His parents never stopped talking about how smart she was, how beautiful and graceful, how she was sure to be successful. Like Tiernan was the ugly step-sister.

Ella laughed, short. "If we could get through one dinner without your name coming up, it would be a miracle." She shook her head. "They don't hate you, you know."

"They just hate who I am. Did they even come?"

She pursed her lips and he knew the answer. He hadn't expected them to, but somewhere, deep down, he hadn't been able to stop himself from hoping. "It's their problem," she said instead.

"They're never going to change, are they?" he asked finally. He was way over his five minute limit. Coach was going to murder him.

"And you can't make them," Ella agreed. "So forget about it and the wedding, and go be happy with Nik. He seemed like a nice guy."

Tiernan grimaced as he remembered the way Nik had looked at him: betrayed and disgusted. He doubted Nik would ever forgive him.

"The wedding didn't just piss off Mom and Dad," he said when she waited for a response.

"Well, don't be stupid," she said bluntly, adjusting her scarf. "Take responsibility for yourself and fix it."

She was right, but that didn't mean Tiernan enjoyed getting the responsibility lecture again. Maybe he deserved it. If he'd been responsible before, he wouldn't have led Nik into an attack. He'd have Nik with him right now, and he wouldn't feel so terrible.

"I gotta get back," he said instead. "I'm late for the press room. Coach is going to kill me."

Ella stepped forward and offered him a hug, brief but warm. "No matter what happens in finals, you'll always be my stupid little brother."

"Good to know," he said, but some of the pressure inside him released. "Thanks for coming."

"I wouldn't be anywhere else."

Tiernan left her in the hall, heading back for the locker rooms. Coach was definitely going to have his head, but Tiernan couldn't bring himself to care and he smiled as he threw on his clothes and hurried for the press room.

Josh snuffled in his sleep, twisting and turning, but not waking. Tiernan glanced over, but Josh just mumbled something unintelligible and turned over again. It was still dark out, though sunrise couldn't be far away. Tiernan's alarm was set for six AM, but he still had a good ten minutes until it went off.

He couldn't sleep, and not just because finals were today. Butterfly anyway, and that was the one he was most worried about. He couldn't sleep because every time he closed his eyes, he saw Nik's face.

Slipping out of bed, he grabbed his phone and stepped into the hall, careful to shut the door quietly behind him.

The hall was bright but empty, ugly grey carpet underfoot as Tiernan walked to the end of the hall. There wasn't really anywhere to go aside from the lounge downstairs, but Tiernan didn't want to risk running into anyone there, so he stopped by the stairwell and brought up Nik's name on the phone.

It rang too many times. It was going to go to voicemail again, but just as Tiernan was about to hang up, he heard the phone pick up.

"'Lo?" The answer was slurred, half-awake.

"Shit," Tiernan said, then grimaced. It was almost midnight in New York. He hadn't thought of that. But Nik had answered. "Hey."

"Tiernan?" Nik asked, still sounding half-asleep.

"Yeah, hey," Tiernan said, softer. He hadn't actually expected Nik to pick up. He'd been letting it go to voicemail for days. Now that he had, Tiernan's words got lost, jumbled up in apologies and explanations that he couldn't straighten out. "Sorry, I forgot about the time difference."

Nik didn't reply, but Tiernan could hear him breathing, slow and steady, like maybe he was falling back asleep.

Sucking in a breath, he steeled himself. He had to get this out before Nik decided to hate him forever.

"I just called to, to say I'm sorry," he said finally, pushing a hand into his hair and tugging at the ends. "I should never have asked you to come to the wedding. Not because I didn't want you there. Because I knew my parents would do that. I shouldn't have put you in that situation. I was stupid."

There was no other way he could put it. Tiernan had *known* what would happen, but he'd done it anyway, without thinking.

"I just want you to know that I'm sorry, and I didn't ask you to get back at them. That was never what I meant to happen. I mean, maybe on some subconscious level, I was trying to get back at them. They've always just refused to accept who I was and I thought maybe... But I shouldn't have taken you there where I *knew* that would happen. When you asked me that, at the hotel, I just, I couldn't think. I like you so much and I couldn't believe I would be so stupid."

Nik didn't reply. Tiernan listened for a second, unsure he was still on the phone, but he could hear breathing, a rustle of sheets. There wasn't anything he could say to take it back, to make it go away. He hated that he'd messed up so badly. The only other thing he'd screwed up so much was the last Olympic trials, and that had been about guys too. Maybe he just wasn't cut out for relationships and feelings. Without them, he'd only have swimming to focus on. That might get him a medal, but it wouldn't make him completely happy.

"And what I said about your family..." His stomach sank as he remembered the words he'd spit at Nik, accusing him of using him back. "I had no idea. I should never have said anything." He sighed. "Look, I know you probably hate me, but the truth is I really like you. More than I've ever liked anyone, and I fucked it up. I really did. I just hope you don't hate me forever. You don't deserve that."

His phone beeped. Six AM.

Nik still hadn't replied, and Tiernan didn't expect him to.

"I have to go. I hope everything works out for you."

He hung up the phone with a slight pause. It had been a long-shot, that Nik would even listen to him, let alone forgive him. He'd tried was all he could say, but it didn't feel like enough. If he hadn't been competing in the Olympics, he might have done something crazy like fly to New York, but Nik didn't want to see him. He didn't even want to talk to him.

Tiernan returned to his room, shutting the door as Josh snuffled and mumbled something else. He tossed the phone on his bed and grabbed his clothes. It was over now. Now, he had to focus on the one thing he knew he could do, and that was swim.

Chapter 27:
The Deep End

"Mike wants copies of this for the Board meeting."

Julianne dropped a stack of papers in front of Nik, taking up what little space he had on the table. He really didn't have a place to work, mostly using empty conference rooms when he could, but it didn't matter since he was largely running around making copies and ensuring the coffee pot was full.

Julianne swept her long brown hair over her shoulder and sighed down at him. "I can't believe you gave up Paris. What I wouldn't give to be there right now, reporting on real shit, instead of picking up dry cleaning and proofing puff pieces."

It wasn't the first time another intern had told him that, and Nik didn't reply, shuffling the papers into something more organized. He hadn't tried to explain why he'd left. They wouldn't understand. Besides, he wasn't even sure if he should have left, not after last night.

Tiernan's phone call felt fuzzy, like it hadn't really happened. It had been late, and he'd been mostly asleep when he'd answered the phone. He wouldn't have, if he'd taken the time to check who was calling. Nik would have been sure it had been a dream if Rae hadn't asked, "Am I hallucinating or did someone call you in the middle of the night?" the next morning.

Nik couldn't remember exactly what Tiernan had said, only that he'd woken up with a guilty knot in his stomach. He remembered Tiernan apologizing, something about the wedding being his fault, that he still liked Nik.

He didn't know what to think. He'd spent the past week and a half trying to get Tiernan out of his head, convincing himself that

Tiernan was an asshole who didn't care about anyone but himself, but now he was starting to think he'd made a mistake. He hadn't really given Tiernan a chance to explain, had just jumped on him after the wedding, taken his parents' words and thrown them back at him. Insecurity, Rae would have called it, projecting his own issues onto Tiernan. He didn't need her voice in his head when he thought about Tiernan.

"Jesus Christ, he is hot," Julianne said, breaking into Nik's thoughts, interrupting the spiraling feeling of guilt taking over him.

The television in the corner was permanently switched to the Olympic coverage. Twenty-four-seven, Nik was surrounded by the sounds of the Olympics, a reminder of what he'd given up. And for what? His brothers barely acknowledged he was there, and he still hadn't worked up the courage to see his mom. The only person happy to see him was Rae.

Tiernan appeared on screen, a promotion this time. Shots of him against a black background, wearing his USA swim suit, goggles perched on top his head, video of him swimming, slow-motion waves around him as he crashed through the water. His voice rolled over the images.

"I've been working for this my whole life... If I swim my best, I'll be proud... Swimming is my life. It's my passion. It's everything... Win or lose doesn't matter. It's about the support of the American people, of my friends and family, and everyone who's worked hard to get me here."

The promotion ended with a shot of Tiernan gazing into the camera, intense, Olympic rings stamped across the bottom of the screen.

"No way I would have left if I got to stare at that all day," Julianne said as the screen changed to a live feed, the competition pool.

Nik hoped she would leave, but instead, she took the chair next to him, kicking up her feet and turning to the television. Swimmers milled around the edges of the pool, and the announcer was talking. Stats appeared on the screen and Nik automatically searched for Tiernan's name, next to the little American flag. He was in fifth place currently, two spots below the other American, Dylan.

"The men's butterfly has been little contested this year," the announcer said, and Nik felt his stomach drop. Butterfly hadn't been

Tiernan's best event. "Dylan Hoffman is this year's favorite. He's swum well in the preliminaries, but going into the finals, it's Tiernan Pace who will be looking to move up."

"Is he as hot in person?" Julianne asked as the camera flashed to Tiernan. Tiernan ignored the camera in his face, adjusting his suit.

Nik gazed at Tiernan, the tiny lines on his face so obvious this close-up. He wasn't smiling, for once, listening to whatever his coach was saying, nodding along, eyes narrowed at the pool. Nik could almost see the wheels turning, grinding to a stop as he moved to the starting block.

"No," he said finally, eyes not leaving the screen. "He's hotter."

"You're an idiot," she told him matter-of-factly, and Nik had to agree.

He'd let himself get carried away in feelings of uselessness, doubts that someone like Tiernan could actually want to be with him. Now, he'd missed out on his chance. Tiernan probably thought he hated him. He had to figure out a way to apologize for being such an idiot.

The swimmers climbed on their blocks and the announcer was still talking about statistics, but Nik's eyes were trained on Tiernan in lane four. This was Tiernan's chance to prove his family wrong, everyone who'd said he wouldn't make it. Nik couldn't help feeling nervous for him, ignoring Julianne's comment about swimmer's packages.

"And they're off," the announcer said as the swimmers snapped from the blocks, gliding smoothly into the water. It was different, watching it on TV, Nik thought, listening to the roar of the crowd behind the announcer. He didn't care what the announcer had to say about the other swimmers. He only cared about Tiernan.

Nik felt like he blinked and it was over. Scores popped up on the screen and his heart dropped. Fourth. Tiernan finished fourth.

The cameras didn't even flash to Tiernan, skipping instead to Dylan, who was yelling and pumping his fist. Nik stared at the TV. It couldn't be possible. Tiernan had worked so hard. He trained every day to be good enough, but he'd still lost. By one place.

"Shit," Nik muttered to himself. He should have been there to tell him it was okay, to make him believe all the things he'd said in that voice-over.

He caught sight of Tiernan once as the cameras focused on Dylan. Tiernan had walked forward to shake his hand and say something the mic didn't pick up. He flashed a brief smile, polite, nothing more, to Dylan before vanishing.

Nik felt as if he'd just lost, crushed under the weight of all those expectations. He couldn't even imagine what Tiernan felt.

"Okay, I lied," Julianne said, oblivious to Tiernan. "*He's* hot."

Nik made a face as she nodded at Dylan. "I have to make these copies," he said instead, grabbing the papers off the desk.

"Make sure they're collated and stapled," she reminded him as he left and headed for the copy room.

The copy room was thankfully empty, and Nik set the papers on a table, staring unseeingly at them. Tiernan had lost the one thing he'd been working so hard for. Nik grimaced. If it had been because of him, he would never be able to forgive himself. If he'd just realized how stupid he'd been earlier, had accepted Tiernan's apology...

He had no answer that didn't make him feel guilty and he was almost glad when his phone rang, interrupting his downward spiral. He was relieved to see Brooke's name on the screen. He hadn't talked to her at all since he'd left except to respond to her text about how Paris was, only to correct her that he wasn't there.

"Hey," he said. Maybe she could put things into better perspective.

"Hey," she said, and by the tone of her voice, Nik knew she knew. "I just saw it."

"Yeah," Nik agreed, leaning against the copier. It was quieter in here than the rest of the office, an office where Nik didn't quite fit in. He'd never really felt like he fit in anywhere, so it was nothing new, he supposed.

"How do you think he's taking it?" she asked and Nik couldn't even imagine. The Olympics were the only thing Tiernan was working towards, and to have a medal so close within reach...

"I don't know." Nik wished he did know. He wished he hadn't been so stupid. "Do you think I completely fucked up?"

"Fucked what up?"

"Everything." He shook his head as a lump formed in his throat. "I should be there, shouldn't I? I shouldn't be making copies and stapling documents. I should be there for him."

"You're there for your family," she reminded him, and Nik didn't argue. He'd come home for Rae. He hadn't given Brooke all the details; just that his mom was sick and he couldn't go to Paris. He felt torn, torn between wanting to be there for Tiernan, to make everything right the way he should have done weeks ago, and being here with Rae, who needed him more than anything. It wasn't like he could go around changing his mind every five minutes. He'd decided to come back, and he still had to make it up to Rae.

"You're right," he muttered. Rae was more important right now. He'd have to find some other way to fix things with Tiernan, though he didn't know how at the moment.

"How is she?" Brooke asked after a minute.

Nik still hadn't been to see her. Every time he got to the door, his body froze up on him, and he couldn't make his feet move. He had to see her, he knew that, but he couldn't force himself to do it.

"I don't know," he admitted. Rae went to the hospital every day, and Nik tried to go along, pacing up and down the block, bracing himself for the moment she told him it was all over, the day it would end. It might never end, he knew. She might hang on for months, years more. "I'm... afraid."

"Of what?"

Nik didn't know why it was easier to talk to Brooke about this. He didn't know her any better than he knew Rae, who would have been the logical choice to expand upon his worries. Rae had always been there, always known what he was thinking before he even said it. Maybe that was why. Rae knew his excuses and ways to counteract them. She had answers to every problem; he didn't want an answer this time.

Nik's head jerked up as someone passed by the door, but no one stopped to ask what he was doing, why he wasn't working.

"I don't want to forgive her," he said finally, shoving a hand through his hair, turning from the door. "But she's sick and everyone expects you to forgive people who are sick, like because they might die, they somehow deserve it now." Nik didn't want to see her looking frail and weak. He didn't want to have to face her, to listen to what she had to say on her deathbed, as though it might make up for everything he'd been through.

"Death doesn't absolve people's sins," Brooke said when he didn't continue. "But maybe you need to see her anyway."

"Why?" Nik asked, exasperated, staring at the paper cutter and biting his lip.

"Maybe it's not about forgiving them for what they did. You can't change it. Maybe you just have find some closure."

Nik wasn't sure he'd ever get closure even if he talked to her, even if he forgave her for everything she'd done, everything she'd put him and Rae through.

"How's the website?" Nik asked instead of answering. He didn't want to think about his mom right now. There was nothing he could do to make a difference.

Brooke paused, but she let him change the subject. "It's good. The feature did really well. Got lots of comments on your stuff, even a few shares, which is great. I'm hoping mainstream media might pick it up if it gets enough publicity. Or I could not so subtly anonymously submit it to an online journal."

Nik smiled briefly, the knot in his chest lessening. "Isn't that cheating?"

"In the journalistic world, it's called marketing. I give it a little push and who knows where it could go. Sometimes I do it with the pop culture stuff. Gets me a lot of hits, if the research is done right."

"That would be great," Nik said, but his heart wasn't in it. He couldn't bring himself to hope his career might take off, not when so much else was going on. "Listen, I have some copying to do. I'll call you later, okay?"

"Sure," she agreed easily. "Don't take life too seriously, Nik."

"I won't," he assured her, but he sighed as he hung up the phone. He rubbed at his face, the tension in his forehead. He needed to just stop thinking about all the things he couldn't control. His mom, Tiernan, Andre. No good came of any of it.

As he lifted the top of the copier, his phone vibrated in his pocket and for a brief second, his heart jumped excitedly — it might be Tiernan. It wasn't, though. Rae's name appeared on a screen and he hesitated a second before answering.

"Hey," he said, but she cut him off before he even got the word out.

"You need to come to the hospital," she said immediately.

Nik's heart contracted sharply. "Why?" he asked, though he didn't want to know. It couldn't be good.

"Just come."

E.E. Grey

She hung up before Nik could ask anything else. He didn't give himself time to talk himself out of it and left the papers behind.

Chapter 28:
Drowning

By the time he reached the hospital, Nik was pretty sure his heart was going to climb right out of his throat, and he tried to catch his breath as he found Rae in the hallway, pacing back and forth in front of the door.

"Rae, what is it?" he asked, grabbing her arm, forcing her to stop.

Her hair was messy, eyes a little wild, like she wasn't sure what to do. "She crashed. The doctor's stabilized her, but they don't think..." She couldn't even finish, taking a deep breath and shaking her head.

Fucking Christ, Nik thought as he stared at the door behind her. It was really happening. Somehow he'd thought his mom would always be around. Around, but never there.

"Where's Andre?" he asked, looking around for them, but the hall was empty except for a few passing nurses. "Where's Seth, Dan?"

"They're on a job," she said desperately. "They're not answering. I left a message with the company."

"Shit," he muttered. They were on their own this time. He looked at Rae, but her hands were shaking and she didn't meet his gaze.

Nik felt sick like he never had before. His stomach was awash with nausea and he couldn't bring himself to do anything other than stare at the door beside him. Somewhere behind it, his mom was dying.

"I don't know what to do," Rae said, pulling her arm from his grip. "There's nothing to do. It's over."

"It can't be over." She couldn't die. For all the times Nik had told himself he didn't care, he couldn't lie to himself now, facing the solemn door. She was still his mom, despite everything that had happened. Suddenly he was eight years old again, showing her a drawing he'd done in school, waiting for her to praise him or just acknowledge him. Sometimes, she had, and he'd clung to those moments for so long.

Rae had given up. He could see it. The way her shoulders slumped, gaze cast to the ground, exhaustion etched into every feature. How long had she been like this and he hadn't noticed? Too wrapped up in himself?

He wasn't going to let Rae take this on all by herself anymore.

He took a breath, heart thudding against his ribcage, stomach broiling as he faced the door. "I'll go in there."

Rae met his gaze, a pause, but she said nothing. He half hoped she would come with him, but she took a step back as he reached for the door, hugging her stomach.

He was six years old, going to school for the first time, and the building towered over him like a foreboding castle. The front door glared at him, chained and terrifying. There might as well have been a dragon.

Taking a breath, he held it as he pushed the door open and stepped inside.

He didn't know what he'd been expecting, but instead, he was met with the quiet beeping of machines, the sterile whiteness of the floors. A bed sat near the window, covers tucked in tight, like a straightjacket.

The woman on the bed stirred and a machine whirred to life. A steady drip came from the bag hanging next to the bed, and Nik forced himself to go in further.

"Nik?"

Her voice trembled, weak, and Nik stopped a few feet from the bed. Her arms were thin, veins winding their way over her skin. Her light brown hair spread out on the pillow, scraggly, unbrushed. He'd never seen her like this, so helpless.

It should have made him feel bad, but instead, he just felt angry. She'd done this to herself, to them.

"Is that you?" she asked, blinking slowly, as though she couldn't quite focus.

"It's me," he said, staying where he was. He didn't see how this was supposed to help, what Rae expected to happen. That they'd just patch everything up and it would be fine? That he'd just forget everything she'd done, or not done?

"You came," she breathed and the heart rate monitor beeped. Nik followed the little red line on the screen. "My baby."

"I'm not your baby," he said sharply, crossing his arms. He could feel his heartbeat against his throat.

"You are," she said, gazing at him from the pillow, and Nik shied away from it.

"You didn't seem to think so when you drank until you couldn't walk, when Rae and I had to lie to teachers about why you didn't come to conferences, when we needed you. You weren't there."

She licked her lips, cracked and dry, and nodded, surprising Nik.

"I know," she said. "Your brothers, they did what they could."

"This isn't about them," Nik said, and he knew he shouldn't be getting mad at someone so sick, but he couldn't help it. She didn't deserve his forgiveness, or anyone else's. "They shouldn't have had to. I shouldn't have had to grow up that way. How could you just abandon us?"

Nik had never understood. How could she have just stopped caring? Didn't he matter?

He hated the tear that came to her eye. She wasn't allowed to be upset. She'd done this to herself.

"I wanted," she said, trailing off as though speaking was too much effort. "I wanted…"

"You wanted alcohol," Nik finished for her. "That was always more important."

"I wanted not to feel," she said finally. "I wanted your father back. I wanted a normal life."

She wasn't allowed to do this, Nik thought as he swallowed down the lump in his throat. She wasn't allowed to explain things, to make it seem like she'd had a good reason for turning to alcohol, for becoming numb to the rest of her life.

"So, what?" he asked sharply, avoiding looking at how skinny she was, hardly even a person anymore. "Now that you're sick, you feel bad? Now you care? You never cared when I needed you to."

"You didn't need me," she breathed with a huff. "You were strong by yourself. You and Rae. My little birds."

203

"Only because we had to be," he snapped, feeling the emotions building up inside him — anger, annoyance, fear.

"Then I did my job," she said, her eyes fluttering. "You made it through."

"No," Nik said, tears gathering, threatening to spill as he took a swift step forward. "You don't get to take credit for what we've become. You trapped Rae here. You drove me away. You made everything harder than it should have been. And you don't get to swoop in at the last minute and pretend you did anything for me. I did everything. Me and Rae. *We* made it through."

He couldn't help the hot tears spilling out now, the anger shaking his body as he stared at her. He was so *fucking* angry. He'd always been on his own, always been the one singled out, the reason everything went wrong. Andre blamed him for this, for everything. For so many years, he'd wished she would come back and be a mother, and when he'd finally gotten out, she'd dragged him right back in.

"Nikos," she said, voice tired, and the machines beeped louder, faster. "Don't live in the past. It'll only turn against you."

Nik shook his head, wiping away the wetness on his face. She lay there, unmoving, eyelashes fluttering against her cheeks, so much paler than he remembered. He didn't want her advice or her apologies. He realized now, as he watched her chest moving up and down in shallow breaths, her eyes searching out his, that he didn't need it.

The heart rate monitor beeped again, once, then it flat lined.

"Mom?" he asked, taking another step forward, but she didn't stir, her eyes staring at him blankly. "Mom?" He reached out and shook her arm. Her skin felt like paper, like it would rip if he pressed too hard. His heart jumped in his throat as he realized. "Shit. Shit!" He jerked back. "Rae!"

Rae burst in the door behind him, eyes wide in panic.

"What happened?" she demanded as she saw the tears on his face, how he stepped back, stumbling, hands trembling.

"I don't know," he said, shaking his head, unable to process. "I don't know. I don't fucking know."

"I'll get a nurse," Rae said, bolting from the room as Nik backed into the wall, still shaking his head. His body shook as he doubled over, unable to stop the tears, unable to stop anything as he let go and just gave in.

He felt empty. He had no more emotions left. No more tears. Nothing.

Sirens blared out the window, but neither he nor Rae spoke, sitting on opposite ends of the couch. A door slammed in the hall.

Nik hadn't expected to feel this way. He'd already run the gamut of emotions in the last hour, and now there was nothing left. Somehow, he'd expected it to be like passing a dead pigeon on the street where you went, "Huh," then kept walking.

It wasn't like that at all. He felt as though he'd been punched in the gut, like somehow he'd still thought she might come back from it and be around to piss him off for years to come.

Rae hadn't asked him what their mom had said. She wouldn't ask. She'd just wait.

They both jumped when the door opened and slammed shut. Andre threw his keys at the counter where they bounced off onto the floor. Seth and Dan came behind him, dragging their feet, looking as exhausted as Nik felt. He exchanged a glance with Rae. It was never good when Andre was in this mood.

"Why didn't you call?" Andre demanded without so much as a pause for breath, zeroing in on Rae, and Nik felt a ripple of annoyance.

"I did," she said, frowning. "You didn't answer."

"Why didn't you try harder?" He crossed the room, rounding the couch to glare her down.

"You were on-site," she said, as though confused why he was attacking her. It wasn't usual. Usually, it was Nik Andre went after. "You never answer your phones on-site. I told the receptionist."

"So we miss seeing Mom before she dies? That's bullshit, Rae!"

"Leave her alone," Nik snapped, standing to face Andre. "It wasn't her fault." The last thing he wanted to do was get in a fight with Andre, but it seemed to be coming whether he liked it or not.

Andre turned his glare to Nik, and Nik stiffened. "You're both the reason Mom's like this — was like this." He gave his head a jerk, like he couldn't quite process it. "If you hadn't come along, everything would have been fine."

"I know," Nik said, voice rising angrily. "Dad would still be here. Mom wouldn't have become a drunk. Your life would have been perfect." He'd heard it a million times before, but he was so fucking sick of being blamed for things he couldn't control. "If only we hadn't been born. You should have just dropped us off at the fire station. All your problems would have been solved."

"You fucking little piece of shit," Andre growled, and even Seth looked apprehensive now — Seth, the one who didn't give a shit about anything. "You'd be dead if it weren't for me, and have you ever appreciated what I did for you? Have you ever said thank you? I kept you clothed, fed. You wouldn't be at that pretentious fucking school if it weren't for me. You'd be nothing."

"I didn't realize I owed you for common fucking decency." Nik was shouting now. The neighbors would bang on the wall in a minute, just like high school all over again. "I'm so tired of being your scapegoat. You *hate* that I left. You blame me for taking away your life. It kills you that I might actually get to live my life. That's why you wanted me back. Without me, there's no one to blame and you have to face the truth. Dad was a deadbeat and Mom couldn't handle it. But I'm not the reason you're so unhappy."

Nik didn't see it coming, and he heard Rae's cry of, "Andre, no!" right before Andre's fist slammed into his jaw.

Nik stumbled back, hitting the couch and falling onto it. Pain exploded on his face, a sharp sting that blurred his vision in his left eye.

"What the fuck is wrong with you?" Rae demanded, shoving Andre back. Andre blinked, but he didn't say anything as Rae pulled Nik off the couch.

Clutching his face, Nik let Rae pull him up. Andre had never punched him before, not like that. He'd always deemed Nik too weak to take a punch.

"Next time I leave," he said as Rae grabbed the first frozen thing she could find in the freezer and shoved him in the bedroom. "I'm never coming back."

Rae slammed the door shut behind them, locking it for good measure.

"I'm fine," Nik assured her as she forced him to sit down on her bed and pressed the pack of frozen broccoli against his face. He didn't think he could hurt more than he had today. The wedding seemed like a laughable situation now. He'd been so stupid to think that was the worst his life could get.

"Yeah, your face'll be fine tomorrow," she said, rolling her eyes, but she sighed, and Nik knew she was barely holding it together.

He took the broccoli from her and she sunk onto the mattress, leaning into him instead. His skin felt like it was buzzing, and the coldness of the broccoli didn't do much to soothe it, but he kept it pressed to his eye.

"I can't believe Andre," she said, but Nik shook his head.

"He's always blamed me." Without Mom, he wasn't sure what Andre would do. He'd probably blame Nik forever, but Nik knew now that he didn't need to carry that around. He wasn't responsible for Andre's anger, and he couldn't use it as an excuse to run away. "I don't know what he'll do without her, but I know what I'm doing."

Rae glanced up at him but said nothing. Their room was dark and messy, unchanged since the last time Nik had been home. His old mattress was still in its usual spot on the corner, walls covered in photographs he'd ripped out of library magazines. The tiny window faced a brick wall barely three feet away, a crack in the pane that had been there as long as Nik could remember.

"I'm going back to Chicago. I'm gonna figure out a way to fix things with Tiernan. And I'm never coming back here."

Rae sighed, but she didn't try to convince him that Andre was just upset, that he'd get over it, that there was anything for him here. They both knew it wasn't true.

"But you have to come with me."

Nik took down the pack of broccoli, watching Rae. He wasn't going to leave her here, not again.

"Nik," she said, reluctant, but Nik shot her a look.

"What's keeping you here? Andre? Seth? Dan? They don't care."

"They do," she argued, but it was weak. "In their own way."

"Maybe they do, but it's your life. You can stay with me. You can go to school or get a job." He didn't care what she did as long as she did it away from Andre. He'd left her for too long already; look how well that had turned out. He wasn't going to leave her behind, not again. "I just don't want you to be stuck."

"I have friends here," she said, but she wasn't really arguing anymore. Just going through the list of excuses until they got to the end. Scooting back, she slumped against the wall and Nik joined her. It was just like old times.

"There are people in Chicago. I have two really annoying roommates. You can be friends with them."

She almost smiled. "Be friends with people who annoy you?"

"You always are." Nik hardly ever understood Rae's choice of friends, but maybe that was because he barely had any of his own. Other people just got in the way. He preferred being on his own or with Rae.

Rae sighed and reached for his hand, forcing him to press the broccoli back to his eye. He tried to smile behind it, hopeful. Things didn't have to turn out terribly, not all the time. He could change his life, just like she could.

She leaned back against him as they sat there. There was no noise from the living room and no one tried to come in. Nik hadn't expected them to. Dan and Seth always did what Andre told them to.

"So you're going to fix things with Tiernan?" she asked finally, and Nik knew they'd found the end of the argument. She was saying yes.

"Gonna try," he muttered, though he had no idea how to do it from halfway across the world.

"Flowers are always good," she said, "or sex."

Nik didn't want to know how she knew that. "Don't think that's going to work from here."

She made a noise of agreement. "So show him you care. Show him he still has a chance."

Nik wasn't sure how to do that, but he felt better knowing he was going to try, despite the stinging in his eye and the bruise surely forming on his face.

Chapter 29:
Butterfly Bandage

Fourth. Fourth *fucking* place.

Tiernan's stomach felt hollow, like there were no nerves left to coil up, to leave him feeling anything but empty.

Two-tenths of a second and he would have placed. He would have been an Olympic medalist. Instead, he watched as everyone else swarmed around the winners, cameras swooping over him like he wasn't even there, like he didn't even matter.

"Protocol," he heard in his ear, a low mutter, and Coach's hand pressed the small of his back, urging him forward, toward where Dylan preened like a peacock.

Tiernan edged past the other swimmers and offered his hand to Dylan, a brief smile, enough for the cameras to catch it.

"Congratulations," he said, forcing the words past his lips. For once, Dylan was too happy to even offer a biting retort, and Tiernan slipped away.

It wasn't anger he felt as he met Coach, only disappointment. Dylan had been faster. They all had. It was no one's fault but his own.

Coach seemed to see the thoughts rolling through his head as he handed Tiernan a towel.

"Fourth place is not the end of the world. It means you're the fourth best butterfly swimmer in the world."

Tiernan wasn't sure that was supposed to be reassuring. He could imagine his parents, sitting at home in their freezing cold house (they always kept the AC on, like they wanted to live in Antarctica), watching him lose, saying, "I knew it."

"But guess what? You're the top backstroke swimmer in the world, and you've got a hell of a shot in freestyle too. This was one defeat but you're not going to give in to it."

Logically, Tiernan knew he was right. It was just one event. It wasn't the end of the world. He had two more events to go, two more he had much better odds in. Still, he couldn't shake the feeling of inadequacy that stole over him as Coach shooed him off to the locker rooms. He should have been better.

Distractions, he told himself as he grabbed his bag out of the locker and pulled out the USA jacket. He'd let too many distractions get to him. It was exactly what had happened last time, except backwards. He'd been so focused this time, so determined not to get distracted from competition that he hadn't seen Nik coming. He hadn't seen how much he would care when Nik wasn't there anymore.

Straightening up, he shut his locker with a snap. That was over. He couldn't waste time thinking about Nik anymore, not when Nik wouldn't even talk to him. He had to accept the fact that he'd messed up and there was nothing more he could do to fix it. If he could get past that, just forget about Nik, he would only have swimming to focus on.

Coach would have deemed it a good idea, but Tiernan just couldn't shake the feeling of disappointment as he left the lockers and headed back to his dorm. He just hoped Josh wouldn't be there and he'd have a minute to decompress. Backstroke finals were in a couple days, and he needed to be ready for the million press interviews that came with it.

Tiernan thought he was pretty used to the press process by now. They mostly asked the same questions over and over again. He just had to remember to smile and be charming for each one. He was always a little relieved to see Jennifer in the press room, almost as if she was a friend.

He hadn't asked about Nik since that first day, and he tried to put it out of his mind as he sat down with her at a table. The other reporters grumbled about waiting, but Jennifer ignored them and pulled out her phone to record.

"I hate to say it," she said as they sat there, and Tiernan felt his chest contract slightly in anticipation. "But you didn't place in the butterfly."

Two days, and Tiernan still frowned whenever anyone brought it up. All the reporters had already asked. All except Jennifer.

"I didn't," he agreed, hoping they wouldn't have to go over the why and how he planned to turn this loss around.

"Can I just say, off the record, that it really sucked. I know how hard you worked."

"Thanks." No other reporter had said that. They were all focused on getting their stories.

She smiled and straightened up. "We won't talk about it again. So tell me about the backstroke. It's your best event."

He relaxed slightly and smiled. "Yeah, I think I'll do much better today. Training has been intense since we got here. Everyone is really talented."

Compliment the other swimmers, his coach said. *You don't want to come off as a pompous jerk.*

Tiernan would have done it anyway, except maybe about Dylan. Most of the other swimmers were great guys who just wanted the same things he did. Even Josh, with his unbridled enthusiasm, had a place in Tiernan's heart. He wondered how much more fun they would have if there wasn't so much pressure.

"Did your family end up coming?"

"My sister came by for the semi-finals. It was really great of her actually."

"So she's over the Bridezilla phase?"

Tiernan laughed. "Don't use that word. I got in trouble last time."

Behind Jennifer, a young reporter sniffed impatiently, tapping her nails against her phone case. A bored-looking guy with a camera lingered beside her. Tiernan wasn't sure what was so important, but Jennifer ignored the girl.

"Okay, no references to Japanese monsters. Did the wedding go alright then?"

Tiernan paused. Alright wasn't the word he would use. "It was beautiful," he said instead. "Very purple, very white. Very hot."

Jennifer smiled and scribbled something down. "You should be used to that, training in Phoenix. How's it been being in France? Quite a change."

"It's nice. I haven't really gotten out much, but it's nice stepping outside and not roasting alive." Unfortunately, his training schedule didn't leave much time for sight-seeing. He'd thought about sticking around after the Olympics ended, but those plans were still up in the air. He didn't really have time to think about it.

"Excuse me." The girl behind Jennifer interrupted with a small cough and a pointed look at Jennifer. "We had an interview scheduled five minutes ago."

Jennifer smiled back at her, overly polite, and Tiernan didn't try to hide his amusement. Jennifer didn't seem the type to be talked down to by an overly-made-up twenty-something.

"My apologies," she said graciously, rising from the chair. "Tiernan, good luck today. I'm rooting for you."

Jennifer stepped past the girl with a pointed look and the girl shook her hair back. She didn't dwell, though, immediately taking Jennifer's vacated seat while the camera guy set up the shot. Her lipstick was too dark for her skin tone, and she held out a delicate hand to him.

"Tiernan, my name is Carissa Jenkins with *Twenty-One* magazine."

Tiernan had heard of it — some post-teen magazine that focused on make-up tips and produced their own web series news clips to try to seem relevant. He merely smiled at her. This wasn't the first online news clip he'd done. It just meant being more charming than usual.

"Nice to meet you," he said, shaking her hand and watching her primp for a second before turning to the camera and sweeping her long, blond hair back.

"Hello, and welcome to the 2024 Olympics in Paris, France!" she greeted the camera, almost obnoxiously perky. "I'm here with Tiernan Pace, one of the United States' best swimmers, and I'm going to get all the dirt on what makes him tick."

Tiernan barely remembered to put on his press face as she turned to him. Her brown eyes were big, like she could trick him into revealing personal secrets with just a look.

"Tiernan, you're the favorite to win the backstroke this afternoon. How do you deal with the pressure that goes with such a competitive sport?"

This was easy, Tiernan thought. He'd answered this question a million times. "It's all about management," he said simply. "Time management, pressure management, relationship management." He winked at her, but she didn't blush, not like they usually did. Instead, she tilted her head to the side, her smile sweet and deceptive.

"How do you manage those relationships? Friends, family... boyfriends?"

"Part of it is that they have to understand that you're an athlete first. A lot of my time is taken up with training. It's not something I can control, so it's important for them to manage expectations as well."

"Is that hard on potential boyfriends?" she asked, not looking as sweet as she watched him, and he paused.

"I guess. To be honest, it hasn't really been a problem yet." He smiled winningly, and she echoed it, though just for a second.

"What about Nik?"

Tiernan blinked, caught off-guard for the first time. "What?"

"Nik Cali," she repeated as though she almost had him. "You were in a photo with him on Instagram."

Tiernan didn't even know Nik had an Instagram. He had never bothered to cyber stalk him — he'd never thought about it.

"Uh, I don't," he said, but she whipped out her phone, the picture already pulled up. It was the one he and Nik had taken at the lake that day, kissing on the shore. For a moment, he stared at the screen, his heart swelling, then confusion took over. Nik had posted this? How had she found this? Nik hadn't even tagged him.

"Nik's a photographer for Hot Shot Sports magazine," Carissa went on, less like an interview and more like an interrogation. Tiernan heard the camera zooming in on his face, and he tried to school it into something less like confusion and more like he knew exactly what was going on. "The magazine that's had an exclusive with you all summer."

"Intern," Tiernan said before he could stop himself. "He's an intern." He didn't know why that mattered, but he couldn't think of anything else to say. What was she getting at? What did it mean that Nik had posted *that* photo? There was no caption, no tags. Had he expected it to be found?

"Is he your boyfriend?"

Even Tiernan was surprised at the bluntness of this girl who was probably an intern herself.

"Uh, well," he said, trying to buy time, to figure out what to say. The real answer was no, but Nik wouldn't have posted that if something wasn't going on. Nik had been so worried when they took it, that Tiernan might post it somewhere. "It's kind of complicated."

"Aren't all relationships?" she said, her tone reassuring, but Tiernan was far from reassured. She turned to the camera without letting him try again. "There you have it, everyone. An exclusive reveal from Twenty-One news source. Tune in next time for more exclusive content and personal in-depth news."

The red light went off on the camera and Carissa hopped off the chair.

"Get that edited ASAP. I want it on the website before anyone else finds out."

"Wait," Tiernan said as she stepped away. "What the hell was that?"

She tilted her head again and tossed her hair over her shoulder. "It's my job to tell our readers the truth."

Tiernan couldn't even reply, left floored as she swept away. What the fuck had just happened? Had he just confirmed to the world that he and Nik were "complicated"? The press were ravenous dogs.

He didn't call Coach for damage control, though. Instead, he whipped out his phone and immediately looked up Nik's Instagram.

There it was, filled with artistic-looking photos of Arizona sunsets, a lizard on a rock, New York City at night, a blurry dark picture of something tagged as #endofchapterone. And the photo. It was one of the few selfies on his account, though Tiernan didn't go back years to check. It was the only recent one. There it was, so innocent, untagged.

What did Nik mean by posting it? There were no other photos of Tiernan, though Tiernan was remembering some of the photos Nik had taken that day, photos far more incriminating than a kiss.

It had to mean something, but it couldn't... Tiernan shook his head, scrolling through the photos now. It couldn't mean that Nik had forgiven him, that maybe there still was a chance. It would be too much to hope for, and Tiernan couldn't afford anything other than concrete fact right now. Competition was the only thing to focus on.

Still, his chest ballooned with hope as he put his phone away. He couldn't help it.

He had to get to lunch, though, before Coach got upset about shirking the schedule again, and Tiernan tried to push aside the millions of questions running through his brain. As he left the press room, he passed the gymnast from the Center, Auden, he thought. Auden seemed to recognize him as well and smiled in greeting. Tiernan didn't miss the silver medal around his neck, and returned the greeting in kind.

At least someone was doing well.

The Olympic complex was so big, it took Tiernan a few minutes to reach the cafeteria, and even longer to navigate the line to the front. Most tables were filled with a random assortment of country-colors, but he caught sight of Josh sitting with a few other guys from the USA team and he headed over.

Josh appeared engrossed in his phone and his eyes widened as Tiernan sat down.

"What?" Tiernan asked after a minute as Josh just stared at him.

"Dude, it's all over the internet."

"What is?"

Josh shoved his phone at Tiernan and Tiernan's heart sunk as he saw article after article.

Secret boyfriend? Olympic swimmer admits to affair — Tiernan Pace's adorable boyfriend on Instagram! — Who is Nik Cali? All the details here!

"Fuck," he breathed and let Josh take the phone back.

"It's everywhere," he said, scrolling through more. "They pulled a ton of photos from your Insta. Mostly shirtless."

"Of course," Tiernan muttered. Nik would hate this kind of attention.

"'Olympic swimmer, Tiernan Pace, has always been a player,'" Josh read, and Tiernan wanted to disappear right then. "'The story of his defeat at Olympic trials four years ago is well-known, as are the steps he took to numb the pain — '"

"Jesus Christ," Tiernan said, shoving a hand through his hair. This was exactly why he hadn't posted the photo in the first place. It would be different, if he had Nik here, if Nik could back him up, but he didn't. He didn't know where Nik was, if this was what he wanted, if he'd done it to get back at him? Nik wouldn't, he assured himself. He wouldn't be that spiteful.

"Man," Josh said, shaking his head. "They act like you're the biggest fuckboy ever."

Tiernan had been, back then. He wasn't anymore, and even if he was, it wasn't the press' problem.

"'There's been no comment from Nik Cali about the photo,'" he read finally. He put down the phone. "Must suck."

Tiernan sighed. "It's the press. You get more well-known, they'll go after you too."

Josh didn't look excited at the prospect, but he lowered his voice. "So is he really the boyfriend?"

"Was," Tiernan replied, pushing at his food. He needed to carbo-load for the competition, but he'd been put off his appetite.

"But he posted that this morning," Josh pointed out.

Tiernan didn't know. He didn't know what was going through Nik's head. He knew what he hoped, but he couldn't be sure.

"I can't think about him right now," he said instead, glad when Josh put his phone away. "I've got finals in a couple hours."

"You're better than me," Josh said, digging into his plate. "If it was me, I'd be freaking out."

Tiernan didn't say it, but he was. He was freaking out, but he couldn't let himself get distracted, not again. He was going to win this match and afterward, afterward, he'd allow himself to hope, but not right now.

Tiernan took a deep breath, tuning out the rumble of the crowd, the bustle of movement on the sidelines. Even his coach said nothing as Tiernan walked out to the block. Tiernan waved at the camera and climbed on the block, adjusting his suit, rubbing down his arms and carefully setting his goggles on. Down the row, all the guys adjusted swim caps or goggles until the whistle blew and they jumped in the water.

Positioning himself, Tiernan focused himself on the feeling of the water encompassing his body, the warm embrace that he'd always counted on growing up. This was a safe place where he knew he could succeed.

"On your mark," came the official's voice. Tiernan pushed himself up, hands on the bars of the block, feet pressed flat to the side of the pool. "Get set. Go!"

The crowd exploded, but Tiernan heard only the rush of water as he propelled backwards, a quick dolphin kick until he broke the surface of the water.

He was in fourth place again going in. He just had to keep it and move up a few places. He wasn't thinking about placement as he swam, though, making the turn fast, arms hitting the water and propelling him forward. He was lost in the count, the way his body cut through the water.

His focus wasn't on the crowd or the other swimmers. He was alone, just him and the water.

The second turn came quickly, and now was the time people fell behind. Now was the time where the lanes looked like flocks of geese with one leader at the head of the pack. It had to be Tiernan. He felt a burst of excitement, of adrenaline, as he hit the wall for the last turn and pushed with everything he had.

The seconds flew by, as if they weren't really there, and Tiernan's hand hit the edge of the pool as he let his body drop. Panting for breath, he tore off his goggles, finding the screen.

First.

Stamped across his lane was the number. For a second, he couldn't believe it, staring at the screen, struggling to get his breath back. It couldn't be right.

"Congrats," his lane-mate said, a Brit whose name Tiernan couldn't remember.

"Thanks," he got out finally, out of breath, in disbelief, but happiness filled him as he floated there trying to catch his breath, still staring at the screen. It wasn't a mistake. He'd just won gold.

And in that instant, it didn't fucking matter that he'd placed fourth in butterfly. Screw butterfly. *This* was his event. This was what Tiernan was good at. From now on, he'd always be an Olympic gold medalist, no matter what else happened.

He pulled himself from the pool finally, the screams of the crowd coming back and he smiled at a poster someone held up that said, "Don't 'Pace' Yourself! Go For Gold!"

E.E. Grey

He waved at the person holding it and she about fainted. Coach met him back in the locker rooms, giving him that rare smile as Tiernan grinned at him.

"You just won a gold medal," he said simply, as though it was as common as finding a penny on the ground. "What are you going to do next?"

Tiernan grabbed a towel and smiled. "Swim the freestyle."

"That's right," Coach said, but Tiernan couldn't deny that the swell of happiness in his chest didn't also have something to do with the thought that Nik hadn't given up on him, and that was why he'd really done so well. He didn't need his parents. He just needed Nik.

Chapter 30:
One Stroke

"Sit down."

Nik sat down slowly, facing Marion's desk; scattered with papers and pens, two computer monitors. For once, he didn't feel nervous, confident despite the fact that this was an 'exit interview.' He hadn't exactly followed the rules set out for him at the start of the internship, but it had been one of his most informative summers ever.

Marion turned to him and smiled. "At the end of our internships, we like to talk to you and get feedback and give it as well. First, how did you find your time with *Hot Shot Sports?*"

A lot had changed since the first day Nik had been introduced to Jennifer, the first time he'd taken photos that would end up online with his name attached. He'd been a meek, naive, amateur photographer.

"It's been amazing," he said. "I never thought I'd learn as much as I did, and not just about photography."

"Oh?" Marion asked curiously, setting her chin on her fingers.

"I learned about interviewing, about when to back down and when not to, how far you actually need to go to get what you want." He'd always been afraid of pushing too hard, of standing out in any way. Even in college, away from Andre, he still hadn't tried to be the best. He'd lingered in the background; that was what a photographer was supposed to do, he'd thought. They weren't supposed to get in the middle of things. The camera kept a distance between themselves and the world they were photographing. The good photographers, though, they weren't afraid to get dirty, to get in the middle of conflicts and show the truth.

"I'm glad you learned so much," Marion said, glancing down at his file on her desk. "You were a special case. Normally, we don't send interns out to do projects like this, and it's unfortunate you couldn't go to Paris. I remember your application packet." From under the pile of papers, she pulled out a portfolio. It was the one Nik had sent in with his application in a desperate hope he wouldn't get stuck making copies all summer. The photo she took out was one of Rae, one he'd taken before he'd left for college. "This is what you're good at," she said, "bringing this kind of emotions through your photos."

Rae had been trying to be happy for him. He could see the frown behind the smile, the tiredness of her eyes. Even then, she'd just been trying to keep everyone together, sane, happy. He owed her so much.

"Now," she said, sitting back and smiling at him fondly. "We've seen a lot of your work this summer and you impressed our photo editor, who is not an easy person to impress. If you're interested, we'd be interested in extending this internship."

"Extending?" Nik didn't understand.

"I know you have school," Marion said, "but how would you like to be a sort of freelance photographer for us? We have articles that sometimes need to be shot on-site, and Chicago is a big hub. It probably wouldn't be a lot of work, but I want to keep an eye on you."

Nik couldn't find words for a moment, too surprised, overwhelmed with gratitude. "Really?" he managed to stutter finally, staring at her, sure she was going to say she was joking.

Instead, she smiled. "And when you graduate, you come see me about something more permanent."

"I, oh my God," he said, shaking himself. "That's amazing, I, it's, no, it's too much."

No one ever did things like this for him. Nik wasn't lucky. He never had been. This was too much to offer.

"It's a couple years off," Marion reminded him. "You start with this freelancing, then you call me."

Nik didn't even know what to say, shocked. He just shook his head, staring past her at the city rising, silver and gray buildings glinting in the sunlight, New York winking back at him.

"Thank you," he said finally, heart swelling with gratitude. "I, I just... thank you."

"It's my pleasure," she said, rising from her chair and he did the same. "You take care of yourself, Nik."

"I will," he promised before he left, not bothering to bite down the grin that blossomed as the door shut behind him. He couldn't wait to tell Rae.

"Are you sure you don't want to pack this?" Rae asked, holding up a green stuffed dragon. Their room was messier than usual with half of Rae's things packed in suitcases.

"I told you," Nik said, taking the dragon from her and pausing as he gazed down at it. "We're not packing anything you can leave behind. I'm not coming back here, and I don't have room for stuffed animals."

"But it's Bucky. He was your favorite."

"It was a Captain America phase," Nik said, but he shoved the dragon in his bag anyway. He was packing for the last time, clearing out everything in their old room he wouldn't be sorry to see gone. It was helpful that he hadn't had much stuff growing up; it made getting rid of it a lot easier.

Rae laughed as she dumped a drawer of her clothes into a suitcase. "I knew you were gay before you did, the way you were always staring at Bucky."

"He was really hot," Nik said in his defense.

A door slammed out in the living room. He and Rae looked up, but neither said anything. Andre had been stomping around all week since Rae had told him she was leaving, but he hadn't argued with her. He hadn't tried to make her stay. That was one good thing he'd done, at least.

Rae grabbed a book off her nightstand and dropped it into her bag. "I'm kinda nervous."

"You don't need to be nervous," Nik assured her. "My roommates won't care, especially if you can help with rent."

"Not about that." She sighed at her bed scattered with bits and pieces of her life. "I've never lived anywhere but here. I don't know how to do anything."

"That's ridiculous," Nik scoffed. "You know how to do everything. You're the one who taught me how to do laundry and cook more than mac-and-cheese."

"That's not important stuff," she said dismissively.

"My roommates don't do laundry," Nik pointed out. "It's kind of important." He knew what she meant, though, and moved over to the bed, sitting down on a pile of magazines. "My first year in college was terrible," he admitted. "I didn't know how to find classes, or the right way to email professors, or how to make friends with normal people. Some days I thought I should just give up and come home. But I didn't. Mostly because I didn't want to give Andre the satisfaction, but also because I knew if I didn't stick it out, I'd never learn anything."

Rae gazed at him for a second, then shook her head. "It's weird when you sound smart."

"Funny." He rolled his eyes.

"You're right," she said, though, yanking the magazines out from under him and tossing them in the trash. "You were brave enough to leave, and so can I."

Nik didn't say it, but he'd always thought Rae was much braver than he was. Andre had only ever called him selfish, but since he'd been back, since their mom had died, he thought that it wasn't selfish. Getting out of a bad situation wasn't selfish.

"No more stuffed animals," he told her as a knock came on the front door.

He crossed the living room quickly with a glance at Andre's room. Andre didn't come out. At the door, Nik pulled it open and stopped short.

Tiernan stood in his dingy hall, gazing toward the stairs, but he jerked around when Nik opened the door. For a second, he didn't say anything, and Nik didn't either. Nik just stared. Of all places he'd ever expect to find Tiernan, his front door hadn't been one.

He hadn't heard a word from Tiernan about the picture. He'd posted it on Instagram over a week ago, then called up Brooke and asked her to post it on her website and make sure it hit the webzine communities. He'd seen the aftermath, the deer-in-headlights interview with Tiernan that magazine had done at the Olympics. It had been all over the internet within hours, and Nik had finally turned off his phone when it kept ringing. He hadn't talked to any of the press, waiting for Tiernan. He'd waited for Tiernan to call, to do something other than stutter out an answer to a reporter's questions during an ambush interview.

Tiernan had been all but mute on the subject. Nothing on his Instagram or other social media accounts. He hadn't called either.

"What are you…" Nik said finally, unable to finish as Tiernan smiled at him, and it was like the last few weeks hadn't even happened.

"What happened to your eye?" Tiernan asked, frowning at the bruise on Nik's face. It was healing now, lightening from purple to yellow, but still very obvious.

"It's nothing." Andre hadn't said a word about it, and Nik didn't expect him to. That was how things were in their family, but Nik wouldn't have to deal with it for long. Without Mom, he had no obligations to his brothers, and they would probably be just as happy to be rid of him.

Tiernan shook his head, but didn't push. "I got your message," he said instead with a small shrug. "Or at least, I think I did."

"Yeah, well," Nik said, because he couldn't think of what else. They stood awkwardly in the doorway, Tiernan still in the hall, but he didn't ask to come in.

Tiernan licked his lips and sighed. "I'm sorry about what I said about your family."

"I didn't exactly offer," Nik replied, almost smiling at the way Tiernan swept his hair back, a nervous gesture.

"And you were right," Tiernan admitted to the floor. "Maybe I was using you in some weird way that I didn't even realize."

"I said some stupid things too," Nik said simply. He couldn't deny he'd overreacted, had taken out his insecurities on Tiernan. He'd let himself get too far in over his head to see clearly.

"Maybe we could just start over," Tiernan suggested, looking up hopefully. "The photo… Was that, I mean, did that mean what I think it means?"

"What do you think it means?" Nik leaned against the doorframe and tried to look cool, like his heart wasn't beating out the Samba on his ribcage. They'd both made mistakes, and if they could both admit it, they could move forward.

"I was thinking maybe it meant that you forgave me for being such an idiot."

"You're wrong," Nik said, and Tiernan frowned, confusion skittering across his face.

"Oh," he said, shaking his head and taking a step back. "I — "

"It was an apology," Nik interrupted before Tiernan could get too much of the wrong idea. "I overreacted about the whole wedding thing. I was upset and stressed out, and I took it out on you. So I posted that picture and had my friend post it on her blog and get it to the magazine so you would see it and maybe not hate me."

"I never hated you," Tiernan said, his smile coming back, brighter now. "You're the reason for that terrible interview? I'm a meme now, you know."

Nik smiled. "I've seen it." He suppressed the nerves rising as they stood there. "So you forgive me for ruining your butterfly?" He wasn't actually sure he deserved forgiveness, since he'd probably been part of the reason Tiernan had lost.

Tiernan's eyebrows furrowed and he shook his head sharply. "You didn't ruin anything. I lost because I wasn't fast enough. Plain and simple. You can't blame yourself for my failings. God, please, don't do that. I do it enough to myself."

Nik felt a weight come off his chest. "And you did win a gold medal."

"Or two," Tiernan reminded him cheekily.

Nik smiled and stepped back, finally. "You wanna come in?"

"Love to," Tiernan replied, stepping towards Nik, but not to come in. Instead, he backed him up against the door frame and kissed him.

Everything Nik had felt over the past few weeks melted away as Tiernan kissed him — 9the stress of his brothers, conflicting emotions about losing his Mom, worry over Tiernan. It was all gone as they stood there, Tiernan's hands on his jaw, Nik's around his waist. He'd spent so much time worrying about the internship, about Rae, about life. He'd never stopped to appreciate how much better life was with Tiernan. He'd never make that mistake again.

"You must be the swimmer," came Rae's voice from behind them, and Nik broke away quickly, wiping his mouth.

Tiernan didn't seem bothered at being caught and smiled widely at Rae, who arched an eyebrow at Nik and smirked.

"You must be the sister," Tiernan said, and Rae shrugged.

"The one and only."

Tiernan slid an arm over Nik's shoulders, and Nik couldn't stop his smile. For once in his life, everything was working out. Everything was going right, and this time, he wasn't going to wait for the other shoe to drop, because it wasn't going to.

"It's nice to finally meet you."

Rae shot Nik an approving look and held out her hand to Tiernan.

"Nice to meet you, too."

"When you said your roommates were annoying, I didn't think you meant *that* annoying," Rae said, coming unannounced into Nik's room. Nik looked up from his textbook and out the door to the living room where Ty was doing yoga in his underwear.

Rae shut the door with a shudder and flopped down on his bed.

"They're art students. When you get a job, maybe we can kick one out."

Rae smiled up at him. "I went down to that restaurant," she said. "They're hiring servers. I could make a lot of money as a server."

"It'd give you good flexibility, when you go back to school."

"Let's not get ahead of ourselves," she warned. "I haven't applied yet."

Nik knew she would get in. They'd missed the deadline for fall classes, but she could get in for second semester. He was just glad she was thinking about it. She'd make a great psychiatrist someday.

Rae rolled over onto her stomach and closed the book Nik had been trying to read. "Heard from Tiernan lately?"

Nik couldn't help smiling despite himself. Even the thought of Tiernan made him happy. It was a weird feeling, but one he didn't hate at all.

"He's supposed to get back to the training center today," he said, thinking of the text Tiernan had sent. It had come with a picture Nik would *not* be posting on social media this time.

"More training? But Olympics are four years away."

"There are other competitions," Nik pointed out. "And he likes it. It's what he does."

"And you do photography," she replied. "So when is he coming out?"

"He's already out."

Rae rolled her eyes. "Ha. I meant, coming to visit? You haven't seen each other in a month."

"He can't just come out whenever," Nik said, setting his book aside. He wished Tiernan could, but Nik had school and Tiernan had training. It was his first long-distance relationship. Fuck, it was his first real relationship, and he wasn't always sure what he was supposed to do, but he trusted he and Tiernan could figure it out.

"I'm sure you'll see him soon," Rae said reassuringly, patting his arm. "He really likes you."

"Yeah," Nik said with a sigh. It would be nice if Tiernan were nearby, if he trained in Chicago, but Nik wasn't going to ask him to. It was too much to ask.

"We should go the park later," Rae said, sitting up. "Take some photos. Do a photo shoot."

"With you?"

"I am a great model," she said seriously. "After all, it was your photo of me that got you that internship."

Nik should never have told her that. "Only because you looked sad."

"I was sad," she admitted. "But I'm not anymore."

"Me neither," Nik said, and it was true this time. He sat back in his chair and glanced around his room. It seemed so much bigger now, even with Rae's stuff piled in a corner. Maybe it was just the freedom from nagging thoughts that made everything seem so much brighter, now that he was back in Chicago. He'd even stuck up some photographs on the wall behind the bed, including one of Tiernan on the beach.

"They're moving," Rae said after a minute, watching Nik. "Dan said they got a new place closer to work."

"Good." Nik hadn't talked to Andre or Seth or Dan since they'd left. He doubted he would ever be close to his brothers, but Rae kept up with them. It was good she did, but Nik didn't have to, and he felt better than ever about that.

"Nik!" came Ty's voice from the living room. "Door!"

Rolling his eyes, Nik climbed off his bed and Rae followed him out to the living room.

Tiernan stood in the doorway, a grin already on his face as Nik's mouth dropped open.

"Hey," he greeted Nik as Nik scraped himself together and shook his head as Tiernan crossed to him and gathered him into a hug.

"You're supposed to be in Phoenix," Nik said, staring up at Tiernan, who shrugged.

"I could go there if you want."

"No," Nik said sharply then laughed. "What are you doing?"

"You know," Tiernan said vaguely. "Sight-seeing, shopping, clubbing."

"And here I thought you might have come to see me," Nik said, and Tiernan laughed, pressing a kiss to his lips.

"What gave you that idea?"

"Staying long?" Rae asked from where she leaned against the couch and pointedly looked away from Ty's yoga poses.

"Maybe," Tiernan said, but Nik looked up at him sharply.

"What about training?"

"I think I deserve a little bit of a break," he said. "And Chicago seems like the perfect place to take one."

"It's lovely in the fall," Rae commented, but Nik ignored her.

"You're not avoiding training or anything?" He didn't want Tiernan to avoid it on his behalf. They weren't going to go through that again.

"I've been training non-stop for two years," Tiernan pointed out. "I just won two gold medals for my country, and I want to spend a month or two with my boyfriend because I miss him. If that's avoiding, then I'm avoiding."

Nik smiled, ducking his head. No one ever missed him. Well, except Rae.

"I guess it wouldn't be terrible to have you around."

Tiernan grinned. "Good, 'cause I don't have anywhere to stay."

"You don't want to stay here," Rae said with a significant glance towards Ty, who was standing on his head, scrawny legs in the air.

"The more, the merrier," Ty said from the floor.

"There's plenty of space in my room," Nik said, grabbing Tiernan's bag from where he'd dropped it by the door. He wasn't going to let Tiernan get away this time. No, not this time.

227

E.E. Grey

If you enjoyed this story, you can sign up for a free membership at
ForbiddenFiction.com and discuss it with other readers and the
author at the Backstroke story page at
http://forbiddenfiction.com/story/EEG-1.000308.
We do our best to proof all our work, but if you spot a text error we missed,
please let us know via our website Contact Form at
http://forbiddenfiction.com/contact.

Author's Notes:

Like *Vaulted* and *Tumbled* before, I stuck with the Olympics theme for our continuing Olympic Passion series. *Backstroke* came to me as a thought that there's a lot that goes on outside the Olympics, mainly media coverage. I'll be the first to admit that swimming is not my favorite Olympic sport (I'd rather watch diving), but swimming gets a lot more hype in the media, largely thanks to swimmers like Michael Phelps and Ryan Lochte. I pictured the next biggest swimmer, the best swimmer ten years from now, the one everyone swoons over. That, to me, was Tiernan. He's good-looking, handsome, charming, an all-American boy who just happens to find Nik, our resident hipster, adorable. Of course, it isn't just about competition; it's about emotional struggles our heroes go through.

I've always found it difficult to make my characters "likeable," so it's important to make them relatable instead—what's the difference? Well, anyone can be likeable. Be nice, charming, funny, smart. Those people are likeable, but they're not the characters you really care about. My favorite characters tend to be the dark, sarcastic, and generally not-so-moral. I relate to those characters, the ones who have to struggle. I struggle with making my characters likeable because what I like is not what everyone relates to. A relatable character is someone readers can identify with, someone who they see themselves in. Both Tiernan and Nik struggle with self and familial acceptance. Self-acceptance is a big issue for a lot of people, so it's nice to see characters going through the same thing and coming out better for it in the end, something I hope we all do when we face adversity. I like characters I can see myself in, and that might not mean they're likeable. They may be stubborn and argumentative and make bad choices, but so does everyone else.

About the Author

E.E. Grey has been writing for over ten years, from short stories to novels and everything in between. Now Grey has completed eight novel-length works and over three hundred short stories. When not writing, Grey enjoys traveling, having visited over twenty countries. Grey's other favorite pastimes include baking and home-improvement.

Other Works by E.E. Grey:

Brush with Death

By the Hour

Checking Out

Cigarette Burns

From the Storm

Stage Dreams

About the Series

Olympic Passions

It isn't easy to win both love and gold. To be an Olympic athlete requires incredible passion. There are other passions, however, which rise in young men training in such close quarters. When these passions swell, an athlete's dedication can waver. It's hard to keep your eyes on the prize when your friend's finely muscled back is so distracting...

Will it be love over gold? Will these young men choose each other over the Olympics? Or can they find a way to win it all?

Works in this series:

1. Vaulted

2. Tumbled

3. Backstroke

About the Publisher

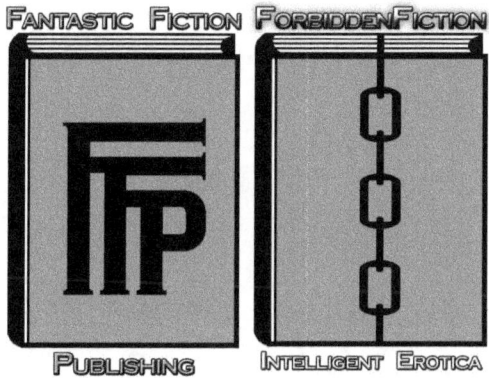

ForbiddenFiction.com is a publisher devoted to writing that breaks the boundaries of original erotic fiction. Our stories combine intense sexuality with quality writing. Stories at Forbidden Fiction.com not only arouse readers through sensations, but also engage them emotionally and mentally through storytelling as well-crafted as the sex is hot.

ForbiddenFiction.com is also designed to be a social reading environment. You'll have fun even if just reading the latest post each day, yet you will have the chance for so much more. Readers and authors can be part of ongoing discussions of specific works and individual authors as well as more general topics.

Sign up for a FREE Membership today at ForbiddenFiction.com